HERE THERE BE DRAGONS

Tom Frye

Copyright © 2022 Tom Frye

All rights reserved.

ISBN-13: 978-1-958557-12-9

Published by White Cat Publications, Lincoln Park, MI, USA.
No part of this may be reproduced or copied without written permission from the author. This is the fourth book in the Emerald series.

For Lance, who walked
many moonlit trails
with me.

And Carol Beem,
whose own trail
crossed path with
many of my
new readers.

1

* * *

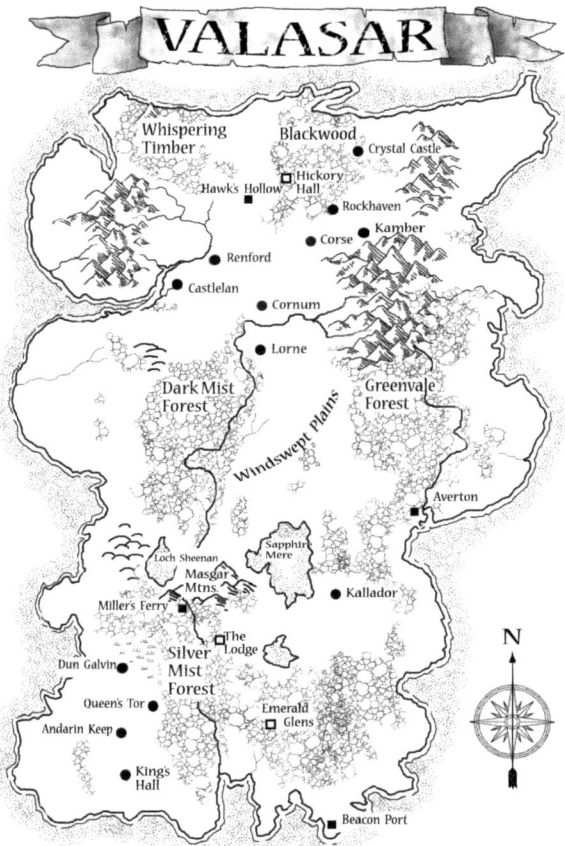

Tucking wild strands of his blond hair beneath his black bandanna, twelve-year-old Lucas Holland slid from the shadows and into the moonlight. He imagined himself a Ninja pirate, dressed all in black and creeping around at 2AM when no cars or people were in sight. He stealthily raised the wooden baseball bat he carried, moving back to the edge of the sidewalk, giving himself plenty of room for what he planned to do.

Before him, the Emerald took up the entire block at the center of Havelock Avenue. The Irish pub was a legendary steak house there in the small suburb. Patrons included Irish railroaders, Husker foot-ball fans, and dozens of biker clubs on Poker runs, fund-raising for one good cause or another. The entire rough crowd were all drawn there by its home-brewed ale and its fine Nebraska beef.

Lucas faced the huge stained-glass window that dominated the pub's front wall. It was a central focal point along the five-block business district, depicting a black dragon in flight, red flames erupting from his mouth contrasting sharply with the green emerald clutched in his talons. He narrowed his eyes for he could have sworn the flames slowly unfurled as he faced the building, and if he squinted just right, he detected a slight flutter of the dragon's wings. He froze there on the sidewalk, creeped out by the emerald pulsating with an eerie green light within the six-by-six foot circular window.

Old man Billy Connors should have never interfered in his dad's business. By doing so, the old Irishman, owner of the Emerald, had placed Stone Holland, president of the Elder's Den, in deep trouble. Since teaming up with the anti-terrorist agent, Khalid Karim, Stone had already gotten in way over his head in his hunt for the extremist, Achmed Waziri. Lucas knew that someone needed to arrest the man, he just didn't want it to be his father to continue the hunt to do so. Besides, now that Waziri was still in the States and not in the Middle East as first rumored to be, Lucas knew his dad was on a wild goose chase. He wouldn't find Waziri over there. The man was right there in the USA. And now that Billy had captured the souls of Molech and Baphomet, imprisoning them inside of two jewels, the old Irishman had sent them on through a portal to the Valley of Kings in Egypt. Billy claimed Khalid could best deal with the two demons, and yet he had placed Stone in even more danger by sending their entrapped souls through the portal. Now Lucas was determined to get even with the old Irishman for putting his dad's life at risk.

He dug down inside his jean pockets for one of the black rocks he'd stuffed them with earlier on his way down to the Avenue. He plucked out one sleek, black stone, tossing it up into the air a few times. Remembering what his Uncle Nate had said about putting a bullet from his .357 directly through Billy's prized window, Lucas determined he would beat his uncle to it. He thought about stealing Nate's big pistol, but he knew he'd probably get caught and throttled for such an infraction, so he resorted to the next best thing besides bullets: Rocks.

Satisfied that the one he'd selected would do, Lucas tossed it up into the air, took hold of his bat with both hands, and swung at the falling rock with all his might.

Thock! The satisfying sound echoed up and down the Avenue, bringing a smirk to his face, and his powerful swing of the bat sent the rock flying directly at the illuminated window.

Prrrrrfht! was the sound that came from the panes of the colored window as the rock struck it. Where Lucas expected shattering glass and a domino-effect of complete destruction, figuring the entire window would cave in, he blinked in astonishment. The rock struck the glass, and was literally sucked inside the stained-glass window.

"What the holy hell!" he gasped, staring at the ripples that passed through the entire artistic creation. In the aftermath of what he expected to be a satisfying crash, he stood there watching the dragon shudder as the warbled, rippling effect flowed over it. Lucas tried another rock. He tossed it high in the air, swung the bat two-handed, and *Thock!* sent another sleek, black rock at the stained-glass window of the Emerald. *Phhhhrrfring!* echoed shrilly in his ears.

He blinked again as this rock, too, simply vanished within the deep greens of the emerald clutched in the dragon's talons. The same ripples spread swiftly across the face of the backlit window.

This time when they reached the dragon's flames, there came an airy *Poof!* And the flames flickered as if they had been splattered by cold water. "No way!" Lucas growled. "No way in hell!"

He gripped the baseball bat in both hands, swung it back and over his shoulder, and charged at the window, determined to shatter it to smithereens. The bat struck the glass with considerable force, passed completely through the window, and the momentum of his charge, carried Lucas forward and on into the pub.

He landed just opposite of the stained-glass window on a bearskin rug spread out before an enormous stone fireplace. He cringed and closed his eyes, fully expecting the entire window to come crashing down on him, showering him with a bright burst of colored glass as it shattered into a million pieces.

But when he opened his eyes, the window behind him remained intact. Not even a crack to show he'd came through it. Lucas's brow furrowed deeply as he stood up. He shivered as he realized he had just passed through the multi-colored glass without a scratch or even the slightest cut on his hands and arms. He shivered again, just thinking how he should really be plucking slivers of sharp glass from his skin, and yet there he stood, unharmed.

He reached up, removing the bandana from his head, golden hair spilling down past the collar of his black T-shirt. He used the bandana to wipe the sweat from his brow, and a few tears from his cheeks. He couldn't help himself, the tears came out of his amazement. There was no way he could have fallen through that window without breaking it or cutting himself to bloody ribbons.

Blinking away tears to clear his vision, Lucas looked to the seven stag-heads mounted above the fireplace mantle. Streamers of green Christmas lights hung from the antlers of the proud-looking deer, resembling fireflies drifting through the darkness of the pub. Just be-neath the mounted stag-heads was a wooden plaque, one that Lucas had heard so much about growing up in Havelock, the Irish-Catholic community founded by Irish railroaders back in the 1800's. The oak plaque was engraved with words and sported two perfectly round bullet holes above the words. Those holes had been left there by another Havelock kid, determined to take Old Billy Connors out of this world. From the story Lucas had heard, the old Irishman refused to involve the Irish mob in an act of revenge for a young girl that the boy had fallen in love with.

That was the mushy part of the story, the part that hardly interested Lucas. But he did, however, like the part that the boy had stolen that same gun earlier that night while car-shopping. It just so happened that the gun had been used to murder the young girl that the boy demanded vengeance for. The kid used it to try and shoot Billy late one night. Evidently, he had failed, yet left behind two bullets in the plaque above the fireplace. The ballistics had linked the gun to the murderer and served to put the shooter away for his crime.

Hesitantly, Lucas raised his hand as he tried to touch the bullet holes. Being only 4 foot 10, he had to stand on his tiptoes to reach the plaque. As his fingers grazed the two round holes, he read the words of the plaque out loud: "Dedicated to William Connors, for his ser-vice to the Sinn Fian."

He said, "Sin," pronouncing it the wrong way, and seconds later a gruff voice came from the shadows at the back of the pub: "Shinn Fayn, lad. It means, 'We Ourselves,' and is a left-wing Irish political party in both the Republic of Ireland and Northern Ireland."

Old Billy Connors stepped out of the blackness just beyond the pub's pool tables. Dressed in a three-piece suit, his long, silver hair fell loose about his slender shoulders, while beneath his hawk-like nose was a thick, white mustache. His amazingly blue eyes pierced Lucas where he stood, nailing him in place.

Greatly reminding Lucas of Mark Twain, the old Irishman quietly asked, "Do you have some quarrel with me, laddie?"

Unable to muster any words that would make sense, Lucas searched the room, frantically looking for an escape route. To the right of the fireplace was a dark hallway stretching toward a round oak door standing closed at the end of the ten-foot hall.

Above the door was another wooden plaque that read:

Here, there be Dragons.

A strange bright light leaked out from beneath the door and slithered into the hallway, illuminating its walls with a greenish light.

Lucas turned and ran toward the door.

"Don't!" Billy shouted at him. "Don't you dare go in there, boyo! I swear to you, no good thing will come of it!"

Ignoring the old man's ranting, Lucas pulled on a rusty door latch, swinging the door open. The fresh scent of mint washed over him and a slight breeze ruffled the strands of his unruly hair.

Keenly aware of the solid footsteps behind him, he ran through the doorway and the door slammed shut behind him, cutting him off from this world, and sending him to the next one beyond.

2

Lucas found himself standing in a round, stone vault with an array of stained-glass windows taking up the entire front wall of the chamber. "A church?" he whispered, staring at the light flickering beyond the panes of each window.

He counted six of the colored windows, with an oak door situated beneath them. It reminded him of Saint Patrick's church down the street from the Emerald, with its ancient stonework, its oaken doors, and its own windows, usually illuminated by candlelight.

Twin birch trees stood on either side of him, their lower branches creating a framework for the window-like screens in the front wall. Swift movement behind the first window on his immediate left caught Lucas's eye, and he stared in amazement as the shadowy forms of two dragons slammed into each other, locking together in fierce combat. One beast was sleek and black with green eyes, while the other was white as snow with deep blue eyes. Flames burst from the mouths of both beasts as they tumbled through the skies, disappearing from the view that the window-screen allowed Lucas to see.

Looking at the second window, Lucas saw a bird's eye-view of a massive castle under siege by a vast horde swarming across its green-way. Thousands of antler-crowned warriors converged upon the fortress, while above the high towers of the besieged castle black banners unfurled, revealing a winged, white lion.

The third window showed a herd of wild horses fleeing across a wide-open plain, their eyes wide in terror as sleek, black wolves pursued them. Hundreds of horses appeared there on the screen before Lucas. He cringed as the dark beasts drew closer behind the steeds. Suddenly, a pack of shaggy gray wolfhounds sprang up from the long grasses, and hounds and wolves crashed into each other, while the horses ran on, their lives spared by the attack of the noble dogs.

Lucas looked over at the fourth window where a company of child-like figures drew twin swords from sheaths depending from their shoulders. The impish warriors were cloaked and hooded in black leather. As each blade was drawn from shoulder-sheaths, a brilliant display of multicolored light burst at the base of each sword, and like electric eels slithering beneath the surface of dark waters, scintillating colored hues of blue, green, red, and violet traveled down the length of each blade, bursting from sword tips with a crackle of blue-white lightning.

"Those wee woodland imps," came the voice of Billy moving into the chamber behind him, "are the Jewel Folk. And fierce is the fight within them, Children of the Woods that they be."

Lucas wheeled around, his blond shaggy bangs whipping wildly as he turned to gape at the Irishman. Rumors of Billy's cruelty whirled through Lucas's mind, especially the one where Old Man Connors once caught Reason Nelson stealing pop off of his loading dock, and put a knife to the back of his knee and threatened to hamstring him, making his own grandson a cripple for the rest of his life.

Not checking to see if Billy even carried a knife, Lucas bolted and ran, placing distance between himself and the old man. "No!" Billy shouted. "Don't. Go. In. There!"

But Lucas paid no heed to the Irishman's warning, and he swung open the door beneath the windows. He darted through, pulled the door closed behind him, and ran into what could only be described as a Hobbit hole.

In full flight mode, Lucas passed through a rounded room, lit up by a small, cozy-looking fireplace to one side of the room. A cheery blaze crackled inside its hearth, and yet its bright red glow was enhanced by a row of lanterns lined up on the mantle above. In each globe of the lanterns were lime-green specks of luminous lights that cast a deep green aura about the rest of the room. He noticed a tea pot on the small table between two high-backed chairs situated before the fire, then glanced down at a small figure seated there. At the sight of the fair-haired kid racing through the den, the tiny fellow let out a startled yelp of surprise, his steaming cup of tea flying from his hands, fragrant mint tea splattering over the hearth stones.

As Lucas ran past him, he muttered, "A Hobbit! As if dragons weren't bad enough? And I don't even do drugs!"

Skidding to a stop before a round green door, he reached for the latch and heard the small fellow behind him say, "Not a hobbit, but Chaykin, lad! Chaykin of the Jewel Folk fame!"

Without bothering to even look back, Lucas pulled open the door and sprang outside onto the porch situated before an enormous hill. In fact, both the porch and the round green door were directly in the center of a large mound of earth, similar to what he imagined a hobbit hole at Bagend would look like.

"Holy Moses!" Lucas gasped as he ran beneath the luminous fireflies flittering through the evening air and listlessly drifting through a woodland clearing. Only these fireflies were as large as doves, their tails lighting up so brightly that the surrounding trees were splotched here and there by a lemony haze.

A horn sounded from the distant woods. The sound of galloping horses came from deeper in the hills beyond the clearing. Lucas scanned the darkened trees, his heart beating loudly within his thin chest. He wished he'd carried his baseball bat with him, for being armed against whatever was coming seemed to be wise.

Whatever was coming down from the high hills was not there to be friendly. He had trespassed into a different realm. He was certain there would be consequences for his actions, even if he had only been trying to escape from Old Billy Connors.

His eyes were drawn to a flicker of red flame at the end of a pathway winding up the wooded hillside just opposite of the one he'd exited. A tall, pale figure mounted on a large black elk sat there, a fiery sword held above his head. The rider's long, silken white hair danced wildly about his shoulders in the night wind. His red eyes matched the fire of his blade, and as they locked on Lucas standing there on the porch, he felt a malicious rage and hatred pass through him as though the pale-skinned rider had cast a spell at him.

The silver-haired swordsman spurred his mount into a run. The elk sprang down the path, carrying his rider gracefully down the opposite hillside. As the black elk picked up speed and brought the swordsman closer, Lucas could clearly see that his heavily muscled bare chest and arms were covered in blue tattoos, a mix of predatory beasts, tiger, panther, bear, leopard, all dominated by a horned devil inked across his thick chest.

Each tattooed creature emanated a strange bluish glow as the rider closed the distance between them. And yet, Lucas continued to peer up in alarm at the enraged glare the swordsman held within his eyes.

Like an arrow sent swiftly down the hill at him, words were sent to him by the tattooed swordsman: "I was drawn here by your rage, boy! Your anger and the fires and storms of your own making, shone like a beacon in a dark night, drawing me to you like a lodestone! And I have come to feast upon your red-hot soul!"

Within the seconds that it took for the elk to reach the bottom of the hill, Lucas suddenly found himself surrounded by a small pack of winter-white wolves. Green eyes glowing, all nine of the large beasts turned to face the approaching swordsman, fierce growls of challenge rising to meet him.

The silver-haired rider raised his fiery blade and snarled, "White Wolves of Masgar dare thwart my hunt? Surely you jest!"

Hearing a sound behind him, Lucas glanced back to see an enormous Wolfhound come bounding across the clearing. The huge, shaggy dog raced past him and took his place at the center of the wolf pack, joining the white beasts as they faced the rider and his elk mount. The swordsman swayed back in his saddle. "What's this?" he said. "A Hound of the Chieftains? This is my hunt, Hound! This is my feast, Dog of the Gypsy-kin!"

Lucas shuddered at the word feast. He had already been alarmed by the swordsman's claim that he had come to eat his red-hot soul. He did not like what that implied, since he figured the rider was speaking anything but figuratively. No, Lucas surmised that the red-eyed rider meant to literally eat his soul, though he had no clue how he intended to do that. He immediately thought of Mange and how Molech had drained him of his soul, and he shuddered to think that this swordsman intended to do the same thing to him.

Suddenly, the entire clearing between the two massive hills lit up with a brilliant light, and Lucas turned to see a small band of hooded warriors riding horses down into the clearing. As the riders formed up on either side of the silver-haired swordsman, long, slender glowing swords appeared in their hands.

One of the hooded riders said, "Well met, Traxx Dire, King of the Shadow Realm! The Stealth are here to serve!"

Traxx Dire gestured wildly with his flaming blade and beckoned with his free hand, saying, "The wolves are yours! The hound, as well! But the soul of the boy is mine alone!"

3

The large wolfhound raised his shaggy head and let out a long, mournful howl. Standing there within the semi-circle of the wolves, Lucas heard the haunting trill of pipers from the far end of the vale. Above the bagpipes a pleasant voice rose in song:

Kissed by the sun,
    embraced by the morning,
    the Forest sheds
    her cloak of night.
    She slips into
    a gown of mist,
    she wove herself,
    by morning light.

In amber rays,
    the Forest dances.
    In hidden glens
    within the hills.
    Barefoot, she glides
    through open meadows,

tip-toes her way
past silver rills.

Her gown of mist,
  trails behind her,
  fluttering in
  the morning wind,
  adorned with gems
  and sparkling jewels,
  the rising sun,
  did surely send.

The song ended and a herd of dainty black stags appeared on the slope in the distance. The tiny sable stags were no bigger than fawns, and yet they each sported a full rack of glistening antlers. All of the creatures had large blue eyes that glowed with a strange illumination. A moment later, the herd of stags gracefully bounded down the green slope, scattering fall leaves in their wake. Within the mad swirl of colorful leaves, a company of child-like riders appeared there at the crest of the slope.

To Lucas's surprise, all of the wee riders were mounted on dozens of the dainty black stags. At first, he thought the riders were small boys, but then he saw that beneath their long, black riding coats, they were clad in leather armor and heavily armed, with sheathed swords strapped to their saddles. Most of the small folk wore their various shades of long hair either loose or in single, braided tails, but some wore wide-brimmed, deep-crowned hats adorned with jewel-encrusted broaches or bright red feathers.

It was a strange company for sure, and Lucas was quite startled when one little rider let out a riotous whoop, sending the entire band galloping down the distant hillside. The stag-riders rode in loose formation, their black mounts leaping in chaotic patterns across the valley floor. Then all at once, like a flock of swooping swallows, the wee riders fell in behind the leader, forming an orderly charge directly toward the clearing where Lucas stood.

Suddenly, their leader, the long tails of his coat flapping wildly, rode hard toward the green mound. Lucas noted that beneath his long coat, the small fellow was dressed in shiny, black leather armor. He also wore a black beret, adorned with a single red feather, and the locks of his raven hair swirled back over his slender shoulders, revealing gold hoops dangling from the lobes of his ears.

When the diminutive rider was a mere twenty feet away, Lucas could clearly see that he had a tiny, upturned nose, a slight cleft in his chin, and a faint dusting of freckles on his dimpled cheeks. The rider brought his mount skidding to a halt, sprang from his saddle, and nimbly landed in front of the white wolves and the wolfhound. While his stag raised its head and gazed at Lucas with its blue eyes, the wee rider removed his black beret and dropped to one knee, declaring, "Greetings, Advocate of Woodwalkers! The Black Foxes are at your service! I am their commander, Peyton Ring!"

Peyton Ring kneeled there, strands of hair swirling down on either side of his brow. He rose to his feet and drew twin swords from his stag's saddle sheaths. Both blades were illuminated by a violet light that reminded Lucas of a winter sky before nightfall. He looked on in amazement then as the entire company of stag-riders drew their own glowing blades and shouted, "Hail, Advocate of Woodwalkers-!"

Stepping in between two of the wolves, Peyton leaned forward and whispered, "Lad, now would be a good time to retreat back inside the Lodge. If we should lose this battle, you will be on your own."

That said, the small woodland warrior wheeled around and remounted his stag. He then joined the twelve other Black Foxes as they advanced upon Traxx Dire and his Stealth allies.

The fight that ensued was brutal. Traxx's fiery blade swooped down only to be met by the shimmering jewel-blades of Peyton Ring, his violet swords ringing as they deflected the fire-blade of the silver-haired swordsman.

Lucas could hear the snick and flick of blades as the small riders were met by the hooded band of warriors. Where Lucas expected to hear the humming and whirring of light sabers, much like those wielded by Jedi Knights, instead he heard the worrying blades of the Black Foxes ringing, sending shrill echoes off into the black trees.

He had watched many sword-fighting movies back at home, The Lord of the Rings, The Thirteenth Warrior, The Kingdom, and The

Princess Bride, but never had he seen the speed and skills displayed now by the Jewel Folk, their moves so graceful and fluent that it was more like a well-rehearsed dance rather than a bloody, savage battle.

And there was blood involved.

Much blood, as the Stealth were swiftly eliminated by the glowing blades of the Black Foxes. Some died with silent screams erupting from their mouths, others fell with loud gasps or pain-filled grunts as the shimmering blades of the Foxes slithered in past their guards, or sank deep within their bodies, spilling them from their saddles.

Peyton Ring forced the elk to back up as his own small steed sprang up so that he could exchange sword strokes with the wielder of the fire-blade. Quicker than the eye could follow, the woodland warrior delivered dozens of loops and whirls of his flashing blades, and yet they were deflected by Traxx as he expertly parried and blocked each attack.

With a loud bellow, Traxx's elk mount skidded to a sudden stop, lowered its head, and with the wide spread of its antlers, caught and lifted Peyton's stag, tossing both high into the air. Peyton somersaulted backwards, landing twenty feet away on his feet. His black steed, however, struck the ground hard and collapsed into a crumpled heap, the blue glow slowly leaving its eyes.

Stirred to wrath by the loss of his steed, Peyton started back across the clearing, but before he could renew his battle with Traxx, the huge swordsman drove his fire-blade into a hapless Fox closing with him. The fiery blade crackled as Traxx lifted the sword-skewered warrior up and out of his saddle. The Black Fox screamed in agony then as the red blade literally sucked his soul from his small body. Looking on in horror, Lucas watched as the Chaykin's face melted, his eyeballs popped, and his body collapsed like a wet paper sack, dropping to the ground with a wet-sounding thwack! Laughing wildly, Traxx withdrew his blade from the dead forest warrior, and sent the blade cleaving into a second rider within his reach. This small Chaykin died horribly, too, his body flopping to the ground like a landed fish as the fire-blade sapped his soul from him.

Traxx took out four more of the Jewel Folk before Peyton finally reached him. And then, the wielder of the fire-blade was knocked from the back of his elk mount as the Chaykin warrior sprang up high and barreled into him, slashing and hacking with his jewel-blades.

Traxx landed on his feet, his sword sizzling as he fended off the small swordsman's twin blades. Finding himself hard-pressed to win against the highly skilled Peyton, Traxx removed his left hand from his hilt and with a wild gesture, he cast a spell at his fierce attacker.

A strange blast of force blew Peyton off his feet, sending him cartwheeling across the clearing, his violet blades flashing as he rolled to a stop before the wolfhound and the wolves.

Lucas could see that the little swordsman was dazed by the sudden blast. He had also dropped his glowing swords, and as he pawed frantically at them, Traxx came on, his own flaming sword raised above his head, his red eyes locking on the wolfhound as the great, noble beast moved to defend Peyton.

4

Lucas shouted, "No! Don't kill the dog!" He then ran between the two wolves on either side of him and snatched up the violet-shaded jewel-blades. "No, lad!" cried Peyton as he tried to rise to his feet. "You don't stand a chance against—"

Arroooo! erupted from the mouth of the noble hound, and a shimmering blue field of force appeared between Lucas and the falling blade of Traxx, stopping the flaming sword from descending.

A tall, well-built figure suddenly moved in front of Lucas and said, "Traxx, return to the Shadow Realm!"

Traxx was flung backwards by the large figure, who stood there sadly shaking his shaggy-maned head. Traxx and his fiery blade were then gone, vanishing into an ethereal cloud at the edge of the forest.

The heavily muscled figure turned to stare down at Lucas. He had the large body of a man, yet the head, the face, and the long, scraggly mane of a lion. His smile was dazzling, and the light in his blue eyes caused Lucas to cringe as the lion-man fixed him in his gaze.

"Tawn," said Peyton, rising to his knees, "Chief Messenger of the One. Is this the Chaykin Advocate?"

Tawn shook his head, his mane trailing over his huge shoulders. "No," he said. "Not this one."

A movement across the clearing caused Lucas to look to the giant elk as the creature moved to stand over Peyton's fallen stag. Lowering its head, its great rack of white antlers glistened in the moonlight as it sniffed at the dead stag. "Leave it alone!" Lucas snapped.

Tawn gently said, "Hush, child. He means no harm."

As Lucas lowered the twin swords, he watched Tawn approach the elk. The lion-man ran a hand down its flank and said, "You are free. Go. Run the forests again, no more to serve such a master."

With a soft chuff, the elk sprang away, vanishing into the night. Tawn knelt beside the fallen stag. Peyton staggered to his feet and moved to join him. Smiling down at the raven-haired Chaykin, Tawn reached down and placed his hand on the head of the dead steed. A strange green mist drifted out between the fingers of the lion-man's hand. It swirled round, evolving into a thick emerald cloud that slowly covered the entire body of the small, black stag.

Lucas actually gasped when he saw the ethereal form of the stag settling down on the prone body, blending with the undulating mist, now sparkling with tiny bursts of lime-green light. With an audible click! the soul of the fallen stag entered back into its body, and the once-dead creature's eyes blazed a bright blue as he lifted his head, staring up at Peyton, now kneeling beside the lion-man, tears of relief streaming down his face.

The white wolves darted across the clearing, reminding Lucas of excited puppies as they snuffled and whined, each garnering attention from Tawn. Some rolled over on their backs, exposing their stomachs to the lion-man, while others burrowed their heads into his outstretched arms as he hugged them to his massive chest.

Studying the lion-faced man, Lucas noted the gold hoop hanging from the lobe of one ear, barely concealed by the silvery white strands of his mane. The beast-man was dressed in a leather vest and pants, and yet he was bare-chested, his bare arms rippling with muscle. He reminded Lucas of his dad and his uncle, both bikers who had similar proportions when it came to physical appearance. It then occurred to him that this beast-man was a warrior. In this realm there were no bikers, but simply warriors who relied on their muscles to conquer their enemies.

Tawn peered in alarm at the western sky. "Drakvoren is coming!" he whispered.

"The Drak?" Peyton said. "Coming here to the Lodge?"

Tawn's eyes locked on Lucas. He said, "The Drak is drawn here because of him. He radiates turmoil, rage, and distress. He's a walking wound that desperately needs healing."

Peyton said, "If he is not the Advocate of our kin, send him back, Tawn. There is really no other recourse."

The black-haired Chaykin moved to Lucas, retrieving both of his jewel-blades. "Sorry, lad, no offense, but you cannot stay." Sliding his glowing swords into sheaths on either side of his stag's saddle, he cried, "Boyos, you must ride from here now!"

Vaulting into their saddles, the Black Foxes rode out of the clearing and away into the eastern vale beyond the Lodge. The white wolves trailed behind them, and within seconds, the band of Jewel Folk and wolves vanished into the dark night.

With one last glance at the western skies, Peyton led Lucas to the porch of the Lodge, the wolfhound trailing behind them. The dog whined as it appeared to be fully aware of the danger coming their way. Lucas asked, "What is the Drak? Why is it coming here because of me? He's a dragon, right?"

But Peyton simply pulled open the large, round door of the underground haven, and ushered both Lucas and the dog inside.

"I'm sorry, lad," he said, sorrow in his eyes, "you are not the one I have come here for. You must return to your realm. It would be far too dangerous for you here. Your raw emotions attract evil beings of all sorts, and I'm afraid you would be like a magnet. Nothing for you then, but to go back to your world."

A thunderous roar came from the sky beyond the wooded vale.

Peyton glanced back, alarm in his eyes. Lucas looked past the lion-man to see a dark dragon coming swiftly through the night sky, angry flames bursting from his open mouth. Peyton stepped into the Lodge behind Lucas and pulled the round door closed behind him.

Lucas looked across the den to the fireplace where Billy Connors knelt as he picked up pieces of the cup Lucas had caused the Chaykin to drop on the hearthstones.

"Sorry," Billy said, "the wild child got past my guard. He should have never trespassed into the realm of Valasar. I'm sorry he made such a mess. I should have been a bit quicker on my feet."

Suddenly, a deafening roar erupted from the outside in the forest. Pieces of shattered glass fell from Billy's hands.

"Sweet Jesus!" the old man gasped in alarm.

As he and Peyton hurried to the round window overlooking the clearing outside, an answering roar exploded from the grove beyond the window. It had a deep, throaty harshness to it, and reminded Lucas of the roar of an African lion. He imagined that Tawn was now battling with the dragon, and he had little hope that he would win such a combat. Bright flashes of red light illuminated the panes of the window glass, and while Billy and Peyton were distracted, Lucas made his move to escape.

He darted across the den, his sights set on the oak door he'd come through to enter this realm. As he raced past the fireplace, he glanced down at the Chaykin now seated in one of the high-backed chairs, a leather map clutched in his hand.

Impulsively, Lucas snatched it up, crumpling it up in his grasp.

"At least, I'll have some proof," he whispered as he reached the door. "Hobbits with glowing swords! White wolves! Tawn the Lion-Man! A dragon named Drak! When Alex laughs at my story, I'll just shove this map in his face as proof I've been here!"

5

Boone Nelson seated himself in a high-backed booth there in the Emerald Pub. He picked up the steaming cup of black coffee situated on the table in front of him, sipping it slowly. He smiled and fondly thought of his grandfather who had sat in that very booth for over forty years, sipping at his own cups of hot black coffee. Billy Connors once told him, "I've settled for the lesser of two evils, one being the booze, the other being the bean that makes goats kick up their happy feet and literally dance after they've consumed a score of the little black beans!"

In contrast to the days Billy was an alcoholic, his coffee-drinking mellowed the Irishman, proud owner of the Emerald, considerably.

Boone studied the Emerald's rustic woodwork, its white-washed walls, oak beams, high-backed booths, and tall stools situated before a bar with brass foot rails. Tapestries on the walls depicted castles, and dominating the west wall, was a red banner with three black lions wearing gold crowns. The most eye-catching sight in the pub was the enormous stained-glass window at the front of the building, facing out onto Have Ave. The dragon carrying the lime-green emerald in its talons had cost the old man a pretty penny. Boone remembered the first night he'd set foot in the pub. Billy met him inside the entrance.

"Thanks for coming," he'd said. "I'd like you to watch the meeting from a surveillance console in my office. Maybe you can detect if your little brother is telling it true or lying."

Old Will Connors had then led him to his office at the back of the pub. Tall and scarecrow thin, Billy's snow-white, collar-length hair trailed back over his ears in wavy wisps, and the tips of his thick, white mustache were waxed and twisted into tight curls. To add to his noble appearance, the old Irishman wore an expensive three-piece suit, but as Boone looked into Billy's ocean blue eyes, he detected a dangerous rage roiling beneath the surface of his regal-looking exterior. He reminded him of an old, gruff lion.

"I know you are reluctant," he told Boone, "to eavesdrop on your brother, but perhaps by you watching from a distance, we can resolve this issue."

The issue was, Reason, his troubled little brother, at 13 had gone to a party. During a bust of said party, Reason had a collision with private investigator, Jessie Dalton, and a drug dealer named Brooks. In the aftermath of their floundering around on a shadowy kitchen floor, Reason had snatched up what he thought to be his leather jacket. Instead, he came away from the party with the jacket of Brooks. Later, after hiding out in a doghouse behind the party house, Reason discovered a strange blue key in the pocket of this jacket.

Jessie tracked him down, and there at the Nelson house, the private detective had shared with the boys and their mother, Rose, that the key belonged to a safe-deposit box at a Havelock bank. Inside the box, was evidence that would solve the murder of a state patrol informant named Kelly Drake. Jessie warned the Nelsons that Brooks, the dealer who had murdered her, and a dirty private eye named Quinn, badly wanted this key to prevent the evidence from falling into the hands of the local police.

Reason, plagued by a bad case of oppositional defiance disorder, refused to cooperate with Jessie and stubbornly kept the key for himself. Jessie enlisted old Billy Connors to talk sense into Reason. Boone had watched the meeting between Reason and Billy from the pub's security system, and unknown to Reason, he saw right through his lies.

Jessie had escorted their mother, Rose, Reason, and his friend, Vince, into the pub. Patrons looked up from their meals to curiously stare at the rugged-looking investigator leading the lady and two boys across the room. Reason walked over and stood beneath the heads of seven deer mounted above the mantle. The numerous strands of tiny, green lights wrapped around the antlers of the bucks caused them to resemble fireflies floating above their heads. Reason shifted his gaze and peered at the wooden plaque on the mantle beneath their chins. Before he could read the inscription on the plaque, Reason turned to face Billy.

It all played out inside of Boone's head as he sat there:

Reason asked, "Is that the plaque the Sinn Fein gave you? According to my mom, the IRA were terrorists, and yet you believed they were patriots, and you sent lots of money back to Ireland to finance their war against British oppression."

Billy said, "Never mind that, you little scoundrel!"

"This," Rose snapped, "coming from the King of Scoundrels, the great Irish Godfather of Havelock?"

"Godfather!" Billy snorted. "Does he know his proper history? Nelson means Neal's son, which is derived from Niall, High King of Ireland! You've got the blood of kings in you, lad! Your ancestor founded a powerful Irish dynasty. Niall's raids into foreign lands resulted in a young lad coming to Ireland in the third century. And do you know who he turned out to be? Saint Patrick! Ironic, don't you think? Your ancestor brought Patrick to Ireland, and now you live one block away from a church named after the great saint, yet you fall so short of what you could be. It's tragic and disappointing."

The old Irishman lit his pipe and slowly blew out several puffs of smoke. Quietly, he then said, "Tell me, lad, do you know what happens to a fly caught in a spider's web?"

"Yeah," Reason replied. "He gets killed by the spider."

Billy said, "And like two little flies, you boys got tangled up in a web of conspiracy the night you found that key. If Jess had that disk, he could bring Brooks down. But unfortunately, it hasn't resurfaced yet. So, I'm offering you both a safe haven." -

Removing two pamphlets from inside his jacket, Billy slid them across the table in front of Reason and Vince. Reason snorted, "A treatment program? Treatment is only for kids who have drug problems! Thanks, Mister Connors, but I'll pass. I quit drugs."

Billy snorted, causing the tips of his mustache to quiver. "That's what folks say when they're in denial. Checking you into treatment will keep you safe until all the mad dogs involved in this mess can be rounded up or put out of their misery."

"Is that your answer to everything?" Rose scoffed, gesturing to the plaque above the nearby mantle. "I'm well aware of what that award symbolizes, Will Connors, so don't think you are fooling me with your goodwill gesture. My boy does not need your help!"

Billy's entire crass demeanor changed then, and Boone, seated before the surveillance monitor noted the sorrowful look he offered Rose. "Fine, Rosie," the old Irishman said, quietly. "I was only trying to help." He switched moods then, taking on the mantle of his former gruff attitude. "Jess, I gotta go be friendly with the rest of my guests, but I'll check in with you before you leave."

Glaring at Reason, he added, "And as for you, if you so much as fart in my booth, I'll be booting your scrawny butt out my door!"

Only later did Boone and Reason find out that Billy was their grandfather, and Rose's estranged father. In Billy's checkered past of running guns and other nefarious deeds, one deed came back to haunt him. He broke away from the IRA and as a result of this, his wife was killed in a car accident in Ireland. Due to her death, Billy turned to the bottle, and Rose had wanted nothing to do with the old Irishman ever since. Rose did, however, allow her two boys to establish a relationship with the old man and though she never forgave him for her mother's death, she was cordial and polite to William Connors, the Godfather of Havelock.

And now tonight, as previously planned by Billy, Boone came down to the Emerald. He had been greeted by four boyhood friends, all members of his old boxing team, who served as Billy's bouncers. Doug "The Kid" Kaluza, Tony "The Tiger" Menefee, and Joe and Anthony Mendoza. The four had retired from the ring, but stayed on there at the Emerald as security staff. Although Boone had walked away from the MMA years before, he still stayed in touch with the four Havelock tough guys. Tall, blond-haired Doug had greeted him at the door of the pub. "Welcome, Bossman," he had said with a lop-sided grin.

Dark-haired Tiger handed him two ornate keys. He glanced down at them, finding one to have a rampant, full-maned lion on its end, while the other was adorned with the same emerald that dominated the window of the pub. The tiny gems inside the lion's eyes were blue, while the emerald was a deep green. Before Boone could examine them, the Mendoza brothers ushered him into the dining hall of the pub and seated him before the massive fireplace.

Joe Mendoza said, "As secrets go, the boys and I have had a hard time in keeping this from you, but tonight, despite Billy's mysterious absence, the Emerald Pub is being deeded over to you."

Doug pulled a chair out from the table opposite of Boone. Tiger came from the bar, carrying a bottle and two shot glasses. He placed one glass down in front of Boone, and moved around the table to place the other one before Billy's usual spot at the table. He then opened the rather ornate bottle, with a label depicting a dragon connected to a knight by the lance driven into its side.

"A shot of Dragon's Breath," Tiger said, pouring from the bottle and filling both jiggers to the brim, "to seal the deal."

Doug stared down at the golden liquid and said, "Now, although Billy's not touched a dram for over 40 years, and I know how you feel about spirits yourself, Boone, but to make this official, indulge us."

Placing the keys on the table next to the jigger, Boone stared down at the swirling gold liquid for several seconds before picking it up. Boone killed the drink, taking the liquid down in three solid gulps. He had never tasted anything like it in his life. The gold liquid stirred images that rose slowly like a fish rising sluggishly in murky waters. He saw in his mind's eye: The marble statue of a lion-man in the tall spire of a castle's tower. In his raised fist, an emerald pulsated with an inner light that sent shimmering rays shooting across a lush landscape, dappling a forest beyond with sparkling light beams.

The second swallow of the liquid stirred a second image: A silver dragon soared across a stormy sky, lightning crackling all around her outstretched wings.

The third wash of the gold liquid going down his throat produced an explosion of images: He was mounted on a black stallion. In his hand he held a glowing blue sword, and he was dressed in some sort of black leather armor with a roaring lion emblazoned on his breast. A swarm of antler-crowned warriors with fluorescent braids of hair surrounded him, and Boone raised his sword and he swung...

Boone sat his shot glass down with a solid clink!

"Fear not, Boone," Doug said. "It's not liquor, at least not as we know it here in this realm. That brew of Dragon's Breath comes from the Inn of the Howling Moon in far away Valasar. Delivered in person by Creed Blackstag, Bard Chieftain of the Order of the Lion."

He gestured at the keys. "The emerald key opens the door to the Emerald. The lion's head opens the door located in the back room of the pub. The door that lies beside the sign, which states, 'Here, there be Dragons.'"

He tossed a pen to Boone and slid the deed across the table in front of him, and said, "Sign it, my friend, and the Emerald is yours."

Silently shaking his head in disbelief, Boone signed his name to the deed.

Doug, Tiger, Anthony, and Joe shook his hand, clapped him on the back, and left, vowing they would see him tomorrow evening, serving as security staff as they had done for Billy these past several years.

6

Boone was disturbed by a rather large, heavily panting pit bull that came bounding into the Emerald. It was a beautiful dog, with black fur masking his face, and the same black fur trailing down his back, blending with his broad white chest. All four of his paws were black, as well. The dog gave him a gentle head-butt and proceeded to slobber and drool all over his pant leg as its head came to rest on his leg.

"Well," he said, rubbing behind the pit's thick neck, "nice to see you, too, Lobo. Is your master with you?"

Lobo let out an excited whine as Reason Nelson came through the front door of the pub. The bearded man sporting a long, braided ponytail, carried something in his hand. He approached the booth and placed the item on the table in front of Boone, then thought better of it as Lobo tried to snag it out from under his fingers, and he simply handed it to Boone.

"You were right," Reason said, taking a seat across from his older brother and grunting slightly as the rambunctious pit bull tried to scramble up into the booth and join him. "Manners, Lobo. Remember your manners."

Boone peered down at the black bandana in his hand. Reason proceeded to pet Lobo as he settled down beside him on the floor.

"Lobo's nose-work led me straight to Stone Holland's place. How did you figure that bandana belonged to Lucas?"

Boone said, "The bandana and the baseball bat. I just put two and two together. And it was you who told me your foster kid had quite a temper."

He paused, took another sip of his coffee, then said, "Evidently, Lucas came here for payback."

Reason asked, "Payback? This had to do with Billy sending those two gems through the portal? Gramps did involve his dad in this mess, so you think the kid came here seeking revenge?"

Boone said, "He brought a baseball bat with him for some reason, and I don't think during the wee hours, he was playing ball."

He grimaced as he said, "Granddad has been missing for two days now, and tonight I learned that he deeded the Emerald over to me."

He slid the deed across the table. Reason studied it a moment, then said, "But that doesn't answer any questions."

He looked past Boone to the oak door at the end of the hallway running back to it. "You don't think Billy went in there, do you?"

Boone turned in his seat, his gaze lingering on the doorway leading to the chamber beyond. "After all the preaching Gramps did about never opening that door? I doubt very much if he would ignore his own advice. Whatever lies beyond the 'dragon door,' I don't think Billy would seriously consider using it under any circumstances."

When Reason spoke, Boone turned back around to face him. "Even if he used it to escape a beating by the Holland clan?"

"It had crossed my mind," Boone said, solemnly.

"So," Reason said, "do you want me to track the kid down, get him alone somewhere and ask him what he was doing breaking in here, or should I put the same question to Nate?"

Boone shrugged. "Frankly, I don't know what course to take. I know Nate and the Den are a troublesome lot, but I can't see him doing anything this serious or severe. If the other clubs ever found out he'd harmed Gramps in any way, they would shut the Den down in a rapid heartbeat. They all love and respect that old Irishman. But I could see the kid coming in here to cause mischief. I know you don't want to believe it, having him in your care as a foster kid, but I don't have the same feeling about this little hot-head Lucas."

At the mention of Lucas's name, Lobo sat up straighter and gave a low whine. Reason nodded as if the dog had silently communicated with him. "Lobo, it seems, has the same opinion of the kid as I do. After all, it was Lucas who rescued my dog from his uncle Nate when he tranqued him and stole him from my yard. El Lobo thinks pretty highly of the temperamental kid."

The two sat in silence for long moments. Boone sipped at his coffee. Reason gently stroked the head of his dog, his eyes continuing to drift down the nearby hallway to the door beyond it.

Finally, he spoke. "Maybe he's in there, Boone. Maybe, against his own advice, he discovered a reason to enter the second chamber. Has he never said anything to you about what lies beyond?"

Shaking his head, Boone ran a hand through his dark, collar-length hair. "No, why would he allow you access to the place? I thought all this time, he kept it locked, barring access to both chambers beyond that door."

Reason frowned. "It's a complicated story, brother."

Boone said, "If you want me to use my investigative resources to find him, any information you might add may be critical to finding Gramps. Share away, little brother."

Reason asked, "Ever heard of virtual reality?"

"Virtual, what?" Boone asked.

Reason repeated himself: "Virtual reality. Alternative realms. All the video games you played, and you've never heard of Virtual gaming? It's the computer-generated simulation of a three-dimensional image or environment that can be interacted with in a real or physical way by a person using special electronic equipment, such as a helmet with a screen inside or gloves fitted with sensors."

"Oh," Boone said. "Yeah. Never played one myself. Guess I'm old school with Guild Wars and even Legend of Zelda."

Reason said, "The environment is similar to the real world or a Fantasy realm, creating an experience not possible in physical reality. Augmented reality systems are considered a form of VR that layers virtual information over a live camera feed into a headset giving the user the ability to view three-dimensional images. Current VR tech commonly use headsets, sometimes in combination with physical environments, to generate images, sounds, and sensations that simulate a player's presence in a virtual environment. A person using

VR equipment is able to look around the artificial world, move around in it, and interact with virtual features. The effect is commonly created by VR headsets consisting of a head-mounted display with a small screen in front of the eyes, but can also be created through designed rooms with multiple screens. VR systems that include sensations to the user through a game controller are known as haptic systems. This information is known as force feed-back in gaming apps."

Boone said, "Sounds like a cool system. But what does this have to with why Gramps is missing?"

Reason said. "Gramps discovered a way to be involved in my youth work that has just been approved by Judge Sully at juvenile court. It took a lot of legal wrangling, and case studies offered by therapists and several psychologists, as proof that it might succeed."

"Succeed?" Boone asked, his nose scrunched up, one eye showing beneath his shaggy black bangs.

7

"So," Boone posed the question, "what does juvenile court have to do with the gaming world? I thought most video games were frowned upon by therapists, psychologists, and even a lot of parents. Grand Mobile Killing Fields doesn't inspire most kids to rise to become responsible adults. Why would Judge Sully be asked to condone gaming here at the Emerald? Doesn't make sense to me."

Reason smiled. "Oh, says the private investigator who has been stealthily doing surveillance on the bad guys and rotten hombres from the sidelines. What do you really know about kids?"

Boone's laughter caused Lobo to stare curiously up at him. "All I ever wanted to know about kids, I learned from trying to stay one step ahead of my troubled little brother back in the day when you ended up with that damned key. Other than that, I know little about what makes kids tick. Only that violent video games tend to make kids more violent. That was proven during the Columbine shooting."

Nodding thoughtfully, Reason said, "All the things that plague at-risk kids is what I've been dealing with for the past ten years. Drug abuse. Teen suicide. Runaway and throw away kids. Anger and rage management. Truancy which leads to probation. Probation that leads to institutions. Institutions that lead to parole. Parole that leads to prison. These are all just endless Celtic hoops that many kids find themselves trapped in once they enroll in the juvenile court system.

"So, Gramps proposed a new program, using one kid as a test pilot to instigate a video program that not only curbs delinquent behavior, but builds self-esteem and character through leadership skills. Something new in the field of youth work."

Looking down the hallway to the oak door, Boone's eyes opened wide as he realized what Reason was now talking about. "Wait a sec," he said, "Gramps doesn't even know what this secret chamber is all about, and yet he approved of you putting a kid in there? Not even knowing what plane of existence that kid would end up on?"

Reason said, "But remember what I said about the screens? The effect is created by VR headsets consisting of a head-mounted screen, but can also be created through specially designed rooms with multiple screens. Evidently, inside the chamber are six windows, where images flash, depicting scenes from different locations of a realm."

Boone leaned forward, his muscular arms resting on the table. "You're telling me there's an alternate dimension beyond this door?"

Reason said, "I'm not sure what lies beyond that door, but based on some far-fetched story Gramps shared with me, he created a game script that aligns with the scenes that appear on those windows. He submitted it to Game Wizards, and the Grand Techs there designed a virtual reality game that can be played with the use of a headset and hand controls, connected to that room by a single cord.

"Remember when I was on probation in Judge Sully's court? Sully and I have a long history. He was really pleased when I got involved in youth work. In pitching this new VR game designed to help delinquent kids, I presented all the costs involved in the programs to help kids. Scared Straight. DARE. Big Brothers. Big Sisters. Medications. Psycho-therapy. Foster care. Group homes. Drug treatment. Confined institutions. The Juvenile Justice department spends millions each year with all of their combined programs, some that work and others that are worthless. I just proposed to Sully a method to boost a kid's self-esteem through a role-playing medium that will build leadership skills, and if the kid wins the game, to save and rescue an entire new realm. What kid wouldn't be intrigued by that?"

After speaking with Boone at the Emerald, Reason and Lobo returned home, where they found Lucas watching TV, Grunge and Goblin sprawled beside him in the den. Reason placed the base-ball bat against his desk, making certain Lucas saw it.

Purposely ignoring the bat, Lucas asked, "So, have you made a decision on which kid will test pilot the game?"

"Not you," Reason said. "You're still on probation, so not a likely candidate. Besides, during the time you've lived with me, I watched you play video games. You flipped out whenever you didn't win, and if a challenge became too overwhelming, you ended up throwing your controller against the wall. You're not the most patient gamer."

Still purposely ignoring the bat, Lucas asked, "Is it Alex then?"

Reason said, "Alex Thorn is your best friend, so maybe you can encourage him to keep his cool when he sits down behind the console tomorrow afternoon."

"Yes," Lucas said, "I can tell him not to have blow-ups like I do."

"Good," Reason said, noting that Lucas stared intently at the bat. "That would be a great help on your part. Alex will need a lot of support if I am going to make this gaming therapy a success. And yet, there is something else you could help with."

"Me?" Lucas said, squirming uncomfortably in his chair.

Reason smiled at him. "You know I told my brother, Boone, that deep down you really had a heart. He did not believe me. But I tried to convince him that my dog loved you. Always a good sign when a dog accepts you, isn't it?"

Lucas glanced over at Lobo sleeping beside Reason. He looked down to Grunge and Goblin snoozing at his feet. "Yeah. Dogs always know what's roiling around inside a person."

"That's exactly," Reason said, "what I told Boone."

Lucas went into defense mode. He was well aware of Reason's psychological Chess games he played. When living there in foster care, the long-haired youth worker was always three steps ahead of him. He couldn't get by with anything the way he outsmarted him.

Reason said, "I know you better than you know yourself. I was a conning, manipulator as a kid. I had defiance disorder. I'm surprised I lived through all the tirades I put my brother through. He wanted to pummel me senseless. I was a major brat of the worst kind. So, don't think you invented that mode to travel in, because I'm way ahead of you there, bud. You can't bullshit a bullshitter."

Lucas folded his skinny arms across his chest, shook back his shaggy, blond bangs with a quick flick of his head. "What is your brother accusing me of? Or should I just leave?"

"Leave?" Reason asked, feigning surprise. "We were just having a friendly convo about my new virtual reality game."

Lucas said, "That's to be played by Alex down at the Emerald, the pub owned by your grandpa, Billy Connors, who you know I hate with a mad-dog passion. So what's your point?"

"Ah," Reason said, forcing himself to maintain a smile, "there is that, isn't there? Question is, how bad do you hate him? He's been missing for two days."

He picked up the baseball bat. "This is yours, right?"

Lucas went into full meltdown mode, a defensive move that Reason was prepared for, for he'd seen his performance many times while fostering the volatile kid. He simply sat there as Lucas exploded out of the chair, bounded across the room, and left the den in a major huff.

All three dogs peered curiously at Reason as the back door slammed loudly.

"Damn," Reason said. "Temper, temper."

8

Alexander Thorn crept out of the alley across from the Emerald rather cautiously. After all, he was well aware of the temper of Reason's grandfather, Billy Connors. The cantankerous old Irishman had once thrown a bucket of water on him when he had sailed past the pub on the front walkway on his skateboard.

The shock of the cold water caused Alex to crash into the trash can situated near the pub's driveway, and Billy had chewed him out as he hightailed it away from the Emerald, offering the old man a one-fingered salute to show he did not appreciate the dousing.

At 14, Alex was lean and not overly tall for his age, standing at 5 feet in his socks. His long raven hair hung in tangles to his slender shoulders, and due to his mother's Cingane bloodline, he had smooth complected skin, and yet not overly dark due to his American-born father. He was a rather good-looking kid, with a rounded nose, a dimple in his chin, and large, brown raccoon eyes. Alex could have been a model for magazines, and yet he used his good looks and charm to weasel his way through the juvenile justice system, for he'd been cursed by delinquent behavior since he'd turned 11 when he first moved here to America.

It was 9PM and as he stood there in the alley, peering at the illuminated window of the Emerald directly across the street from him, Alex became even more reluctant to enter the pub. He knew he had an appointment to meet up with Reason there, but he just didn't have any desire to have a confrontation with old Billy Connors. The Irish-man's irascible nature grated on Alex's nerves. And out of respect for Reason, he didn't want to lip off to the old man, yet was sure he would, if push came to shove. It was his second encounter with the old man he was recalling when a harsh whisper drifted out of the dark alley behind him and Alex wheeled around to see who had spoken: "Alex of the Roma, a nomadic ethnic group, spread all across Europe. Romani are known as Gypsies. Not to be confused with Romanians. The term Gypsy comes from gypcian, derived from Egyptian. This title owes to the belief that the Romani were itinerant Egyptians."

Alex stood there, seeing no one. It was as if the raspy female voice came from out of thin air. There were four dumpsters lining the dark alley, with the brick walls of two adjacent buildings taking up either side of the long, dark lane running back to the end of the next block.

Slightly unnerved, he said, "Who is there?"

The voice came again: "In fact, the Gypsies of your line, Alex, were exiled from Egypt as punishment for harboring the infant Jesus during Herod's reign in Jerusalem, when he had all male infants killed to keep the prophecy of a Jewish Messiah from being fulfilled. Another title of the Romani is Cingane, derived from a Christian sect the Romani were associated with in the Middle Ages."

Alex snapped, "Show yourself!"

Soft laughter echoed between the buildings.

A chill ran down Alex's spine. He frantically searched the entire confines of the alley before him, and still could see no one.

The speaker continued: "Little Alexander, born in Wallachia, the Gypsy child of a Romani archivist and an American biker boy. His mother adopted an injured, pregnant wolf, and she had a litter of seven pups. Little Alex was in charge of those pups for the next three years, living in a Gypsy encampment of motor homes. He and his pack roamed the wilds together. Alex loved his wolves. And then his unwed mother moved here to America. Alex was eleven, and he has been struggling to find his true center ever since."

Alex said, "How do you know these things about me?"

More laughter came from somewhere down there in the darkness and shadows. Alex peered hard at each of the dumpsters. He narrowed his eyes and stared at the blackness as if willing someone to appear there. But there was no one there.

"Alex's mom," the unseen speaker said, "refused to take him back. She flew back to her homeland in Wallachia, abandoning her son, because his grandfather demanded she cut all ties with the rogue and scoundrel. The Cingane have their own system. A cat has nine lives, right? Cingane give you just so many chances to succeed. And then, if you fail, you are shunned. Grandpa Petrov ordered you shunned, didn't he?"

A tear appeared in Alex's left eye, and slowly trickled down his cheek. The words wounded him, reminding him of just what he'd lost this past year. His mother's leaving the States was a sore spot with him, one that stirred up a lot of sorrow inside him.

Angrily, he swiped at the tear track, wiping it from his face. "Okay, that's enough! Show yourself! Go on, I dare you!"

The unseen speaker said, "You best control yourself, Alex Thorn. The thing that hurts you the most will become your worst enemy, unless you control your feelings."

Control . . . my . . . feelings? Alex thought. Exactly what Reason told me last night there in the den at home in regards to being a player on this new game he designed. But how could . . .

And as he stood there, peering hard at every shadow before him there in the dark alley, he recalled the words that passed between his caseworker and Reason just before he accepted him as a foster placement several months back:

His casework, Connie, had said, "I was wondering if you might take Alex in on an emergency stay. It would not have to be permanent, simply temporary. As I understand, those two extra bedrooms of yours have been vacant for a long time. Be a dear, won't you?"

"I get it," Alex said. "You don't want me either. I failed you, too. I'm nothing but a loser."

"Failed me?" Reason said. "Failed yourself! I gave you a hundred chances to prove to Judge Sully you could comply with his attendance order. You blew all of those. Don't con me with the 'nothing but a loser' line, to make me feel sorry for you. Because I don't."

Connie offered Reason a concerned look, thinking maybe he was being too harsh on the kid. But Reason knew what he was doing. In the past, he had taken in some of the most hard-core kids. Kids who had reached the end of the line. Kids who burned everyone who had ever taken them in before. He once took in a kid who had ran away from forty-six other placements. He had remained with Reason for two years after his placement there, not running once.

In the course of ten years, he had taken in kids who had hit him, kicked him, bit him, and spat on him. Each one he saw as the one starfish he was going to make a difference with. And he did, putting up with what few foster parents in the system ever would. He endured every assault, every stab in the back, every failure those kids brought upon themselves.

And he never called it quits. Never once called a caseworker and said, "Come and get this little monster. I've had enough."

It just wasn't in his nature to quit.

"Wherever Alex lands," Connie said, "I know he has to be strictly supervised. I know of your past commitments to end-of-the-line kids, I just thought Alex would—"

"I wasn't done," Reason said. He nailed Alex with an unrelenting gaze. "You are not a loser, Alex. You've got a lot of potential, but somewhere along the way you lost hope. I tried repeatedly to give you direction, to steer you down the right path, but you sabotaged every effort I made to help you."

His words hung in the air.

Connie understood that Reason was giving Alex a chance to make his case in order to be accepted at his house, to give him one good reason why he should take him in. Alex struggled to harness his emotions. His eyes glazed over and tear streaks ran in rivulets down his face. "And now," he said, forlornly, "I've got nowhere else to go."

Reason peered into Alex's dark eyes for long moments, as if daring the kid to break such intimate eye contact. He was surprised when Alex merely started back at him, tears welling up in his eyes. Nodding as if some unspoken communication had taken place between them, Reason at last smiled. He said, "Last year, when you were assigned to me through juvenile court, I contacted your mom, hoping she would work with me. Your mom, however, shut me out, refusing to tell me anything about you. And so, I contacted your grandfather—"

"Grandpa Petrov?" Alex asked. "You called him all the way over in Wallachia?"

"Yes," Reason said. "And he asked me to do one thing."

Alex sniffled. "What was that?"

"He asked me to restore your honor."

"My honor? Then I have failed him."
"Yes, I think we both did."
He fell silent. Several minutes passed.
Reason said, "Why don't we see if we can fix that?"

9

Two luminescent orbs suddenly appeared high up on the build-ing on the left side of the alley. They were bright blue, and they appeared to be simply floating through the night air. Until Alex realized he was peering up at a pair of glowing eyes. The owner of those eyes was perched on the old rusty frame work of an ancient sign with the badly faded words, "Barber," painted on the front.

Twenty feet below the bracketing for the faded sign was a door that had been sealed off long ago, but evidently had once been open to the public for weekly haircuts by some long-dead barber who once plied his trade there in the railroad town of Havelock, keeping the rail yard crew shorn and shaved back in the day.

"Jango?" Alex said in disbelief as he looked up at the monkey-like being perched on the sign high on the side of the building.

Seated there on his haunches, the small, spindly black creature sprang to his feet and performed a spin. Alex watched the demon-monkey scuttle to the end of the sign, leap off its bracketing, and nimbly scamper down the building, finding hidden finger and toe-holds in and amongst its bricks. The bald-headed, big-eared little acrobat landed on bare feet on the pavement close to the sidewalk where Alex stood. Never quite sure of the monkey thing's intent, Alex took two wary steps back and away from the grinning creature.

Jango plopped himself down at the mouth of the alley. He turned his small head to the left and right, searching the street for traffic. But there were no cars coming down either side of the avenue at the late night hour. He blinked again, his large blue eyes reminding Alex of the eyes of an owl. It suddenly occurred to him who had been speaking to him. He was totally confused, however, at just exactly where she was hidden at all the time she had been speaking. "Celeste?" he said, "what is this all about? Why did you tell me all those things?"

Jango blinked his large eyes and glanced over one bony shoulder as Celeste appeared behind him, seeming to slip from the shadows. At the look of surprise on Alex's face, her laughter rang out in the confined space between the two buildings.

She then said, "To prep you for the gaming session taking place over there in the Emerald tomorrow, young Alexander Thorn. I was told you needed a nudge on a subject that might needle you. I was told to push the matter in order to trigger off your mad emotions. I would say, I did a good job at that, right?"

She stood there, dressed in leathers, looking like a Vampire Mistress all clad in black. Her short raven hair gave her a boyish look, but nothing could tamp down the catlike glare in her she-lion gaze. In the hollow of her throat was the tattoo of a stag, its great spread of antlers connecting with tattoos of twin wolves creeping up either side of her neckline, their snarling mouths both ending evenly below her jaw line. Alex could have sworn the stag and the wolves moved, both intricate tattoos slightly flickering beneath her pale skin.

Celeste Holland was a force of nature and older sister to Lucas, and between the ages of 13 and 17 she had been a troubled delinquent with a severe addiction problem. Alex knew that Reason Nelson had pulled out every stop in his youth work arsenal, to save her from herself. But in the end, he had written her off. That was the story Celeste told about her relationship with him being her truancy tracker, but the truth was, in order to keep her from heading down the road of self-destruction, Reason had signed the paperwork to get her admitted to the treatment program in Omaha, which changed her life.

Although Celeste still carried a grudge against Reason for performing the intervention that resulted in her admittance to the treatment program, she did admit that his interference had saved her life. She was now determined to see that her little brother did not follow in her footsteps. She had made that very clear to Alex the first time she'd met him, when she threatened to put his lights out if she ever caught him giving Lucas drugs.

Celeste said, "In order to win this game, you must master your emotions. You were not the first choice to be first player."

Slightly annoyed with the gibberish she was spewing, Alex said, "I wish you would make sense, instead of speaking in these stupid riddles. I still don't get why you had to bring up all that stuff about my history. My life is hard enough without reminding me. Besides, who else was Reason considering being the player?"

A burst of laughter came from Celeste. "Not Reason. He chose you. No, no, the old man. He wanted to put Lucas in the hot seat. Lucas was old Billy's choice to be first player."

Consternation placing a furrow in his brow, Alex said, "Why not? I mean, weren't they just looking for some kid to use as a guinea pig for this project? Lucas has probably played way more video games than me, so why not him?"

Celeste said, "Little Luke is a whirlwind of rage, a soul in turmoil, and not easily tamed. If they hooked him up to the censor meter, the needle would go into the red-rage mode, if things did not go his way. Games are not often a friend to little spoiled brats, and you and I both know, Little Luke is a powder keg just waiting to explode."

Alex looked across the street at the stained-glass window of the Emerald. "Meter?" he asked. "Hooked up to a meter? Is there more to this game than just sitting in a chair and putting on the headset?"

Celeste shrugged. "You shall see, won't you? Go. Go now. There is one who awaits your arrival inside the pub. He shall explain things to you better than I could."

Jango came to his feet. He used one hand to shoo Alex across the street, and in unison with his gesture, Celeste said, "Go, now."

Alex peered down at the monkey creature and Jango opened his mouth wide, showing his rows of sharp white teeth. He angrily hissed, causing Alex, who did not trust the little beast in the first place, to quicken his pace as he crossed the street.

As he pulled open the door to the Emerald, shrill laughter echoed up and down the avenue, but when he looked back to the alley, Celeste and Jango were gone, disappeared into the night.

10

Boone Nelson greeted Alex as he entered the dark pub. They'd met once before at Reason's house when Alex had first moved in, but the two had never even spoken to each other. Alex had heard from Reason that his older brother now owned the Emerald, and as such, had retired from youth work. Reason claimed it was Boone who taught him everything he knew about working with at-risk kids. After all, his older brother had to put up with his own behavior disorders all through Reason's childhood.

Boone appeared against the backdrop of the pub's huge fireplace, where green Christmas lights illuminated the heads of the seven stags, their wires entwined within their antlers. Alex noted he was taller than Reason, and wore his dark hair at collar-length. He was dressed in black jeans and a black Harley T-shirt, and Alex's eyes were drawn to his muscular forearms. Reason had once told him his brother had walked away from a career in the Mixed Martial Arts. And yet, it looked like Boone could handle himself in most situations.

"Sorry," he said, with a grim smile, "Reason's searching for our grandfather. He's been missing for two days. The Holland clan—"

"No," Alex said, not meaning to interrupt him. "Not Lucas. It ain't in him to do such a thing. But Nate? He's a different story."

Boone ushered him over to a nearby booth. "That is why Reason and Beef Tory are over at the Holland's confronting the Den about the matter. They purposely left me out of their meeting, due to a former altercation I had with Nate."

Taking the seat Boone offered him at the table, Alex said, "Yes, I heard about that. Something to do with him coming in here promoting a dog fight. I heard you sent him to the ER that night."

Boone said, "You shouldn't believe everything you hear. But yes, it's on account of my tussle with Nate that Reason didn't want me to join them at the Den's clubhouse tonight. Somehow our grandfather got himself crossways with the Elder's Den."

He crossed the floor to the bar, retrieved two bottles of cold pop from the fridge, and returned to the booth, handing one to Alex. "As ex-vice president of the Outlaws, Reason is appealing to the Den to tell him what they know about where gramps is. If they don't get this resolved, my dad, Rain Nelson, is going to be at war with the Den. And there will be blood."

Alex opened the bottle and took a deep swig. He belched softly and listened as Boone said, "Did my brother ever tell you our family history? Reason and Beef Tory are former members of the Outlaws, a club run by my dad, Rain Nelson. Beef quit the club years ago when Rain went to prison on trumped-up murder charges of a crooked cop. Evidently, some judge took another look at the case, and when Rain was released from prison, he asked both to rejoin the club, but Reason, a youth worker, and Beef, a detective, were no longer interested. So, Rain took on a new cause. He and a scattering of his disbanded club started breaking up dog fights in Nebraska, Kansas, and Iowa. And last week, when Ben Black Bull asked for help out at Wounded Arrow, Rain called on the Outlaws, Elder's Den, American Vets, and the Eagles to help stop that whacked-out extremist from killing US service dogs sheltered at the dog rescue ranch. The attack on service dogs was stopped, but Waziri vanished, and God only knows where he's gone to ground at now."

Alex asked, "What if Nate and the Den had nothing to do with Billy gone missing?"

Staring across the table at him, Boone drank from his own bottle of soda and remained silent, his eyes fixed on Alex.

Alex gestured at the wooden plaque situated beneath the seven deer heads mounted above the fireplace. He said, "Reason mentioned that Billy had ties with the Irish Republican Army back in the day. Maybe Billy's old crew came to pay him a visit."

"No," Boone said. "Billy's cut his ties with the Sinn Fian years ago. It would be an ancient grudge if the Irish came calling. I am thinking we are on the right trail with the Den as our prime suspects."

Alex tore his gaze from the bullet riddled plaque given to Billy by the IRA back when he was running guns for the Troubles. His eyes meeting Boone's, he refused to look away as he said, "Check Lucas off your list. He had nothing to do with why your grandpa is missing. The hot-headed little maniac is my best friend, and I would know if he'd harmed Billy. I know about the baseball bat he left behind here at the pub two nights ago. He meant to use the bat on the Emerald's front window. He came down here to smash that window to pieces. But…"

"But," Boone said, "Billy stopped him, took away his bat, and simply sent him on his way? Is that what you're telling me?"

Holding up one finger, gesturing at Boone to hold that thought, Alex reached inside his black leather jacket, fumbling with an item tucked inside the inner pocket of the coat. "The last Lucas saw of old Billy," he said, drawing a rolled-up leather map out of his pocket, "is him talking to two little leprechauns inside of that room."

He gestured at the oak door at the end of the hallway with his free hand, then continued, "I was a bit baffled when I heard about Lucas seeing dragons, wolves, and some lion-dude, who with a whiff of his paws, sent some demon lord backwards into some hidden void. When Lucas told me about it, I said he was loony and loopy."

Alex scooted the leather map across the table to Boone. "He swore what he saw in that chamber had nothing to do with the virtual reality game that Reason designed. The sappy-headed boy claimed he was teleported to another world. He swore he was chased there by your grouchy old grandpa, peeved at him for trespassing into the Emerald."

Boone spread the map out on the table between them, moving his soda bottle aside as he studied the images of forests, castles, rivers, towns, and lakes scattered across the face of the leather map. "Valasar?" he read at the bottom of the drawing. "Where did you get this?"

"Lucas," Alex said, "nabbed it out of a hobbit hole."

He laughed, pointed a finger at his head, crossed his eyes, and said, "Loony and loopy. Despite all of this planning and preparation for me to be the test pilot for Reason's new VR game, evidently Billy wanted Lucas to be first to try this game, not me like Reason wanted."

Boone shook his head in disbelief. He pointed to the right of the map spread between them. There, sat a small black box with an armband attached to it by a series of wires. "Why would gramps want to interfere in Reason's careful planning for his game? I mean, that is why you two came here tonight, right? So, he could connect you to the machine that would gauge your emotions, to actually test the limits of your temperament in order to get the best results possible for when you actually play the game. From all that I've heard about Lucas he becomes enraged when gaming doesn't go his way. He would blow that needle all the way into the red, and the judge, the therapist, and the psychologist who are overseeing this project would deem Rea-son's virtual game a failure. He has to prove that it changes a kid for the better, not the worst.

"Even as contrary as Billy is, he wants Reason's game to succeed, not fail. Your temperament is why you were chosen to be the test pilot. We may have to cancel the initial launch of the game if gramps doesn't return by tomorrow afternoon."

Taking another sip out of his soda bottle, Alex swallowed, then pointed down the long hallway to the door.

"What if he's in there," he said, seriously, "with the dragons?"

11

As Celeste neared the far end of the alley just off of Havelock Avenue, Jango let out a hiss of warning as a band of small, cloaked and hooded figures came at them from out of the shadows. He sprang forward, slashing his way into the band of black-cloaked figures, his razor-sharp talons taking out the first four warriors known as the Naz as they made to attack Celeste.

The stag tattooed on her neck came alive. The luminescent stag launched itself through the air, raking its glistening antlers to the right and left as it plowed into the black mass of hooded Naz who came directly at Celeste in a mad rush. The twin wolf tattoos on her neck crackled and came to life. The two scintillating beasts howled wildly as they careened into a dozen of the impish warriors armed with fiery blades that crackled as angry flames curled down their swords.

Celeste drew her twin short swords from sheaths hidden beneath her long, black duster. Both blades shimmered with an inner violet light, a sparkling purple light that traveled up and down the twin swords, brightly illuminating the band of hooded figures.

Going on defense, Celeste parried over a dozen sword strokes delivered by the swarm of warriors, and although the Naz were well-trained bladesmen, they did not stand a chance against Celeste when she switched to offense. With wild loops of her swords, she cut them down one-by-one, her guardian beasts serving as distractions, while she ran the Naz through with her whirling, twirling blades.

The last Naz to survive the assault was subdued by Jango, who looped an arm around the warrior's throat and yanked off his hood, revealing the creature's frog-like face. The Naz struggled briefly, trying to break free of Jango's hold, but Celeste slid her left hand blade beneath his chin, saying, "Why have the Nazarawnee broken the laws of Valasar and crossed the boundary between the realms? Answer me, and I will give you a swift death. Answer me not, and I shall bind you and turn you over to the White Council."

The frog-faced Naz spat at her, and a fraction of a second later, it cried out in pain as Jango slashed his claws down one side of his yellow-skinned face, leaving four deep wounds that bled black blood.

Celeste used the tip of her sword, tapping it beneath its chin. "You will answer my questions, Naz! Or answer to the Council!"

At the mention of the Council, the Naz hissed, "We were on the hunt. King's Blood. Gypsy Blood. It is strong with he who was just here with you. He needed to be stopped from crossing through."

"Alex?" Celeste said in confusion. "Yes, I know of his Cingane Gypsy heritage, but what do you mean by King's Blood?"

The Naz threw back its bald head and cackled. "The line of the Lion Lords of Valasar, that is his destiny. If he is allowed into the realm, he will restore the fallen Wizard-Warriors of Kallador. We were sent to see that did not happen."

"Who," she snapped, "sent you?"

The Naz closed his gaping mouth, slowly closed his yellow eyes, and silently shook his head. Standing there contemplating its words, Celeste glanced over at the luminescent stag at her left shoulder. The spirit-beast stared back at her silently, giving a shake of his antler-crowned head. Tracers of green scintillating light marked its majestic form. Celeste looked to her right, where the twin wolves sparkled with a bluish light. They, too, stared silently at her.

Her eyes traveled over to Jango, and the monkey creature grinned wickedly at her as he held up his claws, black demon blood trailing from them. She quickly made up her mind then, and drove her left hand sword directly into the Naz's chest. "I kept my promise, didn't

I?" she said, almost sadly.

Just before it passed, the Naz whispered, "My thanks."

Inside of the Emerald, Boone said, "This map is not part of Reason's game. Wherever Lucas found this, it wasn't created as a prop for the VR game. It looks very realistic."

Suddenly, they both looked toward the Emerald's stained-glass window to see bright flashes of light flickering beyond the colored panes. Alex leaped to his feet, saying, "What in holy hell is that?"

As Boone came to his feet, still staring in curiosity at the brightly flickering bars of green and red lights coming from the alley across the street from the pub, Billy's ornate cane slid out from under the table and thumped on the floor at his feet. He snatched it up, hoping it would make for a good weapon if he needed it once they went out-side to investigate the strange bursts of what looked like lightning sizzling and dancing in the air.

Neither he nor Alex were prepared for the sword fight they witnessed as Celeste took the fight to the swarm of small swordsmen. As they made their way across the street, they heard her questioning the last survivor of the duel, both skidding to a stop as she drove her glowing sword into the small fellow's chest, both clearly horrified by the ruthless act on Celeste's part.

A moment later, the wardings of the stag and the wolves returned and melded into her neck and chest, becoming simply tattoos once more. She had just turned to Jango when the boy lunged at her from the shadows. The boy was young, slim of build, and appeared to be a fifteen-year-old kid. He had long red hair, worn in three braids that fell past his slender shoulders. He wore tight-fitted leather armor and gauntlets that covered his wrists and connected to fingerless gloves on his hands. In each hand, he gripped the hilts of twin ornate daggers. One glowed a bright red, the other pulsed with green light.

A maniacal glare came to his brown eyes as he raised both daggers in a threatening gesture, the blades aimed at Celeste's back. He lunged and there came a soft thumping sound as Boone Nelson struck the kid with his granddad's ornate cane he'd evidently left behind him when he departed from this world two nights past.

Boone attacked him without warning. The dragon-head serving as a handgrip came down hard on the attacking kid's head, and he groaned and slumped to the ground, his twin daggers clattering on the bricks of the alley beside him. Celeste wheeled around, whipping her right hand blade up and planting it beneath Boone's chin with all intent and purposes to take out another enemy. She stopped herself at the last possible second, applying just enough pressure with her blade to cause Boone to gasp and rise up on the tips of his toes. The green blade illuminated the surprised features of his face, and as she looked directly into his blue eyes, he grinned rather sheepishly at her and said, "Hello."

Still heated up from the battle she'd just waged against a dozen crafty foes intent on killing her, her angry gaze drifted down to the fallen boy and his two glowing daggers.

"He's Boone," Alex said, coming up behind them and looking down in amazement as one-by-one the slain Naz warriors vanished with loud hisses! "He's Reason's older brother, Celeste. And he just saved your life."

Frowning in embarrassment, Celeste sheathed her swords. "I'm sorry. I did not mean to alarm you. Of course, I've seen you many times before, coming and going to Reason's house. I am Celeste Holland, one of your brother's failed projects."

Boone raised his brows, looking from the tatts on her neck and chest. "I would say you are one of my brother's most unique projects. Could you explain to me what this is all about? Jawas attacking you with fiery swords. Green stag and blue wolves defending you. This Gollum-like creature doing the same. And now, this kid assassin with the glowing daggers. Just what in the hell is this all about?"

Before she could explain any of this to him, the slender reed of a kid with the three red braids came to and sat up. He looked directly at Alex and snarled. "You are the boy with the King's Blood I was sent here to eliminate! I wielded tokens of power to do that, stolen from the hoard of the dragon, Drakvoren, hidden for many years in the Suncast Peaks! You need to die, Mage Lord!"

Alex's eyes filled with alarm. He asked, "What is this King's Blood you speak of? And Mage Lord?"

"Yes!" snapped the boy, rising to his feet. "In a realm where magic is outlawed, only the outlaws shall wield magic! You belong to the Line and the House of Erin, the keep of Rockhaven, from where the King's

Company hails. Accept your fate, and allow me to extinguish your flame and send you to the High One in the Beyonder Realm."

Alex said, "What drugs are you on? House of Erin? Rockhaven Keep? What the holy hell is your deal, kid?"

The red-haired boy heatedly declared, "I am Hunter Synn, son of Cain Synn, warlord of Mint, the Elven kingdom in the Whispering Timber! As his son, I am destined to wipe out wizards and warlocks, and any and all who trifle with magic."

He snatched up one of his daggers and lunged at Alex bringing his blade up for a downward slice. Alex expected to die in the next few seconds. He knew the blade could easily inflict a mortal wound. Hunter Synn was in full-blown attack mode and about to unleash a savagery on him.

Suddenly, Hunter cried out, his features contorted in bafflement as Jango leaped up, placing him in a sleeper hold, and the would-be assassin sent here to kill the one with King's Blood, crumpled and fell to the ground unconscious.

12

Celeste spoke quietly to Boone as the two of them sat before the fireplace back inside the Emerald. "My entire life changed on the night I came down here seeking your grandfather's help in keeping my brother's dog, Grunge, safe from my Uncle Nate. Billy assured me he would be having words with Nate. He then invited me into the pub, where I walked through the door of his dragon room to end up at a Gypsy camp, with motor homes and painted wagons.

"I was greeted by a tall, dark-haired man who introduced himself as the Cingane Chieftain of this particular clan. The man took one look at Grunge and friended him. I fell asleep next to an open camp-fire. When I woke up, by the faint glow of the smoldering fire, I could see Grunge resting peacefully nearby. However, the entire encampment of Gypsies was gone. I then spotted the most wicked tattoo I've ever seen in my life!"

She paused to take a sip of her soda, then continued her story.

"In a nearby river, I saw the reflection of the moonlit waters. I actually gasped when I saw the tattoos left on my throat and neck. The stag in the hollow of my throat had antlers that created the twin wolves that snaked up on either side of my neck. The wide-antlered stag held a fierce gaze in his dark eyes, and the two wolves were facing sideways, their lips locked in mid-howl. It was a fascinating piece of work, and yet I had no memory of the ink being applied. I simply woke up, sort of in a daze. Jango perched on my shoulder and said, 'The Chieftain said those tattoos are talismans that will come to life when you most desperately need them.'

"A voice came from beneath the trees beside the river: 'It is your destiny. You were called to this long before you were born. If you want to blame it on anyone, the Star Children played a big part in not only losing the Lionstone, but the Star Fire crystal, as well.'

"Your granddad, Billy Connors stepped out of the blackness there, and asked, 'Will you become a new Keeper of the Flame?'

"Billy said, 'Our hometown of Havelock is known amongst the White Council, the Tuatha De Dannan, the Unseen Court, the Sidhe, and the Web of the Wise. In our small suburb are Way stations you will need in order to be the Guardian of your little brother. He said their power would be revealed if Molech ever found us.'"

She stopped, her story ended. She looked at Boone, expecting a barrage of questions.

But he simply sat there, a look of bewilderment on his face.

Seated beside Celeste in the booth, Jango affectionately embraced her, wrapping his skinny arms around her. Celeste smiled down at the black-furred Mogrim and patted him gently on his bald head. Jango purred like a kitten.

Finally, Boone said, "Molech? As in the Canaanite god who demanded child sacrifices?"

Celeste nodded. "Yep, the very one. And his sidekick, Baphomet. Both are now revived and wandering around this world."

"Incredible," Boone said.

To which she replied, "More like a colossal tragedy."

Beef Tory and Reason's meeting with the Elder's Den did not go smoothly. The moment Beef presented the wooden baseball bat Lucas had left behind in the pub two nights past, Nate Holland was less than pleased. When Reason flat out accused the Den of having something to do with his grandfather's mysterious disappearance, the two of them knew they'd made a mistake coming to the Den's council table. Ten members of the club sat across from them, glaring at them. Reason had suggested they meet with Gypsy in private outside of the Den's clubhouse. He did not call the meeting to have a fight. He just wanted answers as to where Billy Connors had disappeared to. Gypsy, after all, had once ridden in his dad's club the Outlaws, and with Beef being former warlord, Reason figured the raven-haired biker would show him respect by hearing him out.

Thirty minutes into the meeting, Nate threatened to come across the table and deal out violence to the two outsiders who dared sit at their council table and accuse them of harming the old Irishman. It was then that Lucas barged into the barn there in the Holland's backyard, Grunge and Goblin trailing behind him.

"Sit your butt down, Uncle Nate!" Lucas said, snapping his fingers and pointing at the empty chair directly behind Nate.

When Nate continued to come around the table, offering Beef and Reason a menacing glare, Lucas said, "Grunge."

And the big Brindle pit bull cut Nate off from getting any farther in his pursuit of assaulting the two outsiders. Grunge planted himself directly in front of the biker, and growled softly.

Nate looked to the head of the table at Gypsy. "I would like to know," he said, "why he left his bat inside the Emerald."

Gypsy, who had once won a Tommy Flanagan look-alike contest down at the Trainyards pub, fixed a stern glare on Lucas. "Yes, Little Luke," he growled, irritably, "tell us how these two men ended up with your baseball bat."

Stepping up beside Grunge, Lucas faced Gypsy, trying not to flinch. "Billy Connors insulted my dad. Remember the last time that old man insulted dad? Uncle Nate said we ought to shoot out his colored humongous window? You know, with his .357?"

Gypsy and Nate both remained cold-stone sober as Beef looked across the table at them, not at all surprised by Lucas's information. Neither biker said anything as Lucas continued.

"Well," he said, placing his left hand on Grunge's head, "I knew better than to destroy such an expensive window, knowing that stained glass must have cost gobs and gobs, and so I—"

"Luke," Gypsy said, interrupting him, "if you incriminate yourself before these two men, you will pay in more ways than one. Understand what I'm saying, kid?"

Lucas swallowed hard, yet managed to nod. "Yes. Yes, sir. See the reason my bat ended up with Old Man Connors is, I was in back of the Emerald, on his loading dock, smashing cases of beer with my bat to pay him back for insulting dad. Billy caught me smashing his beer bottles, and I dropped my bat and ran for it!"

Slowly, Gypsy closed his eyes, sighing in frustration.

Despite his living in foster care with Reason, Lucas felt no loyalty to him, especially since his grandfather had crossed the Den. He liked Reason, for he'd been kind to him while living at his house, but his first loyalty was to his dad. He had no way of telling Gypsy and Nate that Billy had transported the gems containing the imprisoned souls of two fire gods over to the Valley of Kings, where his dad had been on a quest to find Waziri. If he told his uncle the farfetched story about Molech and Baphoment being conjured by Waziri, Nate would demand he take a drug test. Or commit him to the looney bin.

If he could, however, convince Nate that he'd been paying old Billy back for insulting his dad, they would be proud of him. And breaking beer bottles sure sounded better than actually failing to shatter the stained-glass window. It was a lie he was most willing to tell, if it got Reason off his case over the disappearance of the Irishman.

Beef narrowed his eyes, staring directly at Lucas standing not three feet away. "So, you didn't assault Billy? Not even by accident?"

"No!" Nate said. "What do you take my nephew for, Tory? He wouldn't have hurt the old man. He knows better. We all know better. We'd have retribution from seven clubs down on our heads if we touched the Irishman. That's why we can hardly believe you're sitting here accusing us of doing the old man harm."

Reason leveled his gaze upon Lucas. "So, last night on the loading dock of the Emerald, Billy caught you smashing beer bottles with your bat. And he what? Just took it away from you?"

Turning his head slightly so he could face his foster parent, Lucas nodded slowly. "Yes. Sort of. See, I slipped and fell when he came out onto the dock, screaming like an Irish banshee. Billy scared me so bad, I tripped and fell, dropped my bat, and then tore out of there as if the hounds of hell were nipping at my heels!"

He paused, refusing to break his stare down with Reason. He then cleared his throat and added, "Billy was alive and well, and madder than hell, when I left him. Swear to God. Swear on my dead mother."

"Luke?" Nate gruffly growled. "Enough of that!"

Looking admonished, Lucas said, "Okay, sorry, Uncle Nate. But since Reason is convinced that old Billy's vanishing act happened because the Den had something to do with it, I thought I would clear this up by telling the truth of what actually happened."

Looking to Beef, Nate said, "You satisfied? Is the Den in the clear on the missing Irishman?"

Beef said, "We're through here."

He looked beside him to Lucas and softly said, "Thanks for the explanation, Lucas. Guess we owe you an apology."

Gypsy raised one eyebrow casually as Reason turned to him and said, "Sorry we caused such a stir here, Gypsy."

Nodding at him, Gypsy said, "What was the insult? How did Billy insult your dad, Little Luke?"

Lucas froze. If he cringed or showed the slightest hesitation in giving Gypsy a believable answer, he was toast. Not only in trouble with the Den, but he would lose the trust Reason had placed in him since coming to live in foster care with him.

"The foster care thing," Lucas said. Looking around the council table at the members of the Den. "Billy said that dad wasn't a very good dad. He said that I'd been in three different placements since him and mom had that fight at the lake. First, the Yardleys, then Ben, and now with Reason. On account of me being in so many homes, Billy said dad was a loser."

He paused, his nostrils distorted for a touch of believability, and said, "I couldn't just let that go now, could I?"

13

Inside the Emerald, Alex sat at the table situated before the pub's large fireplace. Reason had arrived only a few minutes ago, and though he made Alex feel good about showing up there as he'd asked him to, he seemed distracted as he set up the gaming devices needed in order to play the VR game.

Boone mentioned his angry prisoner. In keeping with his role as a private investigator, he had handcuffed Hunter Synn and settled him on a chair in the storeroom. After listening to Boone's account of his attempted attack on Celeste and Alex, Reason called Beef to arrest the dangerous kid and escort him to the detention center. He certainly couldn't set him loose on the streets of Havelock, not after his bizarre behavior. While Boone went to check on the red-headed kid, Celeste and Jango sat in a booth near the pub's fireplace, both curiously watching Reason hook Alex up to the gaming apparatus.

"This is just a test run," Reason explained to Alex as he handed him a headset fashioned of shiny leather. "We just want to gauge your mood during play, and test your ability to keep your cool during some of the most challenging quests. Those boss fights will be the trickiest. If I made them too easy, you'd get bored. If I made them too hard, you might never want to play the game again. But if—"

"So," Alex said, interrupting him, "is Lucas in the clear on this Billy Connors thing?"

Knowing that Celeste, too was concerned about her little brother, Reason said, "Maybe," as he handed Alex a silver torc, which he placed around his neck. It was fashioned with Celtic runes around its length and made to resemble the torcs worn by Irish chieftains. He next handed him leather gauntlets attached to fingerless gloves. Alex slipped them on and flexed his fingers, tapping one gauntlet with a finger and then reaching up to touch the torc.

Reason handed him a long, leather case. "The torc serves as the mood meter, gauging your emotions as you face each challenge. The gauntlets are laced with super-sensitive electrodes which enhance any movements you make during game play. And this?"

He stepped back as Alex reached inside the leather case and withdrew a jewel-encrusted long sword, complete with a red leather hilt. Alex gave it a few test swings, and the metal blade whooshed through the air, very much resembling a real sword.

"Psychologists," Reason told him, "wanted more fluff added to the game, so they suggested a magic wand or a rod of power in order for you to subdue enemies inside the game. But Gramps ruled out, and therefore, we ended up with a nice slice-and-dice sword."

"Doesn't that," Celeste said from her place in the booth, "border on the violence all these experts are complaining about? Bloody guts and swords?"

Reason said, "Cain did not kill his brother with a sack of fluffy feathers. And the pen might be mightier than the sword but Goliath was not killed by David with a pen. No battle was ever won without blood and guts. So, Gramps compromised. Whenever the game calls for sword work to overcome an obstacle or defeat a boss, the end result is sparkle dust. All enemies are filled with sparkling dust, and once Alex skewers them, they explode in a burst of purple sparkles. Gramps jokingly suggested the enemies burst with Skittles, but game designers shot that down, saying Skittles was already a trademarked candy, therefore it would have been a copyright infringement."

Celeste stared at him. "Skittles? You're kidding, right?"

Reason laughed. "Here," he said, handing Alex the last item in his gaming arsenal. It was a pair of VR glasses, that resembled the round-lensed glasses popular in the Steam Punk world. "Those will light up your world and take virtual to the next level. Carefully, snap them into place on the headband, and slip them over your eyes."

As Alex busied himself with the items he had been handed, Reason walked over to the game console situated on a table ten feet behind Alex. He gave a few gentle tugs on a cable attached to the gaming box. The black cable ran from the console, down the hallway, and directly in through the door which had been opened just a crack to access the chamber beyond.

"This is the lifeline," Reason told Alex. "This is the cable that is hooked up to Billy's dragon room, the place where all the bells and whistles are infused into the game."

He paused, before adding, "Collin Young and I snuck in there one day when we were kids. What we saw in those six windows is what gave him the idea for this game. He's been toying with this whole concept for the past ten years. It took Collin Young and a team of geeks three more years to design and place the concepts within the parameters of a game."

Celeste asked, "Where is Collin now days? I heard he won some prestigious awards for game designs, and moved off to Callie to pursue his dream."

"Yes," Reason told her, tweaking the console for a brief round of game play. "He's known in gaming circles as the White Wizard, a title which amuses him, Nerd that he is. Collin always did march to the beat of a different drummer. He will certainly win another award if this game is successful."

Alex turned around in his chair, headset in place, gauntlets on, and sword in hand. He peered at Reason through the round lenses of the VR glasses he wore, and said, "What do I get for being the very first player? Super Geek of the Year award?"

"Hopefully," Reason said, grinning, "you shall be transformed."

Fortunately, Alex got what Reason was saying. He knew from being a client in his truancy program this past year that Reason was determined as a youth worker to change, restore, and encourage kids in his path by any means possible. Alex had read all of his books, each one action-packed thrillers that had an underlying message that empowered troubled kids, inspiring them to make the best of their lives, to turn negative situations into positive ones, and to build the self-esteem of even the lowliest of his readers. Alex knew from late-night talks with the man, that Reason had grown up on the mean streets of Havelock with his own behavior problems.

At 10, Reason had been diagnosed with defiance disorder, ADHD, and anger management issues. At 12, he'd landed his first probation sentence with juvenile court for breaking into the Emerald pub, several years before he even knew it belonged to his grandfather. Ironically, Billy Connors had demanded that the cops perform drug testing on his two young burglars, Reason Nelson and Vince Patrick, and the two kids had tested positive for THC.

As Reason had shared with Alex all of his kidhood antics, he had said for all the things he put Boone and his mom through, he was lucky to still be alive. Reason claimed every thing Boone knew about his own youth work, he'd learned from dealing with him. In fact, some of his major outbursts had instilled in Boone a stubborn determination to never give up on him.

And now, Reason had taken the same stance and was driven by the same never-give-up attitude. Alex had seen this drive in action when watching Reason deal with him, and especially Lucas, who could push anyone's buttons and drive them over the edge.

Transformation is exactly what Reason and his grandfather hoped this new virtual reality game inspired in troubled kids, and Alex's own self-esteem was bolstered by the fact that Reason had chosen him to be the first test pilot of his creation.

He sat back, sighed quietly, and prepared to be transformed.

14

It was the howl that set Alex's feet to running. It came from the misty woods behind him, a high-pitched, wavering howl that caused his eyes to water and his mouth to go dry.

Alex flicked his scraggly black bangs out of his eyes and peered hard into the trees behind him. Silvery clouds of undulating mist drifted among the black trees like luminous dragon's breath, shimmering in some places, yet sparkling with bursts of light in others.

The howl came again. It was closer this time.

Alex picked up speed, his slender legs carrying him down the trail leading away from the woods. As he ran his unruly tangles of hair trailed over his shoulders, while the tails of his long black duster fanned out behind him like a set of wings. The fear coursing through him spurred him on to run like the wind, while the sword he carried remained sheathed at his side.

An answering howl erupted from the trees to his right. The copse of fir trees was some distance away, still he could see dark shapes beneath shadowy branches. They ran. Staying within the tree line. Yet keeping pace with Alex. He saw brief glimpses of pointed ears. Long snouts. Green glints of narrowed eyes. Vapor trails leaking from open mouths. They were beasts on the hunt. And he was the prey.

Alex risked a quick look behind him. Flickering flashes of emerald shot out from beneath the trees. He blinked and realized they were the luminous green eyes of a dozen black beasts streaking toward him.

Wolves! Alex thought. But not wolves of Wallachia! I sense no friendliness in these beasts.

He slid down an embankment, and in the darkness almost plunged into the swift flow of the river separating him from the distant bank twenty feet away. He skidded to the very edge of the narrow river, tottering there five feet from the black waters racing past him into the woodlands. Fallen leaves crackled behind him. Twigs snapped, as well. He turned his head to watch as the pack of dark beasts gathered on the berm above him, emerald eyes fixed on him, menace in their gazes. Fierce growls came from them. In unison, they bulked up their massive shoulders, hunched their back legs beneath them, and pre-pared to launch themselves over the berm and down to the river bank.

The opposite bank was too far. If Alex leaped he would land in the middle of the swift flow, cold waters closing over his head. When he surfaced, he would have to swim madly for the distant shore as wolves splashed into the waters around him.

He glanced back one last time. The emerald eyes of each beast served to illuminate their bulky bodies, and what Alex saw caused his breath to come out in one ragged gasp. Where he expected to see thick patches of black fur, he saw roiling clouds of pitch-black smoke curling around within the framework of each beast.

They were not wolves at all, but some hybrid created of shimmering black vapors. And yet, they had vampire-like fangs protruding from both upper and lower jaws, and looked capable of tearing him to pieces.

The words escaped his lips before he could stop them, and Alex gasped, "Demon wolves!"

A quiet voice came from his immediate left: "An apt name for them, but in this realm of Valasar they are known as sleeth. They hail from the Vale of Shadows, and are a cross between demon and wolf."

Alex looked down to see a long-haired woodland imp stepping in between him and the smoky wolf-beings now coming down the riverbank. The small fellow stood three feet tall. He was dressed in black leather slacks and sleeveless vest, which revealed his bare arms and the tattoo of a snarling lion covering his right shoulder, while a dragon wound itself down from his left shoulder, the tips of both wings coming together to create a Celtic knot-work at his wrist.

The raven-haired imp glanced back at Alex, revealing a tattoo of a rampant wolf on his right temple and part of his cheek. Fierce blue eyes nailed Alex as the small warrior snapped, "Stand back, lad, lest I cut you with my blades!"

He reached over his shoulders in a cross-draw, sliding twin short swords out of weather-worn leather sheaths hanging down his back. The two swords he wielded were two feet of shimmering steel. The luminous blades reminded Alex of sunlight shining through green leaves, for up and down their lengths the blades sparkled with tiny pricks of bright emerald light.

The pack of advancing sleeth reached the bottom of the incline. Alex asked, "Are you a leprechaun?"

"Quiet, lad!" hissed the wee warrior. "I'll need my wits about me once they close for the kill!" In much lighter tones, he added, "Not leprechaun. Simply a Chaykin."

Alex whispered, "A what?" And then he looked on in total amazement as the small swordsman hurtled forward into the ranks of the charging beasts, his shining blades raised above the flying locks of his black hair.

The Chaykin danced. It was not so much a battle of swinging, hacking, slashing, and chopping, but instead a series of graceful movements. This wee woodland warrior wielded his twin blades with great skill. Each time his blades struck one of the sleeth surrounding him, they vanished with airy poofs of sound, like an angry hot wind hissing over red hot coals.

The Chaykin claimed they hailed from the Vale of Shadow, and Alex decided he would take his word for it. He was glad that they had not been wolves. Born in Wallachia, this Gypsy child had grown up among a pack of friendly wolves back in the old country. As he watched the Chaykin wrecking havoc among the sleeth, he was glad he was not actually killing beasts of flesh and blood.

It would have greatly saddened him.

With a last vicious downstroke of his right hand blade, the small swordsman ended the battle, sending the last smoky creature away and out of the fight. Its long howl of defeat echoed across the moorland, and then was abruptly cut off as if whatever awaited it on the Otherside had rewarded its failure with severe punishment.

Waves of shimmering power undulated on the bank above the Chaykin and the Gypsy boy. A tall, dark figure appeared there, stepping through a portal. The Chaykin said, "Cain Synn, former warlord of Mint, fallen from grace with your king, what brings you out of the Unseen Realm?"

The warlord was dressed in black robes, with strands of white hair tightly braided along the sides of his narrow, pale face. He offered the two below him a sardonic grin. "Tanner Silvertree? You medcle in my affairs? Who is this boy?"

Tanner said, "He is the catalyst that shall be your downfall. In him flows the King's Blood, Lord Synn."

15

Cain Synn laughed, a brittle sound that caused Alex to stiffen. He did not like the dark scowl he offered him. The white-haired warlord was not alone. Behind him, moving through the mystical portal was a slender figure who moved with catlike grace. "Sheen of the Fife," Tanner said.

Sheen's eyes glowed with maniacal glee and he snickered, "The Gypsy boy fears us, Cain. I can smell the magic on him, though. Its scent is that of ripe apples doused with cinnamon, flavored by Autumn magic. It crackles around his aura. He does not yet know of the power within him. We must strike now before it is awakened."

"Yes, you are right," Cain said, nodding at the slender, dark-haired Elf. Sheen of the Fife swiftly launched himself down and over the berm, a silver longsword flickering into his grasp. He was met, his forward movement stopped quite abruptly by Tanner Silvertree. The Chaykin's twin green blades fended off more than a dozen attacks as the two exchanged sword strokes too quick for any eye to follow.

If Alex thought the small woodland imp had moved with grace and speed when he'd defended him against the attack of the sleeth, he was even more impressed with the wild dance he was performing now. Despite the rapid-fire sword strokes of the Elf swordsman,

Tanner gritted his teeth and hissed, "Give it up, Sheen of the Fife! For all the legends about you, you could never best me!"

Sheen of the Fife pursued his attacker, backing the small warrior to the edge of the riverbank. The two worried away at each other, their shimmering blades darting in. Slithering out. Slanting up. Poking. Pickering. Flickering from left to right, all to no avail.

Still, both the Swordsman from the Fife and the wee warrior of the Chaykin continued their duel there on the banks of the river. Alex caught a glimpse of a white burst of power as Cain cast a spell down at Tanner. Although the Chaykin kept his concentration on his most aggressive opponent, the tattoos on his face glimmered to life. Wolf, dragon, and lion rose up, forming a network of scintillating lines, each magical creature meeting the speeding ball of light thrown his way by Cain. And though dragon, lion, and wolf vanished a moment later, they served as wardings to deflect the ball of white light before it connected with Tanner's face.

The hastily cast spell fizzled and plunged into the dark waters of the river. Alex looked down in horror as the entire surface of the black waterway turned to a sheet of sparkling ice, locking the river in a freezing embrace. He could only imagine what such a spell would have done to Tanner. A horn sounded in the distance. Sheen faltered for but a fraction of a second. Tanner slapped his left hand blade down hard on the swordsman's blade, driving it point-down into the bank at their feet. Sheen attempted to free his sword's point from the earth, and Tanner slammed both blades down onto Sheen's sword, ripping its hilt from his grasp. His sword now wavered in the air, its point buried in the bank at his feet.

A series of horn blasts rippled through the woods.

Sheen wheeled away from Tanner's whirling blades. Swiftly, he raced back up the bank to his companion, and the two of them mounted steeds waiting behind them. They rode then to join a large dark horde in the vale beyond the river. Alex followed Tanner up the bank. The two stood looking on in wonder at the activity taking place in the deep vale below.

There at the center of the valley, rode a howling mad company of riders, long, pale hair dancing wildly upon their heads as magic sizzled from their glowing blades. They rode boar-like beasts. There were hundreds of them.

"Dark Elves of Loch Sheeann," Tanner said, "And yet, the battle appears to be evenly matched," he added, directing Alex's attention to a pair of riders appearing on the hillside to the right side of the vale. There a slim, golden-haired Elven lady sat clad in white armor, her hair short, her gaze eagle-proud. She rode a white steed. "Lady Kerrin Skye, Priestess of the Unseen War," Tanner said.

To the left of the white-clad, golden-haired Kerrin rode an Elf with unruly tangles of black hair trailing over broad shoulders. He was clad in black armor, and upon his breast was the form of a rampant stag, its antlers forming a network that resembled an entanglement of briars. He was mounted on a gray horse. "Creed Blackstag," Tanner said. "Bard Chieftain of the Order of the Lion."

Riders poured out of the tree line behind the two in orderly ranks. Swords flashed in the air. Huge wolfhounds shot from between the trees. In sharp contrast to the huge, shaggy dogs, a company of white wolves joined the large hounds.

Tanner said, "Blackstag leads the clans of the Gypsy-Born: Boar, Wolf, Bear, Stag, Fox, Falcon, and Owl. As well as the Companies of mercs: Legion of Sorrow. Badgers of Mosk. Wyverns. Red Sabers. Golden Spears. Twelve Lords. Wizard's Kin. Mad Boys. The Silverlances. Wolf Lords of Shadows. The entire host rides to war."

Alex's eyes narrowed as Lady Kerrin Skye drew a glowing sword from a sheath at her slender waist. It pulsed with red light and small, fiery balls of amber shot from the tip, sizzling as they cleaved into the ranks of the Dark Elves closing with the company of riders.

A blue sword appeared in Blackstag's hand, and the Elf cleaved into the dark swarm. Tanner said, "Thane and Silverflame, jewelblades forged in the Dwarven kingdom of Quain long ages ago. Blades that have slain thousands of demons and hundreds of dragons. Ancestral blades of the House of Skye and Stag."

The two forces came together and the horrid sounds of their clash caused Alex to blink in stunned amazement.

Tanner said, "They came to defend you, Alex Thorn of the Gypsykin. Because of their intervention, you are safe for the moment. Come. We must leave these woods behind."

16

Tanner slid his swords home in their shoulder sheaths and nimbly sprang down the bank onto the ice. Alex took a long look at the ice connecting the two banks together and followed the Chaykin down onto its surface. His high-top leather boots made little squeaking sounds as he skidded across the slick, yet solid ice. He followed the Chaykin up onto the other bank. There two trails intersected. One snaked its way into a jumble of briars and thick under-growth. The other looped around ancient oaks lining the river bank, then shot straight up a steep wooded slope. Tanner chose the path leading up into the trees.

He said, "I am Tanner Silvertree, descended from an Elven Queen and a Dwarven King. Famed Legend Weaver of the Jewel Folk, bright gem among the Chaykin."

He then quoted a poem:

King Graenor of the Dwarf Folk,
    kneeled beside a moonlit sea,
    and there he pledged his heart,
    to a fair Wood Elf Queen.

* * *

Defying Ancient Law,
　beneath the stars they wed.
　The first forbidden union,
　their vows in secret said.

Then one autumn morning,
　to them was born a son.
　And two races of the Fair Folk,
　became joined as one.

Thus began the Legacy of
　the Children of the Woods.
　Bright shining Forest Gems,
　a race misunderstood.

For Dwarven sages wise,
　and Elven priests of Light,
　proclaimed these small folk,
　were demons of the night.

Alex said, "It would have been much more simpler had you said you were a leprechaun. But what is a Chaykin? A child of both Dwarf and Elf?"

"Yes," Tanner replied. "Known as Children of the Woods, long before I was born, Elven priests declared that the inter-racial marriage between Queen Chaylendriel and King Graenor was a sacrilege, and any child born as a result of their wrongful union was condemned. During the Crusades, a tragic time in Chaykin history, all small folk were declared demon-spawn, and despite their Fair Folk ancestry they were ruthlessly hunted by Elven and Dwarven Crusaders.

"But then one day, King Finn of the Elven Kingdom of Mint and King Bronn of the Dwarven Kingdom of Quain, found their Host of Kings, trapped in a siege by a vast demon horde from the Shadow Realm. The Horde greatly outnumbered the Host of Kings and yet when all seemed lost, seven wind-ships appeared in the sky above the fortress. These wind-ships landed on the greenway before Mint, and their crew of Chaykin, armed with jewel-blades, waged war on the

Shadow Horde and soundly defeated them.

"At the end of this battle, King Finn honored these Chaykin by ending the Crusades, and forever after, Chaykin were known as the Jewel Folk."

Tanner stopped, looking back across the frozen river. Alex turned and followed his gaze. There, silvered by the moonlight in the far distance, stood the spires of an ancient stone fortress. A castle of immense size and grandeur. "Rockhaven, nestled on the edge of the Blackwood," Tanner said. "Home of the Lion Kings. If not for the kings of that line, the Jewel Folk would have not survived."

Alex said, "That fortress reminds me of the home of the Vlad the Impaler. Not a man you would want to meet on a night such as this. Dracula, known as the name of a vampire, was the ruler of Wallachia. He was known as Dracula in the 15th century, his name originated in the Romanian words Vlad Dracul, Vlad the Dragon, who became a member of the Order of the Dragon. In Romanian, dracul means devil, which contributed to Vlad's bad reputation that he was following the teaching of the Devil. For he captured all the merchants of Braov and impaled them. He became even more evil and gathered 300 boys that he found in all the markets of Wallachia. Of these he impaled some and burned others.

"And when an army invaded Wallachia, they discovered large stakes there on which twenty thousand men, women, and children had been spitted. There were infants too affixed to their mothers on the stakes, birds made their nests in their entrails. Yes, my world, the realm I come from knows evil, too."

"Stakes?" Tanner said, with a slight shiver.

"Yes," Alex replied.

Shuddering from the visions he was forced to see, Tanner drew out a small blue orb and held it aloft. At once a shimmering force emanated from the fist-sized crystal ball, and a pathway opened up through the trees. A myriad of multi-colored fireflies as big as hawks drifted listlessly through the air above the path. They pulsed, casting shades of violet, blue, green, and turquoise through an otherwise dark forest.

"Be not afraid, Alex," Tanner said, tucking the orb away in a pouch at his belt. "Step onto the path, so we may begin the first steps of our journey."

Alex watched the Chaykin walk down the path. "Journey? What do you know of why I have come here?"

Tanner said, "Come. I shall tell you as we walk. I assure you, our quest, is one and the same."

Alex stepped onto the path. As he stared in wonder at the huge fireflies gracing the woods on either side of the trail, he told Tanner, "I am of the Romani or Roma, an nomadic ethnic group. Romani are known by the title Gypsies."

"Yes," Tanner said. "I know. You are of the line of the Cingane, the Gypsy-born who inhabit this realm of Valasar. Fierce horse lords who have proven to be valuable allies to the Lion Kings over the years. We of the Three Races, Man, Elf, and Dwarf call the Gypsy-born the Clans."

Tanner paused, then added, "It is quite a heritage you have, Alex. Though in your realm I know you go by the last name of Thorn, your full title is Alexander Blackthorn. Here in Valasar, your ancestor, Arron Blackthorn, was a wizard-warrior, who aligned himself with the Guardians of the One to call the Three Races of the Seven Kingdoms to war. It became known as the Lion War.

"To read more about him, the book would be a good place to start."

17

Tanner said, "The Lion War, written by my ancestor, Sanjamon Silvertree six-hundred years ago. Only 12 copies were ever printed in the Elven Kingdom of Mint deep in the Whispering Timber. One-by-one, the leather-bound books were destroyed by minions of Shadow. The last book was said to be stolen by Rifkin the Mink, a Chaykin rogue and master thief, and yet retrieved by Loriel, Lady of the Woods. It remained hidden at the Lodge in the Silver Mist Forest, close to the Emerald Glens.

"It was said that six guardians were slain at the Lodge in an attempt to foil the plans of Cain Synn, Elven warlord, fallen from grace and allied with Shadow Princes. Cain and a company of Stealth assassins traveled to the Lodge to retrieve the book. The six guardians, however, did not die at the Lodge. Fearing that Cain would breach the wardings there, these guardians, a company of Chaykin Black Foxes, who once rode with the King's Company, whisked the book away from the woods of the Lodge and carried the book into the Greenvale. Cain had already sent two of his dragons ahead of them to the monastery fortress of Cross-Key.

"The six Black Foxes died defending the book, and thus, Cain came to be its new keeper."

Alex looked off to the shadowy trail ahead to see a troop of fairies fluttering off into a garden of roses, trails of scintillating dust drifting from their wings and speckling the rose petals beneath them with sparkling glints of incandescent light.

Tanner, too, watched the fairies frolicking above the roses. Sprites, brownies, and woodland imps rode beneath their winged cousins, their mounts a combination of rabbits, weasels, minks, and black squirrels. He said, "The Bright Company graces the Vale of Roses this night."

He continued his tale, saying, "Cain wanted the book to control the Dread. In it are seven secret words written in the Chaykin language, that hold magical leashes upon the dragons, leashes that can rule them or slay them, choking the life from them. Of course, allies of the Lionlord desire those words to slay the seven dragons of the Dread. Whereas, Cain wishes to master them to serve him and bring the downfall of the Three Races of Valasar. Your first quest is to find and retrieve the book."

The Chaykin Huntsman and Gypsy boy traveled down the path snaking its way between ancient trees for quite some time. They came at last to a portal on the far side of the ethereal woodland. "There are pathways," Tanner said, "in the Otherworld that connect with locations linked to myth and fate. This one just happens to open up in Oxfordshire England, where we need to be at the moment."

The Chaykin passed through the gateway, and vanished in the undulating fog beyond. Alex gave a sigh of resolve, and followed his companion through to the other side.

They found themselves standing in a copse of trees situated on a high hill overlooking a bridge connecting a river and a sprawling township beyond. Tanner gestured down at the town, saying, "The Year is 1945 in Oxfordshire, England. We travel now to The Eagle and Child Pub, where two friends are discussing a book written by one of them."

Tanner ushered Alex down the hill toward a cobblestone street. They moved down it, buildings on either side of them. Three blocks later, they came to an ancient pub. A sign hung from a post beside the two-story building, depicting an eagle in flight and carrying a baby draped in a blue cloth in his beak.

"Come," the small Chaykin said, "tonight is the night that Trotter becomes Strider in the Silver Man's epic tale."

Alex reached the pub first and opened the door to allow Tanner to step past him and into the smoky confines. A finely polished oak floor stretched before them. A long bar filled one entire side of the spacious room within. The bar was empty. The hour was late, far into the wee morning and all but two of the local patrons had gone home to warm beds for the night. A bartender sat dozing on a stool behind the bar, his chin resting comfortably on his thick chest.

Blue, sweet-smelling pipe smoke drifted through the air in the corner of the pub. Two men sat there in a booth across from each other, both toking on long-stemmed pipes. One was tall and lean, with a shock of silver hair, and a keen gleam in his eyes. He was reading from a thick pile of papers stacked before him on the table be-tween them.

The other man was rather big, buff, and stocky, with a receding hairline and thick jowls, and yet he also had the same keen brightness in his eyes as he listened intently to his silver-haired companion reading from the papers he held. Neither man appeared to be aware of Tanner and Alex as they settled into a booth not ten feet away from them. They were either too involved in their reading session, or as Alex suspected they could not even see them.

"Koalbiters," Tanner said, "also known as Coal Biters, are those Norse story tellers who sat so close to the fire they were said to be biting coals to stay warm. What started back as a group of fellow writers getting together for an evening of talk, drink, and more talk, eventually turned into a group of writers known as the Inklings.

"Here in Oxford, they met evenings in the Eagle and the Child, dubbed the Bird and Baby. This night, Professor John Ronald Ruel Tolkien and Clive Staples Lewis sits quietly in each other's presence while Tolkien shares his work in progress. Both J.R.R Tolkien and C.S. Lewis will eventually become well-known authors, with Ronald's Lord of the Rings and Clive's Chronicles of Narnia.

"Little do both men know that their stories will become quite popular among the children of Great Britain, perfect bedtime stories, read by thousands of parents tucking their lads and lasses in for the night. Thousands of children will drift off to sleep with their fantastic stories whirling around in their minds.

"Jack, as he is known fondly by John Ronald is the big bear of a man with the thinning dark hair. Tollers, as he is known by Jack, is the silver-haired fellow, too tall for the booth he sits in. The two men, yet to be Legendary Giants in the field of literature, are at this time simply good friends who have much in common. Both men draw inspiration from the Ancrene Wisse. The Norse myth of Beowulf, from the Scandinavia Book of the Heroes. Sir Gawain and the Green Knight. The Old Norse, involving Sigurd and the dragon Fafnir. Andrew Lang's Red Fairy Book. The Finnish Land of Heroes.

"In these early years, Tolkien amused his sons by telling them fairy stories. Actually inventing fairy stories for children was a favorite Victorian past time among upper middle class men. A banker, Kenneth Grahme, told his son animal stories, which later became The Wind in the Willows. Scottish playwright, James Barrie amused his children by telling them tales about Peter Pan and Never, Never land where people could fly. And an Oxford don named Charles Dodgson entertained the three children of a married friend with stories. One of these stories became Alice in Wonderland.

Alex looked over at the two men, seated close to the pub's wood stove. Both had pints of beer before them. Jack's glass was empty. John Ronald's was half-full. Both men were dressed in rumpled vests over white shirts, rolled up at the sleeves, neither man having time to change clothing from a day of teaching at nearby Oxford college.

"Tollers," Jack said, grinning at his friend through a wreath of thick pipe smoke, "during the last reading, you had brought the four hobbits to Bree, where they met another wild-looking hobbit named Trotter. I truly want to know more about this new character. Does he save the Ring Bearer? Does he end up as a guide, leading the company to their destination? Who and what significance does this fifth hobbit have do with the tale?"

18

John Ronald narrowed his eyes and offered his companion a boyish smirk. "Jack," he said, "that was a loaded question. One that you will be surprised as I was when I answered it in the wee hours yester morn."

He scrounged through his papers, searching through three sheets before finding what he wanted. "Here it is," he said, his eyes brightening as he read the words scribbled there in the early morning hours in the comforts of his den.

"I took a good look at this Trotter," he told Jack.

Jack said, "And? Does he help or harm the hobbits in their quest? Is he to become a hero or a villain, leading them off into the wilds where he betrays them? Don't keep me in suspense, dear Tollers!"

John Ronald quietly read:

Gold in the earth does not glitter,
    in the Wilds, he wanders not lost.
    A strong, old oak does not wither,
    its roots are not frozen by frost . . .

He stopped, reaching into an inner pocket of his vest. He drew out a stubby pencil, licked the end for good measure, and wrote feverishly for the next three minutes. Jack, used to his friend's quirky ways, sat patiently. He puffed on his pipe, slowly leaking out a haze of blue smoke that hung in the air between them.

When John Ronald looked up from his fervent writing, he smiled brightly. "I suspected Trotter wasn't really a hobbit," he said.

He picked up the single sheet and read:

Reforged shall be sword once broken,
the crownless once more shall be king.

John Ronald said, "Through much thought on this queer little fellow who travels alone in the wilds, who befriends the four hobbits in Bree, I have come to the conclusion that he is not a hobbit at all!"

He placed the sheet of paper down on the pile of other papers. Picking up his pipe, he gestured with it, making a wide sweep through Jack's roiling pipe smoke lingering in the air between them. "No, his real name is Strider, and he has a much grander role to play in the story. Disguised as a lone wanderer, he is actually walking royalty and eventually becomes King of Gondor, King of Middle Earth."

Looking surprised, Jack said, "Now that one I did not see coming, Tollers! Nice twist. Nice plot. An extremely interesting character. But where did this idea come from? This Trotter who becomes Strider?"

Shaking his head, John Ronald replied, "A doorway was opened for me during the first few lines of the poem. It was, well, for better lack of words, magical, Jack. An Elven Lord from Loth Lorien opened a door, invited me to take a peek beyond it, and offered me a new plot line for the story."

He paused to light his pipe. Once it was lit and puffs of blue smoke drifted through the air, John Ronald removed the pipe from his mouth and said, "This Elven Lord gave me a name for this Strider the Ranger from the wilds. His name is Aragorn son of Arathorn. He is of the Dunedin, a race of Man descended from the Númenóreans who survived the sinking of their island kingdom and came to Middle earth, led by Elendil and his sons, Isildur and Anárion.

"The Men of the West were descended from the Elf-friends, the Men of the First Age who sided with the Noldorin Elves. They created fortress-cities along the western coasts of Middle-earth.

"Sauron, a dark wizard of great power, raised mighty armies to challenge the Dúnedain kingdoms, Gondor and Arnor. With the aid of Gilgalad and the Elves, Sauron was defeated, and he vanished into the wild East for many centuries. But Sauron once more began to gather strength, and allied with the chief of the Nine Ringwraiths, the Witch-king of Angmar, began assaulting the Northern Dúnedain kingdoms from a mountain stronghold. Eventually, he succeeded in destroying Arthedain, the last of the Northern kingdoms. After its fall, a remnant of the Dúnedain became the Rangers of the North.

"In the Fourth Age, the Dúnedain of Gondor and Arnor were reunited under King Aragorn, who married Arwen, daughter of Elrond and reintroduced Elf-blood into his family line."

Jack sat there, absorbing all that he had heard. He sucked thoughtfully on his pipe, and after a long exhale of smoke, he said, "That is quite a history for this Lone Wanderer of the Wilds, Tollers."

John Ronald got a strange look in his eyes.

"A history, I might add that was revealed to me by an Elf Lord opening a doorway inside my head. I don't know really how else to describe it. We'd like to think that we create these tales we write, but sometimes I think they were written long ages ago, and somehow are revealed to us at just the right time, Jack."

Jack hmmmed a bit, his pipe stem clenched between his teeth. When he plucked it from his mouth, he gestured at the nearby wood stove with the pipe, saying, "I would call these inspirations, Flames of the Koalbiters. They seem to be hidden inside our imaginations like flames stirred to life by some strange wind, and these flames burn brightly for a time while we see into them with an inner eye that sees to the edge of hidden realms. And yet, Narnia and Middle-earth have come to life by the workings of our pen and ink upon paper. And who knows the impact those flames may yet have?"

Alex did not see nor hear Tanner get up from his seat, and yet the small Chaykin stood at the doorway to the pub, gesturing for him to join him.

Taking one last look at these two potential literary giants, he stood up. Tollers and Jack were still in deep discussion about this surprising twist on this new character in Tolkien's story. Neither man even glanced his way as Alex made his way to the door where Tanner waited for him. Once outside the Eagle and the Child, Tanner said, "I am a Legend Weaver among the Jewel Folk, who can bring images to life before an audience's eyes. I know what secrets the Flames of the Koalbiters hold for those who have the inner eye to see them. I know what fires have inspired many other writers of Fantasy to create their own tales that spiral round and round like a Celtic hoop.

> "Anne McCaffrey and her Dragons of Pern.
> "Katherine Kerr and her Wild Folk and Lords of Wyrd.
> "Terry Brooks and his Shanara heritage.
> "David Gemmel and his Drenai saga.
> "Paul Edwin Zimmer and his Gathering of Heroes.
> "Dennis McKiernan and his Warrows.
> "David Eddings and his Belgariad.
> "Patricia McKillip and her Beasts of Eld.
> "Ursula K. Le Guin and her Wizard of Earth-sea.
> "Raymond Feist and his Riftwar Cycle.

"All of these writers have had doorways opened in their minds, secret passages from whence come bold and intriguing tales. And through the images planted in their heads, they draw millions in with the ability to paints these images in the minds of their readers. It is really a fascinating concept."

Alex stared down at him thoughtfully. "Legend Weaver, huh? Can you teach me the skill?"

Tanner met his earnest gaze. "It is a gift, Alex. Either you have it or not. I can nurture the talent and skill, but it is you who must determine if you have the same gift."

19

Lucas had just smashed his five-hundredth empty aluminum can with a hammer, when Grunge and Goblin awoke from their nap. Despite all the clattering cans Lucas feverishly smashed flat with countless strikes of his hammer, the two dogs managed to sleep through his punishment. The moment he stopped pounding cans to pancake-thin proportions, the two pits stirred to life and sat up.

"Stupid!" Lucas growled, tossing the hammer over his shoulder and listening to it clatter across the horde of aluminum cans he'd smashed. "I should have never told that stupid lie! Now I've got a mountain of smushed cans to sell down at the salvage yards, but at least Uncle Nate and Reason believed my story about the Emerald."

It was nearly midnight. By the yellow glow of the overhead yard lamp, Lucas had worked for the past two hours on his cans, as strictly ordered by Reason as punishment for destroying Billy Connor's cases of beer. It was a lie Lucas could live with it. There was no way he could tell Reason about his real encounter with Billy down at the pub. Nate would demand a drug test, and send him back to the court therapist to talk about his sightings of dragons, little people, and that strange lion man.

Confiding in Alex had been easy. Alex either believed him or he didn't, no big deal in the scheme of things. But telling Reason or Nate the truth about what he'd witnessed in the dragon chamber would certainly lead to more hours in therapy. Maybe even a trip to some loony psychiatrist down at juvenile court.

Grunge gave a soft growl, causing Lucas to look down at the big Brindle in puzzlement. *You should have told Reason the truth, Lucas. After all he's done for you, you at least owed him that.*

Slightly surprised to get a reprimand from his dog, Lucas glanced over at Goblin as he, too, sent his thoughts into his head. *Grunge is right, Lucas. Someone needs to let Reason know where his grandfather has disappeared to. Reason treated all of us fairly when he took us into his home. Don't you think he deserves at least some show of loyalty?*

Lucas planted his hands on his hips, staring down at both dogs. "I already suffered through a butt chewing by Reason, what makes you think I want to hear guff from you two, too?"

Guff? Grunge said. *A ludicrously false statement? Isn't that what you made at the Den's council table? You outright lied to the one person who really had your back. Are you forgetting he took us all into his home while your dad was in jail? He didn't have to do that, and yet he did. You owe him the truth.*

Goblin said, *Don't you feel bad? Are lies that easy for you? Did you see the worry in his eyes? Did you feel the fear emanating from him over alarm as to where his grandfather might be? Lucas, you need to tell Reason the truth.*

Kicking at the large pile of flattened cans, Lucas snorted, "What are you guys? My conscience?"

Grunge and Goblin looked at each other.

Someone, Grunge said to Goblin, *needs to warn him when he's crossed a line.*

Oh, Goblin responded, *we've been keeping him on the right side of the line for months now.*

Grunge said, *His rage flare-ups. His tirades. His sudden outbursts. We actually have been his conscience these past few months.*

"Stop it!" Lucas snapped, his temper flaring.

Goblin lowered his head in a show of mock submission. *Oh, dear, our master is mad again. What shall we do, Grunge?*

Snorting in annoyance, Grunge said, *Cower in terror. Cringe in fear and horror. At least we can take comfort in the fact that he's never struck us during his fits of rage.*

"No!" Lucas growled, balling up one fist. "Not yet I haven't! But if you two don't shut your stupid mouths . . ."

What? Goblin asked, peering up at him earnestly. *You gonna whack us a good one?*

Moving toward both pit bulls in two swift strides, Lucas skidded to a stop, glaring down at both of them, his fist raised.

We love you, Lucas, Grunge said, rather gruffly. *We only want to see you change, move away from these rage-fests you so often throw. We only want what's best for you. We can no longer be subtle with you. That does not work. So, we resort to—*

"I'm sorry," Lucas said, tears spilling down his cheeks, his bottom lip quivering, his hand no longer balled into a fist. "I know I am bad. I know I've got issues. I really believed when I left home and started living with Reason that I would be a better kid. But—"

But, Goblin said, gently licking Lucas's outstretched hand, *that old dragon of rage keeps cropping up his ugly head, right?*

Bowing his head, closing his eyes, and kneeling there between the two dogs, Lucas nodded.

Grunge and Goblin nestled their heads beneath his arms, offering him their unconditional love that all dogs are noted for.

A few minutes later, composed now and prepared to tell Reason the truth about his encounter with Billy Connors, Lucas knocked on the front door of the Emerald. Beside him, Grunge and Goblin peered up at the door expectantly, both waiting for Reason to appear. Instead, it was Boone Nelson who answered the door.

He said, "The little slugger returns to the scene of the crime."

Lucas met Boone's unrelenting stare and evenly said, "I really need to see Reason. Is he here?"

Boone stepped aside, gesturing with one hand for Lucas and the two dogs to enter the pub. They did so and he followed them on into the main room of the Emerald. Reason, Celeste, and Alex looked up from the booth they shared. "Little Luke?" his sister said, somewhat surprised. "What are you doing here so late at night? You should be at home in bed, little man."

Having just finished his session at the VR game, Alex yawned and said, "Bed sounds so good right now. But wait until I tell you about the game, Lucas. It was amazing!"

"Is something wrong, Lucas?" Reason asked, noting his somber attitude and the manner in which both dogs were standing so closely to the little blond-haired kid. "And why are you here? It must be close to 1AM. I assumed you went to bed after smashing cans."

He forced himself to smile at the troubled kid, knowing humor usually broke the ice when he was in one of his moods.

Lucas looked directly at Alex. "Did you give Reason the map?"

A long silence lingered for several moments.

"What map?" Reason finally asked.

"I gave it to Boone," Alex said.

Leaning against the bar, Boone said, "Ah, that map."

Seated there in the booth, Reason curiously watched his brother slip around the inside of the long bar to retrieve the rolled leather map that Alex had given him earlier. With all the commotion regarding the kid with the knives, he'd forgotten all about it.

Boone came around from behind the bar, carrying the leather map and handed it to his brother. "I first thought this was a prop you had made for the game," he said, watching Reason unroll the map and spread it out across the table. "Alex claimed Lucas took it when he was inside the dragon room."

Reason, Celeste, Alex, and Boone all looked to Lucas as he said, "That's the last I saw old Billy. He was talking to a hobbit inside a hobbit hole."

He shrugged and added, "He just never followed me out of there is what I figure. He's probably still inside."

20

Before Reason could ask him questions about where his grandfather mighty actually be, Detective Beef Tory came from the storeroom at the back end of the pub.

"He's gone!" Beef told the others. "The kid picked the handcuffs, opened a window, and slithered out into the night! I don't know whether to call him Jack the Ripper, because of those knives he was carrying. Or Houdini, for the escape he pulled!"

Beef shrugged his brawny shoulders. "If you guys really think he posed such a threat, let's go get Lobo, have him pick up the kid's scent, and track him down."

"Good idea," Boone said. "He was definitely a psycho, who I wouldn't want running the streets of Havelock. He was way off in his attempted assault on Celeste and Alex. I'd say the sooner Lobo tracked him down, the sooner you can lock him up at the detention center. The crazy kid at least needs an evaluation."

Celeste said, "There was something way off about him all right. I would like to know how he knew about Alex's Cingane blood line and what he meant by King's Blood. That part was very strange."

Everyone in the pub looked at Alex as he said, "Hunter Synn was his name. During game play, I met his father, an Elven wizard named

Cain Synn. I would have been toast if Kerrin Skye and Creed Blackstag hadn't showed up to do battle with Cain and his mob."

Beef laughed. "Kid," he said, "I've got a drug testing kit in my cruiser. Do you want to take a test you don't even have to study for?"

"He's talking," Reason said, "about the new game he just tested, Beef. Nothing to do with drugs. I just don't know how this strange kid knew anything about the storyline of the game. Celeste is right, something is off about this kid. The sooner we find him, the better."

He tossed Beef the keys to his house. "Go ahead and get Lobo. When the kid escaped from here, I bet he never figured on an award winning sniffer dog to find and locate him."

The moment the detective left the pub, Lucas confessed to Reason what he'd done there in the Emerald. As he talked, the others simply sat there in stunned silence.

When Lucas spoke of the white wolves, the massive wolfhound, and the small folk with their glowing blades, Boone and Celeste assumed he was talking about game play, that perhaps the little kid had fiddled with Reason's gaming equipment and somehow triggered a reaction to the virtual world he had created. For not one minute did either of them believe Lucas was talking about a real alternate reality.

Alex, who had just ventured into the VR realm of Valasar, also was convinced Lucas was sharing his own experience with the game. He knew there was no way anything the kid was telling them was real, or had actually happened in real time. Alex was sure Lucas was talking about game time, and he was a bit jealous that his friend had met this lion-man and had actually seen dragons. He had enjoyed his time in the game, and was thoroughly entertained by his game moderator, Tanner Silvertree, a Chaykin who was very much like this Peyton Ring that had been Lucas's own game moderator.

But he really wished he'd seen dragons, too.

Grunge and Goblin sent out thoughts to Lucas, loud enough for Alex to pick up on as well, since he, too, had the gift of dog speech.

They don't believe you, Lucas, Grunge said.

Goblin followed up with, *They think you are talking about playing the video game. They have no clue that Reason's grandfather is trapped beyond that door. If everything you told us is true, the old man fell in between the Otherworld. Remember our time with Ben Black Bull? He spoke of the Otherworld quite a bit. And both Ben and

Wolf have traveled in that realm beyond this one, Lucas. Maybe you should mention those two Natives.*

Yes, Grunge said, *they would have an entirely different take on this story you are sharing. Ben and Wolf would know that you are speaking truth, not making any part of this up, as they are familiar with the Otherworld, a big part of Native culture.*

"The thing is," Lucas said, "I wasn't playing the game. I was not hooked up to any of the gaming devices like Alex was. I was really there, in a realm beyond this one, and what I'm trying to tell you is, old Billy is there now, and just never came back."

Boone and Celeste gave nervous laughs, looking from Lucas over to Alex. But Reason nodded thoughtfully and said, "I believe him. I believe you, Lucas. But how do we get gramps back?"

Alex actually gasped out loud when the map on the table began to transform into a three-dimensional construct. Celeste and Reason scooted back in their seats, both looking wide-eyed as trees sprouted up, forming forests, and rocks turned into a mountain range, and lakes and rivers sparkled as if illuminated by magic.

"Holy molie!" Alex blurted, even as he drew closer to the table to see the living map better. "Castles! Stone fortresses! Entire cities and towns! Whoa, this is so cool! How did you design this to do this, Reason? Someone ought to award you for this! This is fantastic!"

Reason simply sat there, shaking his head in disbelief.

The entire leather map stretched itself across the 4 by 4 foot table and turned into what looked like a 3-D diorama, with the forests spreading out to blend with the rivers and smaller waterways, which in turn connected with the fortresses surrounding cities, with golden lettering marking the names of the many locations coming into view.

"The Vale of Roses," Alex said, looking down at the right hand side of the 3-D map, reading the lettering beside a deep vale filled with multi-colored roses. "And look there, just down at the bottom edge of the Blackwood Forest, it's Rockhaven from which—"

"The King's Company hails," Reason said, knowingly. "I know, I created this land. I thought, too, that I had created the concepts, plots, storylines, and characters, such as Lady Kerrin Skye and Creed Blackstag, and yet you've actually met them, Lucas? They don't even come into game play until chapter seven. I am totally baffled."

Celeste studied the map in fascination. "Have you ever heard of cosmic conscientiousness. Cosmic, pertaining to extended in space or time. Conscientiousness, the quality of being in accord with the dictates of your conscience. Some writers believe there is a vast universe filled with concepts, plots, names, characters, and locations that those who create their own worlds and alternative realities, borrow from.

"The mind is a pretty vast arena to bring new creations to life, there are depths, that when explored or tapped into, bring out new worlds as if they are actually real places.

"Lewis's Narnia. Tolkien's Middle-Earth. Raymond Feist's Midkemia. Guy Kay's Fionavar. Kathy Kerr's Westlands. TS White's Camelot. Anyone who has ever read the books of particular authors visits these imagined worlds and places in their mind. The concept of these forests, castles, cities, and even deep, dark dungeons, stretches the imagination so that it actually felt like the reader has been there."

She smiled sadly. "Remember Gus Howard? When I was doing research for him on the book he was writing, his words took me off and away to many adventures. He painted such a clear picture of the places he described, I felt as if I had actually been there, wandering their halls, exploring their caverns, finding hidden treasure that old Gus wanted me, as a reader, to find. It was Gus's writings that awakened in me a visual gift, kind of like he opened a doorway into my mind, to allow me to see, feel, smell, hear, and experience these rare, hidden locations."

21

Lucas zeroed in on the left hand side of the map as green fluorescent footprints appeared through the trees around the Lodge at the center of the Silver Mist Forest.

The pulsing prints left the round door of the underground haven. Ran down the steps of the porch at the front of the large hill. Then meandered down into a heavily forested glen, until they met up with a slender ribbon of trail that snaked up into the hills beyond, heading north where they faded. Then disappeared into the Masgar Mountains.

"That's the Lodge," Lucas told Reason. "That's where Billy chased me to. The last I saw of him, he was in there cleaning up the mess I had made and speaking to this Chaykin seated before a fireplace inside the underground home."

"The Lodge?" Celeste asked, curiously.

"Chaykin?" Boone asked, also very curious.

Without looking up from the map, Reason said, "An underground haven in the Silver Mist forest, a waystation for those allied with the Light. Chaykin are a race of small folk who come from a forbidden union between a Dwarven King and an Elven queen. Queen Chaylendriel was her name, and thus, the kin of Chay. Also known far and wide as the Jewel Folk, or Woodwalkers."

Lucas lowered one hand to the map, and without touching it, followed the faintly pulsing footprints with an extended finger. "Do you think this marks where Billy was going? Do you think he might have gotten trapped inside of Valasar? There was a terrible battle taking place between Tawn and Drakvoren—"

"Tawn?" Celeste asked.

"Drakvoren?" asked Boone.

Lucas nodded. "The lion-man and the black dragon."

Reason pursed his lips. "Game rules forbid Tawn, a Guardian of the One, to enter into battle. Tawn and the other six guardians are strictly messengers, guiding, instructing, and putting things in order. The Seven Messengers of the High One are angelic figures, strictly forbidden to use violence to conquer enemies of Shadow."

"But what if," Celeste said, "the game has gone off the rails? What if this reality has clashed with the virtual reality, do the rules of a silly game still apply?"

"It's not a silly game, Celeste," Alex quipped, offering her a rather sullen look. "Reason's spent a lot of time creating an alternate reality that is designed to help prevent drug abuse and delinquency. Hell, it's already given me a better attitude about myself. So don't call it silly."

Celeste rolled her eyes, made the sign of the cross, and said, "Forgive me for I have sinned. I didn't mean silly. More like an imagined reality that took off on its own and vamped itself up without the creator having any control over it."

Boone looked to Reason. "Is that possible, little brother? No offense, but you did bite off a big chunk of the unknown by producing a game where players actually enter into such heavy role playing."

Shaking his head, and running a hand through the long strands of his dark hair, Reason said, "And what? Sucked our grandfather down a rabbit hole?"

"Precisely," Celeste said.

To which Boone said, "Exactly."

The five of them sat there watching the luminous green footprints loop down and over a hill, then slowly fade until they disappeared entirely. "If those are Billy's footprints," Reason said, "where could he be going? I mean, if he is trapped inside of Valasar, surely he'd be searching for a way to get out, right?"

"Maybe," Boone said. "Maybe not."

They all looked over at him as he added, "What if you were as old as Gramps, and had nothing else to look forward to here on earth, than a nursing home or the grave? Wouldn't it be just like that old Irishman to go off on one last adventure?"

"Maybe," Alex said. "Maybe not. What if he has been cut off from the exit point at the Lodge? What if the dragon destroyed that portal? If Billy is seeking another opening back into our world, shouldn't someone go in and rescue him?"

At this, Lucas snorted, "Well, it certainly won't be me. I was told in no uncertain terms by Tawn that I wasn't fit to walk the land. I think he was talking about my anger management."

"Or lack of," Celeste said, with a sad frown. "Once you blow, you go off like a grounded tornado. But how did anyone inside the game know that much about you, Little Luke? That's downright spooky."

"Or maybe the game censor kicked in," Reason said. "I designed the game to help kids control their emotions, not lose it. If a player had a mental meltdown, as so often happens during game play on many other formats, the censor device should shut the game down as a definite consequence to bad conduct."

"I wasn't welcome there," Lucas said. "Peyton Ring was there to greet an Advocate for the Woodwalkers. It wasn't me. Tawn said, 'The Drak is drawn here because he radiates turmoil and rage. He's a walking wound that needs healing.' Even Peyton said, 'You are not the one I have come here for. You must return to your realm. It would be far too dangerous for you here. Your raw emotions attract evil beings of all sorts.'"

Reason nodded. "That would be in keeping with game play, as the censor is sensitive enough to pick up on your vibes, or for that matter, on Alex's vibes, which is why he was chosen to test pilot the game. It will take a cool head to prevail, conquer, and win."

Lucas said, "And my head is usually on fire most times."

"Something," Celeste said, "we have all been working on. Reason, Alex, me, Dad, and—"

"The dogs," Lucas blurted. "Don't forget Grunge and Goblin."

Both pits raised their heads from their place before the fireplace where they had been peacefully snoozing. Lucas said, "Better than any therapist or counselor when it comes to curbing my anger."

Celeste snapped her fingers and sternly said, "Head home, Little Luke. The hour is late and you need your beauty rest. Or at least a full eight hours of sleep or your attitude goes south in quite a hurry."

And although Lucas mocked her by blowing her a kiss, he got up and headed for the door. Grunge and Goblin came to their feet. Lucas reached the door, and knowing the dogs would be there before even looking down at them to check, he opened the door of the pub, and ushered the two pit bulls outside. Without glancing back at the others inside the Emerald, Lucas followed them out into the night.

Lucas trudged along behind the two dogs, listening to the mental exchange that took place between them as they lowered their heads and walked away from the Emerald.

Grunge said, *Well, I'll be. He actually noticed and gave us credit for trying to save him from his mad little self!*

My heart be still, came from Goblin. *Maybe there's hope for the little tirade-typhoon after all.*

Yes, said Grunge. *If only he thought of anything but getting angry next time something doesn't go his way. Because once the fuse is lit, it's just a matter of time before the spark sets off a blowup.*

Goblin said, *A secret cure? A special remedy? A count-to-ten technique to counter his red-rage spells?*

Lucas gave both dogs an exasperated look. *I can hear you, you know? Quit talking like I'm not there, or here, or wherever!*

Grunge raised his large head and cocked it to one side. *Oh, my, have we offended you, Little Master Luke?*

Goblin said, *Sorry, we were using this new technique of our own to get your attention, remember?*

Lucas sullenly trudged on and muttered, "Sarcasm duly noted."

22

Reason wanted to stick to the original plan. The initial play test was to be on the morrow. He hadn't figured on Lucas having an experience with his virtual reality creation like he had. Lucas was the wild card that Reason didn't know how to figure out. It seemed he'd met a game moderator, Peyton of the Jewel Folk, and although Reason had designed game play to include a guide, he really had no idea who Peyton Ring was. He had not written him into this game script, so the little swordsman with the violet glowing blades was a wild card, as well.

He was not even sure now that he should allow Alex to test the game. He knew that those who were looking over his shoulder at his experiment to prevent delinquency expected positive results. They included Judge Sully, a juvenile judge, Sally Yates, a therapist, Cathy Baxster, a child psychologist, and a board of directors, who had funded the entire project at Billy's urging. All of them were looking for-ward to hear how the first session of the game had turned out.

As things stood, Reason wasn't sure the VR game was going to be a success or a failure. He never expected game play to go so far off the rails. Sharing a solemn look with Boone, Celeste, and Alex, he said, "There really are alternative realities waiting to be discovered out there. I opened a door into the unknown—"

"Portal," Alex said. "Door just don't have the same ring to it."

"Weren't you scared," Reason asked, "when Cain Synn confronted you? That was not supposed to happen until later in the game."

Alex said, "Cain confronting me during game play didn't concern me, I had Tanner to protect me. But I freaked when his son, Hunter, came at me with a knife. I nearly wet myself when Jango sprang on him and knocked him out."

Reason said, "He was not written into game play, Alex. And I've got a bad feeling about him running loose, especially when he targeted you and Celeste. He is totally psychotic. Two missions, you'll have tomorrow when you start the game. You'll need the Lion War book. You will need to locate it, sooner better than later."

Alex asked, "And the second mission?"

Reason said, "Find and rescue Billy Connors."

Boone asked, "So, you still plan to test pilot the game in the morning? I thought the plan was for Billy to pass along an official invite to Judge Sully and the game evaluation team so that they could witness firsthand what Alex would be experiencing during his first session. You're not going to wait for Gramps on this, Reason?"

"I would like to," Reason said. "But since the sensor test went a little off the rails last night, I figured this would be a way to work out any kinks in game play. We can always send Gramps to personally invite Sully and the board of investors later in the week. By then, with the help of Alex, the game will be up and running smoothly."

There came a loud banging on the front door. The four of them looked on then in puzzlement as Nate Holland swung the door open and stepped inside the pub's entryway. He was followed by Gypsy, warlord of the Den, and Diesel, one of the Den's enforcers.

Nate, a big man with a shiny bald dome and a close-cropped red beard, walked up to confront the two Nelson brothers. "You're playing a dangerous game," he said, gruffly. "I want my nephew and niece back home! Now! And if you try to tell me you aren't swapping them for your missing granddad, I call you a liar! And a coward for picking on kids who have nothing to do with the missing old Irishman!"

Gypsy lashed out and struck Nate in the center of his chest with an open hand. "I told you I would talk, not you. Shut your hole!"

But Nate snapped, "Lucas and Celeste belong back in their own home! I know you boys are pissed about your granddad gone missing, but you can't be that stupid to play a game of payback by making sure Lucas has gone missing, too. Or could you?"

Celeste said, "Reason would never harm us, Uncle Nate."

Nate snapped his fingers. Diesel moved across the entryway, coming directly at Boone. Having spent time in the Mixed Martial Arts arena, Boone automatically took up a fighter's stance, despite the fact that he had a rather large biker bearing down on him. He was ready for him, whether he wanted a fight or not.

Reason looked directly at Gypsy, who had once ridden with his dad's club. "Rain," he said, "is not going to like it when I tell him the Den broke protocol by starting a fight in the Emerald. The clubs all consider this pub neutral ground. You want to explain to dad how you didn't even warn your fellow club members they're crossing a line?"

Gypsy moved to cut the advancing biker off, using both thick-muscled arms to do so. Diesel skidded to a stop, glaring down at the dark-haired warlord's hands resting on his chest.

"Enough!" Celeste shouted. "Lucas just left here a few minutes ago. He's walking home. No one could touch him with Grunge and Goblin escorting him. So, what's the deal?"

"I've seen those demon things," Nate said. "I know there is something weird going on here in Havelock. I have also heard of this dragon room here at the Emerald. A year ago, old man Connors came to Stone and asked if he would allow Little Luke to play his lame-ass video game. Stone said no then. And I say no, now!"

It was Alex who caused everyone present to look over at him standing before the Emerald's large fireplace. "This thing," he said, "with old man Connors gone missing, is sort of tied in with Lucas."

Nate drilled holes in the kid standing there unable to look him in the eye. "What do you mean? The Irishman's disappearance has nothing to do with my nephew! You beg to differ?"

"Uh huh," Alex barely managed to say. "And it's my fault, too."

"What's your fault?" Nate demanded to know.

"You best explain yourself, Alex Thorn," Gypsy said.

Alex dug his hands into his jean pockets, his eyes fixed on the stained-glass window directly behind the three members of the Den. "You all know," he said, "about Lucas's temper. I mean, once something ticks him off, he goes ballistic. Judge Sully warned him the last time in court—"

"Kid!" Nate snapped, "We don't need a lecture on my nephew's volatile nature!"

Gypsy said, "Be quiet. Let's hear the kid out."

Alex continued. "You guys know what a partner in sobriety is? You know, kind of like an AA sponsor who is supposed to keep a friend from drinking? Well, Lucas and I made up this kind of agreement, like I was supposed to help him keep his temper in check. Lucas called me his 'temper tantrum referee,' on account of me and the dogs trying to keep him cool. No therapist seemed to work with Lucas. But the dogs always totally get him. They understand what sets him off. So Grunge and Goblin and I tag-team him. And usually, it works. But the other night—"

"Kid," Nate growled, "are you coming to a point here?"

"Yeah," Alex said, a little too boldly. "If you would let me."

Nate moved forward, but Gypsy latched onto his shoulder and forced him to remain where he was. Nodding at the biker, Alex said, "I let Lucas down the night he came here to smash Billy's window."

All heads turned as Alex gestured at the large stained-glass window depicting the black dragon carrying the green emerald across the blue sky. Boone and Reason shared a quick look with each other, impressed with Alex bringing such a peaceful solution to what had nearly turned into a violent confrontation.

Alex said, "Lucas got ticked at Billy for sending two demons over to Egypt, where Stone happened to be hunting for Waziri, placing him in extreme danger. Lucas came down here with a baseball bat to pay the old man back. He was miffed enough, too, to smash that window to pieces. I thought I had calmed him down enough so that he wouldn't come storming down here."

He stopped talking. Alex held up one finger, then walked across the floor of the pub to the pool table to one side of the bar. "I was wrong," he said, breaking the silence as he scooped up the 8-ball from the center of the table. "I should have kept a better eye on Lucas. I failed him."

He walked back over in front of the fireplace, tossing the black 8-

ball up and catching it. "And here's what happened," he said.

He pointed two fingers directly at Gypsy and Diesel, indicating that the two men should move aside, giving him a clear path to the stained-glass window. Staring at him in bewilderment, the two bikers did so, and while the others looked on, Alex heaved the pool ball at the illuminated window.

"No!" Boone gasped as the ball hurtled toward his grandfather's prized window. "No!" burst from Reason, fully expecting that the 8-ball would destroy the Emerald's legendary window. Nate's eyes went wide in shock and awe as the dragon at the center of the window veered up and dodged the pool ball speeding toward it. The 8-ball passed through a spot of blue sky, and sank like a rock thrown into a pool of water. The echo of an airy poof! drifted through the pub.

The three bikers wheeled around, looking from the shimmering window and back to Alex, complete wonder in their eyes. Reason and Boone both warily approached the stained-glass window, their hands outstretched, and yet their fingers stopping just short of touching the colored glass.

23

Words came spilling out of Alex then as he shared the story Lucas had told him after his odd experience two nights ago there in the Emerald Pub. He told them of his attack upon the window with the baseball bat. Of how he literally fell forward and passed completely through the window. He told them how Billy had chased him down the hall and into the dragon room.

Wisely, he omitted the parts about the Jewel Folk, the lion-man, and the dragon, for he knew they wouldn't believe him anyway. So, he stuck to the narrative that Billy had chased Lucas into the forbid-den room, pointing at the Here, there be Dragons sign. He then ended his tale with the fact that Lucas had emerged from the room, but that Billy had not. And had not been seen since.

Diesel darted outside in search of the eight-ball he believed had passed through the window. Nate muttered under his breath. Gypsy continued to stare at Alex.

Alex walked past the bikers, moving toward the glowing window. "Way Station," he said. "Billy claimed this stained-glass window was the sign of a Way Station between realms. He said this one came all the way from a fairy glen in distant Ireland, the Misty Isle, where the Tuatha De Dannan created it. Elves as some would call them, but

Children of the goddess Dana, all the same."

He looked directly at Reason. "Remember when you were a kid and Billy caught you stealing pop off of his loading dock? Well, when I was 11, the Irishman caught me doing the same. He led me inside the Emerald, drug me right up to this window, telling me he knew I was of the Cingane blood line.

"'Way Stations,' Billy said, 'are located in secret locations. This window is the keystone to the station inside the dragon room. Like a mason using a keystone to hold an arched opening together by all the pressure of the other stones on either side of it, this window serves as the keystone to activate the enchantment of that chamber.'

"Billy said that a band of gypsies in Ireland made a pact with the Hidden Ones there in a secret glen, and due to some favor performed by the gypsy chieftain, the Elves gifted him with this window. It was transported out of the deep glen inside a gypsy wagon, and many years later, it was discovered shining in all of its glory in a pub in county Cork, Billy's ancestral home. Billy first saw it as a young boy, and he vowed he would one day own the enchanted window. How he got it here to America is anyone's guess, but Billy only told me about occurrences that happened here in Havelock once he installed it here in the Emerald."

Reason asked, "Occurrences?"

A distant look came to Alex's eyes. He said, "Yes, first the leprechauns came out of the chamber, then the White Elven Ladies all dressed for battle. A company of Knight Templars visited next, and a delegation from the White Council, made up of wizards, witches, and warlocks. And a Catholic priest descended from a Celtic druid—"

"Visitors?" Reason asked. "Billy referred to them as visitors?"

Nate said, "What kind of stuff have you been smoking, kid?"

Nailing Alex with an intense look, Gypsy said, "What does this have to do with Lucas?"

"Well," Alex said, cutting him off, "this tiff between the Elder's Den and the Nelson brothers is all about the missing Billy Connors. So, I think if we find Billy, he might bring peace to this issue."

Nate Holland had heard enough of Alex's mumbo jumbo, and when Diesel came back inside, complaining that he couldn't find the 8-ball outside, the club members left the Emerald in disappointment. As the door closed behind them, Boone and Celeste made to follow the bikers outside. "Where are you going?" Reason asked them.

"Damage control," Boone said. "Someone needs to put this all in perspective before rumors spread through the Den, and beyond. The vanishing 8-ball was a little over the top!"

Alex stood staring at the front door as Boone, Reason, and Celeste closed it behind them. He grimaced, thinking of where Billy could have gone his eyes locked on the dragon sign and the hallway beyond. He walked over to the table situated before the fireplace, fiddling with the game console, the headset, and the leather gauntlets spread on the tabletop. "Seems pretty trivial," he whispered, "to be playing a game, when there is an alternative realm just beyond that door."

Reason would forbid him to even investigate the chamber beyond that closed door. But if they wanted to find the old Irishman, maybe someone should be bold enough to venture into the unknown.

The moment he opened the door, Tanner Silvertree greeted him in the chamber beyond. The Chaykin grinned and said, "Welcome, Alexander Thorn! Adventure awaits us! Hurry and dress, and we shall get this journey underway! A wyndar stag waits for you beyond this chamber! She shall carry you down many trails!"

Staring past the small form of his Jewel Folk guide, Alex took the bundle of clothes and leather boots he handed him and watched the images pass on the six windows above the second door inside the chamber. As he quickly dressed in leathers and a long, black duster, he saw fires lighting up watchtowers on a long a line of distant hills in one window. Rain was falling lightly in a forest clearing in the second window, and snow was falling in torrents in the third window.

Tanner helped him to lift his ample hood into place on his thick, wool duster, and Alex thanked the small fellow for his aid. At a sudden noise behind them, Alex darted to the door at the far end of the chamber, and thinking it was Reason, he swung the door open and leaped through it. "No!" Tanner shouted. "Don't enter without me! I am your guide! Without my assistance, you could become lost—"

And then, the door slammed shut behind him, and Alex stood in knee-deep snow and was nearly swept off his feet in a fierce bluster of wind and mad torrents of snow. Startled by sudden movement in front of him, he gasped in alarm as a sleek, black stag appeared in the flurries. The dainty stag blinked its large blue eyes, gently nuzzling the front of his wool coat. It shook its head, sending a gathering of icy snow off of each of its six antler tines.

Hesitantly, Alex reached out to ruffle the fur beneath its chin. "Hello," he said, softly so as not to spook the creature. "Are you the wyndar stag Tanner spoke of?"

The tiny stag scooted up against him, rubbing her shoulder against him, revealing the leather saddle she wore. When she shook her antler-crowned head a second time, Alex felt the loose reins trailing down from a bit in her mouth as they flitted lightly over his hands.

The small stag brushed up against him again, placing her saddle directly in front of him. "I get it," Alex said. "I'm supposed to ride you, right?"

She blinked her large blue eyes. Once. Twice. Three times, then snuffled his outstretched hands once more, and turned to make her saddle more easily accessible.

Alex mounted up, and rode the small stag through the blustery snowstorm for the next three hours, determined to find a cottage with a roaring blaze in it at the end of his journey.

24

Run!" rang out in the dark woodlands. "Run or fight!" drifted far in the fierce, winter winds.

Alex peered out from beneath his ample hood. Tugging on his reins, he brought his steed skidding to a stop. Swiftly he slid from his saddle, landing in deep snow, reaching out to gently stroke the wyndar's head. He gazed into the stag's large blue eyes. Whispering soothing words, he reached for the short sword situated in the saddle sheath behind her saddle. He slid the sword free of its sheath. Alex then forced a path through deep drifts. Fluttering white flakes nearly blinded him as he stumbled forward. He discovered the rim of a high bluff one step before plunging into the darkness at his feet.

A brilliant flash of light illuminated the naked branches of the woodlands ahead. Alex slid his sword into the crook of a sapling. He then removed his hood. His long, dark hair fell freely to his slender shoulders and began to dance wildly in the wind. Alex quickly tucked the unruly tangles behind his ears and listened intently to the battle in the wooded vale.

The mournful howl of a wolf traveled up from the black depths. It was soon followed by a fierce growling that chilled Alex to the bone. He looked back to his wyndar steed. Quietly, but firmly, he said,

"Stay, girl. Stay. I shall return shortly."

The small stag shuddered, dislodging a blanket of snow from her hindquarters. Tearing his gaze from his frightened mount, Alex retrieved his sword and started down the hill. He flitted from tree to tree, cautiously approaching the sounds of the struggle taking place in the dark, snowy woodland.

Reaching the bottom of the vale, he parted the branches of a cedar tree and looked to the forest clearing before him. Alex watched as a pack of gray beasts warily circled their enemy. A hideous, man-shaped creature stood at the center of the ring of wolves, its bare arms hanging to its knees, its black body corded with rippling muscle. Its bald head hung down between hunched shoulders, turning from left to right as the wolves cautiously circled it. A malicious gleam shone in its red eyes as the bat-faced creature snarled, "Beasts of the woods, I am Dariak of the Realm! I have come for the blade of Gildrian!"

The demon lifted a claw, and gestured to the frozen creek bed behind it. "Four of your kind have died by my flame. Do you all wish to die? If so, come and join me in battle!"

Hidden within the cedars, Alex looked with pity at the four dead wolves the creature had indicated. He then heard the reply of an old, grizzled beast standing a head taller than the other wolves in the clearing. "Before this night, the Gray Wolves of the Blackwood had nothing to do with the battle between Light and Dark. For long ages, my ancestors have claimed this hill as their den. They neither aided nor hindered the Elf Lord Gildrian when one cold winter night he sought shelter within this hill. My ancestors, and now those of my pack, have allowed his bones to lie in peace. Long ages has the light of the Elven Lord's blade lit the deep recesses of our den. We have heard the blade recite Elven history and sing Elvish ballads. We have heard it beg to be taken by our kind to the Elves of the Whispering Timber in the north, to be claimed by one of the Fair Folk. But we have never chosen sides."

Before the elder wolf could continue, Alex heard another of the wolves say, "What has our neutrality gained us? Nothing, Raider!"

Alex peered across the clearing through the falling snow to see the other wolf who had spoken. She appeared to be an elder female, though her angry voice reminded him of a young girl. The she-wolf spoke reprovingly to the grizzled wolf. "We should have listened to the blade of Gildrian. We should have joined the forces of Light long before, and perhaps Evil would not have sent the spirits of our wolf kin wind-riding!"

Raider and the she-wolf both took a stand before the gaping hole in the snow-covered mound behind them. The grizzled wolf leader said, "Yes, Roseleaf. We should have taken sides long ago."

Raider faced the demon and growled, "We contest your right to take the blade of Gildrian. We forbid you to enter our home in the hill. If you still wish to battle, know that it will be a fight to the death! I, Raider of the Blackwood have spoken!"

Dariak of the Dark Realm was swift and deadly in his attack upon the wolf pack. With a tremendous lunge, and two powerful sweeps of his claws, the demon prince drew two of the nearest wolves into his fierce embrace. As his claws sunk deeply, the wolves turned to stone. Dariak blew flame directly at Raider standing his ground before the den. The old wolf was engulfed by flame, and with one long, mournful wail he, too, turned to stone.

From his place among the cedars, tears came to Alex's eyes. Gripping his sword hilt in both hands, Alex watched as Roseleaf boldly rallied the three remaining wolves before the frozen form of Raider. Dariak inhaled, kindling flame within his gaping mouth. With a fierce growl, Roseleaf leaped up into the face of the demon. Taking the full fury of the demon's flame in the center of her chest, she shielded her three brethren. As she turned to stone, the remaining wolves sprang upon Dariak and bowled him over. He went down amongst the furred bodies with a scream of rage. In the end it was Dariak who slowly rose from the bloody ground.

A howl of triumph burst from the demon, but was quickly cut short as a shrill, yipping sound came from the mouth of the den. Then suddenly, a tiny, white ball of fury came charging from the black depths beneath the snow-covered hill. With a leap and a bound, the small, white form sprang past the frozen forms of wolves and latched onto the demon's left leg.

Alex was almost to the frozen creek bed directly behind the demon when he stopped and stared in amazement. He froze as he watched the tiny, white wolf pup tearing viciously at the dark prince's leg. He gasped as Dariak raked the air above the pup's head. His eyes widened in stunned disbelief as the pup dodged two more vicious sweeps of the demon's claws. It darted quickly away and then charged back for a second attack. "No!" Alex shouted as he ran across the slippery surface of the icy creek. "Leave it alone! Leave it alone!"

Dariak wheeled about.

As he did, the wolf pup bit him in the leg again, ripping his sharp little teeth back and forth in a frenzy. The demon howled and reached down to latch onto the fierce little pup.

Even as he raced across the frozen creek to close the distance between himself and the terror before him, Alex wondered why the demon seemed so slow. As he watched the fight between demon and wolves, he had noticed the demon moving sluggishly. And now as the dark prince turned towards him, Alex saw the reason why. There was a deep gash across his stomach, a straight and even cut that could have only been made by the blade of a sword or a dagger.

This demon has been wounded by an adversary on his way to this vale, thought Alex. He has seen battle before his confrontation with these wolves of the Blackwood.

The wound bled freely, stains of crimson running down over the folds of the demon's rippling stomach muscles. And Alex could tell by the pained expression on the demon's face, he was suffering from his wound. Leaping completely over the wolf pup, he swung his sword with all his might. His sword met abruptly with the demon's hideous face. Silvery fragments of steel flew in all directions as the blade shattered. Alex dove to the left, rolling out of the path of flame broiling his way. He continued to roll across the snowy ground, hoping he was well out of the demon's range of fire. When he finally stopped, he found himself face-to-face with the tiny, green-eyed pup. The pup barked fiercely at their foe. Alex launched himself to his feet and faced the dark prince as it lumbered toward them. When the pup spotted the demon coming across the frozen ground, Alex was forced to hook his leg across the little fellow's chest to prevent him from attacking.

Dariak pulled a fragment of the broken blade from the center of his forehead. Spitting in disgust, he snarled, "Gypsy-kin! Foul offspring of Horse Lords! Spawn of an Ranger Queen and an Outlaw King, not even your own kind accept you!"

Dariak stumbled as he approached. To keep from falling, the dark prince used both long arms to steady himself. Alex looked to the wound in the demon's stomach. A red glow emanated from the center of the deep cut. It appeared the wound was taking its toll.

Dariak wheezed and spittle flew from his twisted lips as he lunged forward. Alex moved swiftly. Scooping up the snarling wolf pup, he tucked its body against his chest, and began running fleet-footed across the snow.

As Alex neared the wolf den, he tucked his head against the pup struggling in his arms, and dove into the shadowy depths. He hurtled down the long chute and crashed into a wall of solid dirt. The impact nearly caused him to release the white pup, but he gripped it tighter, fighting to maintain his balance. Yet he stumbled blindly into the darkness and fell further down the long shaft.

It was this fall that saved their lives.

25

Chapter Twenty-Five

Fire lit up the tunnel behind him. Flames exploded in the shaft's darkness. In that amber light, Alex saw with relief, that the wolf pup now sprawled before him in a rather large den. He could also see that the shaft running up to the entrance of the den was too small for the hulking demon to squeeze through.

He had barely slid down it himself.

"I will dig you out of there, you mangy whelp!" shouted Dariak, as he began to assault the frozen ground about the face of the hill.

Scooting away from the entry shaft, Alex drew himself deeper into the shadowy depths of the main chamber.

"He means it, you know," said a voice from the blackness beyond him. "Sounds to me like you angered this being from the Realm."

A blue light suddenly flooded the underground chamber. Alex shielded his eyes. When he lowered his hand he quickly surveyed the wolf den. It was round and nearly as large as the hill that housed it. There were piles of dried leaves and hollowed spaces in the floor. In the far wall were two cave-like openings.

Between the openings, within a halo of blue light, lay the bones of someone long dead. From shining skull to foot bones there were trappings, armor, and weapons laid in a row. The leather jerkin and cloak and pants were covered with webs and nearly crumpled into dust, but the armor and weapons were another matter. The shield, spear, long sword, and battle axe were completely intact, looking as if they had been tended regularly. The silver of the blades and the rim of the shield glistened in the blue light. Not a spot of rust nor a taint of mildew lay upon them. Alex surmised that a magical source had kept them in good condition.

His eyes drawn toward the sparkling little gems enmeshed within the coat of chain mail, he heard a snuffling at his side. Looking down, he watched the wolf pup keep pace with him as he edged his way toward the mysterious corpse.

"Those weapons won't do you any good!" Alex heard the strange voice say. "Draw me from this sheath that has been my home for the past sixty years, and I will aid you in the task you must perform!"

Searching the entire area in consternation, and wondering where the unseen speaker was hiding, Alex asked, "What task?"

"You must slay Dariak, you imbecile! Can't you hear him tearing at the sides of this hill? Did you hear nothing that he said? He has come to destroy the blade of Gildrian the Elf Lord! He has slain the wolves of this den and is now coming for me! Take me to hand!"

Alex was still looking to the weapons displayed before him when the pup launched himself at the metal sheath leaning against the roots in the wall beyond the bones and armor. The tiny, white ball of fury bolted over the skeleton and furiously bit at the slender metal sheath, taking it in his small mouth and pulling it away from the wall.

"Hey!" echoed throughout the den. "Stop that! I'm trying to save your lives, here. Let go of my sheath before you break your teeth!"

Alex's brows furrowed in bewilderment.

If he wasn't mistaken the falcon head on the hilt of the sheathed dagger was actually talking! Snatching the silvery hilt, he drew it from the metal sheath. While the wolf pup shook his head from side to side, dealing out his wrath upon the empty sheath, Alex heard the dagger in his hand shout, "Free at last! Free! Free! Free! After laying point down in that stinking sheath for sixty-odd years, I am free!"

Stunned by the dagger's outburst, Alex dropped it near the other weapons. "What evil token of power are you?" he demanded.

The beak of the falcon on the dagger hilt opened. "Evil token of power? What sort of crude insult is that? Here I am willing to save your life, you obstinate little child of the Gypsy-kin, you insolent Horse Prince, and all you can do is drop me on this cold, hard ground and call me evil?"

Suddenly the entire hill shook with the force of another explosion. Red light filled the shaft leading to the entryway and a haze of amber seeped into the main chamber. Alex looked worriedly over his shoulder. Even the wolf pup ceased growling in the wake of the sudden blast. He dropped the sheath and scooted up to Alex's leg. There he cocked his head and began to quietly growl. "There, there, little tyke," Alex quietly whispered. "That creature can't get at us in here."

"Wrong! Wrong! Wrong!" snapped the falcon head on the dagger. "He will tear this hill apart if it takes him all night!"

"Through frozen ground that's nearly ten feet thick?" Alex snapped back. He then slapped his thigh and sighed, feeling foolish for continuing to speak with an enchanted dagger.

"Wield me!" growled the falcon head. "I was forged by a servant of the Light to slay creatures such as Dariak!"

Alex stood there, watching in amazement as the falcon head cast forth a magical aura. A portion of the den lit up with the glowing, blue light. The blue gems within the falcon's eyes sparkled. Another blast rocked the hill, causing the ground beneath the den to shake. The wolf pup ceased to growl. It now began to fearfully whine. Out of pity, Alex picked the little fellow up, tucking it beneath his left arm. With his free hand, he began to stroke it behind its ears.

"On the wall behind me," said the falcon, "are the last words of my master. Read them, it just might clear matters up between us. I just hope you're a fast reader!"

Cradling the pup in his arms, Alex studied the writings on the smooth surface of the den's north wall. They appeared to be written with a sparkling silver ink. While Dariak continued his fiery assault upon the hill, the Gypsy boy silently read the sparkling words:

To Creed, my son,

I pray that it is you who has traced Falcon-dan-Alisbar to this den of wolves. It is to your keeping that I pray these weapons fall. They have served me well. My last battle was glorious. Before I received my mortal wound by De-Argonon, I did slay Nazash, Targun, and the demon lord, Rohaz. Long did the Horsemen of the Realm chase me. I would not have escaped them if not for the Gray Wolves of the Blackwood. I know that a servant of Darkness shall come to destroy the long-knife, Falcon. I have carried it this far from the forces of the Fallen. If it is you who retrieves this blade forged by Alisbar of the High Elves, put aside your enmity with the Jewel Folk, for before my soul went wind-riding, I received a visitation from a messenger of the High One. Falcon was forged for a mission of one of the Small Ones. See that it is given into their keeping.

With love,
Your father, Gildrian Blackstag.

As he finished reading the inscription on the den wall, there came another tremendous blast upon the hill. As dirt showered down from the roof, a tear appeared near the shaft of the entrance. Fire flooded the dark tunnel. Huge chunks of earth flew from the sides of the shaft. The opening became suddenly larger. When the fire died, Dariak stuck his head through the opening of the wolf den.

Fiery balls of flame burst from the demon's mouth and streaked across the den toward Alex. He thought for certain he was about to be burned alive. Closing his eyes and holding his breath, he felt waves of heat wash over him. Then, with a loud whoosh! it was gone.

Alex opened his eyes. A nimbus of blue light surrounded him and the pup; a shimmering shield with demon-fire sliding off of it and scattering like droplets of red-gold rain. "You can thank me for that, later!" cried Falcon. "I have little strength left to project another such warding. This is a demon prince, after all, and the power of his fire is no little thing! Take me to hand, and slay this dark prince!"

The pup squirmed about in Alex's grasp. With a nip at his arm, he strained from left to right and leaped to the ground. "No!" shouted Alex, as the little wolf leaped forward, baring his teeth. He was surprised to find that the pup obeyed his command, looking from him to the dark prince across the chamber.

Dariak forced his way into the den, using his huge forearms and bulky shoulders to plow through the dirt. "You cannot escape me, child of maggots! I am coming for you and that cursed dagger!"

"Fight!" snapped Falcon. "Don't just stand there gawkin'!"

Alex heard the dagger, and suddenly he was reminded of the words that had drawn him to this battle: "Run or fight!" had echoed through the snowy forest. It had been the voice of Falcon. Remembering that voice now, Alex was reminded of where he had been only a short time ago: Riding his wyndar stag through the stormy woodlands, about his own business, and not mixed up in the affairs of wolves and demons. And now, because of the shouting of a magic dagger, he was caught in a storm of a different kind. He had always imagined himself on such a quest; thinking that someday he would become like the bold heroes of the fireside tales of his childhood. The Cingane were famous for their bold and imaginative tales. But fantasizing about such things was not the same as being there, especially when it came to facing a powerful enemy like a demon. After all, he was no Gypsy Lord. Tales he had heard were filled with heroes of the Cingane, not ones of young boys faced with impossible odds.

26

Dariak blew flame again. The warding of blue took the brunt of the fiery blow, caving inward until it nearly touched Alex and wolf pup it served to protect. "Whew!" gasped Falcon. "Close one! That blast nearly split the seams of my field of force! Now would you just scoop me up and slay this demon?"

Dariak gave a tremendous lunge forward, breaking away the sides of the entrance tunnel. He fell into the main chamber of the den. Before he could regain his footing, Alex reacted. Spinning back toward the wall where Gildrian's weapons lay, he grabbed the nearest one and hurled it at the struggling demon. The spear flew across the chamber, the point of its head piercing the blue warding. The spear lodged in the center of Dariak's chest. The demon gasped in pain. Then with a roar of fury, he pulled the spear from his heavily muscled chest and snapped its haft over his knee.

A silver-blue beam shot from the tip of the dagger, leaving a sparkling trail in its wake. The shaft of light struck Dariak directly between the eyes, exploding with a dazzling brilliance. A loud sizzle came from the center of the demon's forehead.

Alex scooped up Falcon. He then turned, picked up the pup, and ran for the set of shafts near the remains of the Elf Lord. Ducking his head, he sprinted quickly down the shaft on his left. Blue light filled the round tunnel. Fire filled the opening behind him. Dariak screamed in rage at the elusive boy. Alex scurried along the tunnel, the dagger in one hand, the pup in the other. Ahead of him, he could see a circle of white. Huge flakes fell in the forest outside. Cold wind caressed his cheeks. He sighed in relief for the heat inside the den had been stifling. Exiting the wolf tunnel, he sat the pup on a stump, quietly bidding it to stay put. The pup merely cocked his head from left to right. Alex sprinted quickly up the hill of the wolf den.

He skidded to a halt at the top, nearly sliding over. Directly below him was the cavernous opening. As yet, the demon had not emerged. Alex could hear the demon shuffling about inside the hill. Falcon's blue jewels glowed a brighter shade as Dariak emerged from the den beneath the hill, swaying unsteadily. From his place directly above the demon prince, Alex took Falcon in a two-handed grip. But as he leaped from his hiding place, slick snow caused him to slip. And with a startled yelp, he slid over the edge of the hill.

He found himself sprawled at Dariak's feet. Still clutching Falcon, he looked up at the demon prince hovering above him. He then heard the distinct Twang! of a bow string, then the Swish! of a feathered a shaft slicing through air. Twang! Swish! Twang! Swish!

Three red-feathered arrows blossomed in the center of Dariak's chest. Stunned by the force of the arrows, he staggered back against the entrance of the wolf den. Alex peered through the swirling snow, looking to the hilltop where he had left his wyndar stag.

There on the hill, stood a small archer nocking a fourth arrow to his bow string. Even bundled as he was in cloak and hood against the chill winds, Alex could see his luminescent eyes glowing bright green in his childlike face, while vapor trails leaked from his thin lips. The head of his arrow gleamed with an eery violet light. This small, black-cloaked figure drew his feathered haft to his cheek, and fired once more, streaks of purple trailing his arrow. Dariak let out a painful roar as the arrow sank into his mid-section. Alex glanced back up at the hilltop. The archer removed his hood, strands of red hair swirling about his shoulders. He smiled and said, "So, Gypsy-kit, why are you following me? Has the council at Hawk's Hollow stooped so low that they hired a Gypsy-born tracker to stalk me? I see you ride, Racket, the wyndar stag of Tanner Silvertree, and that is a mystery in itself! I could have left it alone but who would play cat and mouse with me as I bear my treasure to its rightful owner? Surely, the council sent more than just you to retrieve the book of the Lion War from me."

The Chaykin on the high ridge released a second volley of arrows, striking Dariak in the thigh. "You're on your own now, Gypsy-boy," said the lean, red-haired archer. "Remember this deed, for, I, Rifkin the Mink, do not offer my help without reasons. It's just a good thing that Dariak encountered the Chieftain shortly before coming to this vale. That old Celt is a wildcat no demon should trifle with!"

He mounted his own wyndar stag, and rode off into the woodlands and faded from sight.

Alex brought his legs up and with one quick leap, regained his feet. He launched himself at Dariak. Taking the long-knife in both hands, he performed an acrobatic twirl. Dariak, slowed by the arrows embedded in his body, was too sluggish to ward off Alex's intended blow. "Now!" whispered Falcon. "Strike now!"

And Alex drove the blade up into the demon's chest. Dariak fell to his knees. With a rapid spin, Alex swung the long-knife cleaving through the dark prince's neck. "No!" he shouted as the pup went running after the demon's bouncing head. The pup skidded to a stop, watching as the dark object rolled onto the frozen creek bed. With a fierce growl, the little wolf padded over to Alex's side. Kneeling next to the pup, Alex stroked it behind the ears. "Easy there, fellow. You did good, little one."

In injured tones, Falcon complained within Alex's grasp. "What about me? Don't I deserve credit, too?"

Alex rolled his eyes in exasperation at the Elven blade in his grasp.

A short time later, Alex drew the make-shift curtain across the entrance of the wolf den closing out the howling winds and the falling snow. He turned to the fire set before the tunnels in the far wall. Smoke was filtering up the tunnel on his left. In a battered pot above the blaze, water was coming to a boil. Alex clucked quietly at Racket in one corner of the den and bent to rummage through his pack on his bedroll. He had to gently remove the sleeping wolf pup from the rumpled backpack. The pup's soft snoring continued even as Alex lifted him and placed him atop the blankets of his bedroll. The wolf rolled over, stretching his legs in the air.

"Getting attached to him, aren't you?" came Falcon's voice from the sheath hanging on the wall above Alex's traveling gear.

Pulling a pewter tankard from his pack, Alex said, "One would find it hard not to find him cute, but I have not changed my mind."

As Alex prepared himself a tankard of Blackcherry tea, Falcon said, "Then why are you still here with this wolf pup?"

Scooping sugar from a small tin and placing it into his steaming tankard of tea, Alex said, "I cannot travel anywhere in this blizzard!"

"If this blizzard should last for another three days," said Falcon, "you'll be here when the wolf pack comes to retrieve the prince."

Alex swallowed a mouthful of tea with a hard gulp. "I have no intention of being here for three days! How do you know there is a pack coming to retrieve the pup? Why do you call him a prince?"

Falcon snorted, "That's all the wolves of this den talked about for days: The coming of the White Wolves of the Masgar Mountains. According to them, an escort is to take him to the high council of wolves so he can be named King of the Wolves of Valasar. Imagine that, you are the sole guardian of the wolf king of the entire realm!"

Nearly choking on his tea, Alex gagged. "Guardian?"

"Look around you," said Falcon with a clack of his beak. "There's no one left to take care of the poor little fellow but you!"

There came a whimper from the sleeping pup. Alex watched the small creature roll onto his back, his splayed paws wind-milling in the air. Then with a sigh of contentment, the pup began to softly snore. "See," said Falcon, "after our battle, the prince should be plagued with nightmares. But he sleeps in contentment, safe with you watching over him."

Alex snapped, "My mission is urgent! I can't be burdened with a wolf pup!"

Falcon's beak turned up in a wry grin. "What will you do? Leave the little tyke here? By himself?"

Glaring at the smiling falcon head, Alex threw more logs on the fire, then settled himself on his bedroll. Being careful not to disturb the pup as he slid his leg against its sleeping form, he stated, "When this storm lets up, I'm setting out after Rifkin the Mink. He mentioned the Celt Chieftain, and this might be the old man I am searching for, though how Billy wounded that demon I have no clue. This Rifkin may be my best chance at finding the old man. And he has the book. My task is to retrieve it. I cannot be delayed waiting for the arrival of a wolf pack!"

Falcon said, "So you'll be taking the little fellow with us?"

Alex sat up. "Us? You're speaking of me and you?"

Falcon's blue jewels shone brightly in the eye sockets of his hilt. "Knowing what I am capable of in combat, you wouldn't consider leaving me here, would you?"

Alex snorted. "A wolf prince and a talking long-knife? Just what I need to take with me on this chase through the woodlands!"

With that, he settled back into his bedroll, cradling his cup in both hands. The falcon head on the long-knife glared sullenly at the Gypsy boy. The wind outside the door howled loudly, causing Alex to peer at the blanket draped before the entryway. Munching quietly on the oats in his feed bag, Racket plodded over and took his place beside him. With gentle strokes up and down the stag's forelegs, Alex said, "Glad to be in from the storm? It's not quite got the comforts of hearth and home, but what better place to enjoy a winter storm?"

After a long moment of silence, Falcon spoke, saying:

Two of the least
  not considered,
  as hero nor
  token of doom,

will shine as bright
  woven threads,
  upon the
  War God's loom.
  Following the rise
  of Seven Kings,
  Falcon shall fly,
  on brilliant silver wings.

A stroke against
  the Darkness,

dealing death to
a King of Night,

Two of the least
   not considered,
   winning victory
   for the Light.

27

The following morning, mounted on Racket, the long-knife strapped to his back, the wolf pup tucked under his arm, Alex rode out of the wooded vale. The snow had stopped falling during the night. The sun now shone brightly. The white blanketing sparkled and crystal specks danced in the air as Alex left the valley. Falcon spoke from the sheath upon his back: "They died so that Range might live."

Alex asked, "They died, so that who might live?"

"Range, the prince snuggled up beneath your arm."

"Your name for him? Or the one the wolves gave him?"

"The wolves, of course. Why? Have you come up with one of your own choosing?"

Alex chuckled self-consciously. "I was thinking 'Whitethorn' was appropriate. White for his color. And the latter because he's tough as a briar patch thorn."

"Not bad," said Falcon. "Range Whitethorn. Sounds royally noble to me. I'm certain the little tyke won't object to it."

A moment of silence passed between Falcon and the Gypsy boy. Racket plodded on through deep drifts covering the forest trail. Shortly, Falcon said, "I am grateful you made the right choice in taking us with you on your quest. You'll find I can be useful. And I am certain the wolf emissaries traveling to the Blackwood will be pleased that you chose not to leave his royal highness behind."

Guiding Racket with his knees, Alex feathered his bangs on his forehead. "Early this morning, I ventured out to the body of Dariak. During our fight, I spotted a deep gash in his belly. I retrieved an ornate blade from his belt pouch. He escaped a previous battle and took the blade that wounded him with him. It is now tucked within my pack. It was this that caused me to take you both along."

Falcon snorted, "It, too, is a talking blade?"

Glancing over his shoulder, Alex laughed, "No, you silly dagger. I doubt if there is any such blade with your gift in the entire world!"

"So," Falcon said, his tone serious as he said, "Destiny and Fate prevented you from leaving us two behind. We would not have survived our battle last night if not for those two forces."

Racket skirted the edge of the trail to avoid a massive mound of snow at its center. Alex was forced to duck as overhanging branches grazed his face. Falcon sputtered in irritation as these same branches scraped his bronze beak.

"Fate and Destiny," said Falcon. "I was destined to fall into your hands at that fateful moment in order for us to slay the demon prince. And you, upon your quest to catch a thief, just happened upon the battle of wolves, and then someone else battled Dariak before we did. I am most grateful to this unknown warrior for weakening the demon. If not for that earlier confrontation, we would have faced a demon prince in his full power! We were saved because of the brave deed of an unknown warrior, someone known as the Celt Chieftain, according to Rifkin. That, I would call the mysterious weaving of Destiny."

Remembering his rash words last night about wanting nothing to do with Falcon or the wolf prince, Alex smiled. "I would not have left either of you behind," he said, softly.

"Good boy," Falcon said. "And as Fate would dictate, you now have two responsibilities. The pup you must take to the wolves of the Masgar as we travel these woods. And you, according to the message in the den, must take me to Creed Blackstag, son of Gildrian. I am glad you listened to the voice of reason. I would not want to be con-fined in that wolf den for another sixty odd years!"

They rode in silence for a time. Racket plowed through deep drifts with playful recklessness. As long as he stayed true to course on the forest trails leading south, Alex gave him free rein. They made good time throughout the morning. The sun continued to shine and the day proved to be pleasant for traveling.

At times, the pathway dropped in to secluded dales where switchback trails ran up and down the sides of heavily wooded bluffs. For the most part, though, the trail remained fairly level and straight. Muffled by the snow, the stag's hooves made little noise. Only an occasional crunch broke the pleasant bird song echoing through the vast reaches of the woodlands. The constant singing kept Alex's spirits high, causing him not to feel so alone. Wildlife was abundant. Large herds of deer cut across Alex's path more than once, offering him and his wyndar mount little more than a passing glance as they hurried on their way.

Later in the day, Alex spotted the bushy tail of a red fox as it darted over a snowy ridge in the distance. Shortly after the fox's passing, a band of cottontails bounced from patches of bracken to clumps of cedars and firs. Overhead, black squirrels scurried along the leafless branches of oaks, maples, and hickories lining the forest pathway.

The wildlife of the Blackwood kept Alex from dwelling on the task ahead. While watching the acrobatic skills of the agile squirrels and the furtive darting of rabbits, he was able to rest his mind along gentler pathways of thought. The winter-graced woodlands gave him a deep sense of peace. Yet, after a time, his peaceful thoughts were invaded by Falcon who broached the subject of Alex's quest. They had just topped the rise of a high hill, with massive oaks standing on either side of the trail like ancient sentinels marking a secret gateway, when the long-knife asked, "Are you sure Rifkin traveled this way?"

Alex said, "No. The snow has covered any tracks he left behind, but we are heading south, the same direction he left the wolf clearing by. I hoped to overtake him before he left these woodlands, although I am not certain I'd fare so well in a confrontation with him."

"Us!" corrected Falcon. "I now ride with you, remember? The blade of Gildrian Elf Lord which has been lost all these years in a wolf den in the center of the Blackwood Forest. Lost because Gildrian fought his last battle in these woods. Yes, I am a powerful weapon, but I would also remind you of what could happen should you fail at your task. The book that you seek might become lost in these woodlands, also. Rifkin will be a challenge, but I am not a fool! If no one survives such a battle, who would retrieve the stolen item?"

Alex felt Racket slide as the pony lost his footing down the steep slope. He shifted in his saddle. Falcon, too, felt the stag slip-sliding his way down into the vale. "Steady there, Racket. Wouldn't do to send us cartwheeling into a cold, deep drift. Not at all. I am a bit too snug and warm tucked as I am in this sheath on your master's back."

Taking up the slack in the reins, Alex guided Racket toward the shallower drifts on the trail.

"I know of this book Rifkin stole," Falcon said. "The book of the Lion War. It has some sort of secret language, riddled with valuable codes. It also contains words of power that will help defeat the Seven Dragons of the Dread."

"Yes," responded Alex, a little too abruptly. His harsh tone caused the wolf pup to stir beneath the blanket and squirm about within the crook of his arm. Falcon click-clacked his beak. "My apologies. I shouldn't have pried into private matters. It's just that the Jewel Folk have been guarding this book for six-hundred years, waiting for the free Races to unite so that one of their kings might wield the words of power it contains. I fear it may all come to no good if this book falls into the wrong hands."

Hearing the calmer tones in Falcon's voice, the wolf pup settled deeper into the folds of the blanket and remained still. Falcon said, "And this thief has stolen the book so the wrong hands might lay hold of it. If Cain wields the words of power, he can control the dragons."

Alex fell silent as Racket reached the bottom of the steep incline. He kept his eyes on the trail before them. Falcon watched the incline behind. Boy and long-knife were aware that something was amiss. Birds had stopped their incessant chattering, and an ominous quiet had suddenly fallen over the woodland vale.

It was then that a stone came flying from a patch of bushes behind Alex, striking him just below the right ear. Without a sound, he slid from his saddle and fell to the snow-covered trail below.

28

The burly man stepped onto the trail in front of the prone Gypsy boy. A red-bearded, wolfish-looking Dwarf slipped from his place behind a tree ten paces from Racket. An Elf appeared on the trail to the rear, a sling dangling from his glove-covered hands.

"Good shot, Master Loftlin!" cried the stocky Dwarf, brushing red braids over his shoulders. "As promised, I get his ears."

At this, the Elf fitted another stone to his sling. "Not so fast, Master Gideon," he said. "The chief of the Black Hearts requested this one be brought to him alive and well."

Gideon glared at the slender Elf clad in snow-white garments. "Be reasonable about this, Master Loftlin. Ears are a small matter."

The Dwarf smiled grimly and an evil gleam came to his dark eyes. He quietly added, "I'm not going to debate this with you."

The man, clad in garments of gray, moved forward. In a blur of motion, a long sword and dagger appeared in his hands. He gestured at the Dwarf with his sword, at the Elf with his dagger. "While you two bicker amongst yourselves, I'm thinking we need to disarm the little bloke before he comes to. I have been instructed by the chief of the Wild Boars that he is to be brought in alive."

Gideon pivoted about ever so slightly, placing his stocky frame in front of the big man. "Take his weapons, Garth. I will take his ears."

Garth's sword point wavered within inches of Gideon's long beard. "I have given long thought to what we would do when we hunted down this kit of Gypsy-kin. I knew there would be a dilemma when we first joined forces at the Wounded Stag in Kamber."

Loftlin toyed with his sling. A light breeze ruffled his long locks. Smiling slyly, he asked, "Your long contemplation has brought you to what conclusion?"

The big man removed his hood and gestured toward Alex with his dagger. "The Black Hearts, whom you serve, the Wild Boars that I serve, and the Oath Bound that Master Gideon faithfully serves, have taken this hire from Cain Synn. My chief and yours, Master Loftlin, are the only two who asked that this Gypsy boy be brought in alive."

Loftlin stood stone still, his dark eyes following the movements of Garth's weapons. "The point is," stated Garth, as he slowly sheathed his sword, "This one we must keep alive. He would live if Gideon took his ears. I say we allow him to do so."

Loftlin said, "If Gideon takes his ears, then the matter of who collects the bounty would be between you and I?"

Carefully fingering the point of his dagger, and calculating the distance between himself and the Elf assassin, Garth smiled. "Yes, Master Loftlin. Why don't we allow Gideon to do some careful carving, then we can decide who gets to take the boy to claim bounty."

With a snort between a laugh and a grunt, Gideon moved directly toward the unconscious Alex. Over his broad shoulder, he offered, "My thanks, Master Garth. So glad the Boars have some sense of honor. I'll be quick about my task."

As the stout Dwarf knelt beside the prone body of Alex, a number of things happened at once. The blanket beneath the boy's left arm seemed to come up off the ground of its own accord, and with a growl and snap of teeth, Range Whitethorn shot from the folds of the plaid material. Gideon reacted instinctively, viciously hacking downward with his short sword. Yet before falling blade could strike snarling pup, a transparent wall of blue light erupted before the Dwarf, blocking his sword and smashing forcefully into Gideon's startled face.

Garth laughed aloud as the Dwarf went sailing backwards, his nose bloodied from impact with the warding Falcon had projected.

The man said, "Little beast nipped your nose, Master Gideon!"

"Magic!" Gideon cursed. "Shield of sorcerous warding struck me, not the teeth of that white devil!"

Loftlin fired a stone at the pup. It skimmed the surface of the blue dome draped over Alex, Racket, and Range, and went spinning off into the bracken beyond. The Elf scanned the surrounding woods. "Show yourself, wizard, witch, or whatever manner of sorcerer that you be! You interfere with the Orders of the Hearts, the Boars, and the Oath Bound. You have just made yourself some very dangerous enemies! Show yourself, I say!"

"Tut, tut, Master Loftlin," said a voice near Alex and the wolf pup. "Don't confuse wizardry, witchery, or sorcery with High Magic!"

Falcon then cracked his beak from his place in Alex's shoulder sheath. Blue jewels sparkled within his eye sockets. The transparent blue aura became increasingly brighter. Loftlin, having overcome his surprise, slipped his sling into a pouch at his waist and drew out a handful of black throwing stars. "I know you," he said. "Falcon dan-Alisbar, blade of Gildrian, lost to our race long years ago."

In rapid succession, Loftlin sent a dozen stars spinning at the dome of blue light. Each hit with little more than a whisper of sound and went spinning harmlessly away. "A warding, then," said Loftlin. "A warding can't last forever. We can wait."

Falcon laughed. "Old and gray is what you'll be if you plan to wait long enough to snatch this boy from my protection!"

Garth hefted his sword. "Could we not chop it to pieces?"

Loftlin shook his head.

Falcon laughed.

Gideon muttered, "Fire? Could we not burn a hole in it?"

Again Falcon laughed.

Loftlin said, "Only a high wizard could harm this warding."

The sound of an approaching horse caused the three assassins to look up. -Loftlin cocked his head to one side, listening intently. "One horse coming from the south. I estimate we have three minutes."

In moments, the trail was empty with the exception of a curious wyndar stag, an unconscious boy, and a bewildered wolf pup.

Creed Blackstag wheeled in his saddle, twisting to one side as an arrow hissed past his face. Only the distinct Twang! of a bow string betrayed his would-be killer. With a nudge of his right heel, the lean Elf-sent his dark steed spinning about on the trail. As the horse turned, Creed reached over his shoulder, drawing his sword. Rays of sunlight reflected off the blade and pin-points of sapphire light danced through the frosty air, illuminating Creed's face.

Clad in black leathers, his dark hair streaming over his broad shoulders, Creed appeared to be a rogue or renegade of the wilds. When in fact, the Bard Chieftain was as valiant and noble as any king who walked the realm of Valasar. Creed Blackstag, serving the Kings of Erin as his ancestors had done before him, rode these woodlands at the bidding of King Corum of Rockhaven. An angry glare came to his green eyes as he scanned the forest. He shared a scathing look with the three assassins lurking in the surrounding woodlands.

Swiftly he dismounted, landing lightly on booted feet. Craft brushed past him with a wild snort. The black stallion took up a protective stance next to Alex's wyndar stag, guarding both the fallen boy and his tiny mount. Creed glanced from left to right, twirling his long sword in one hand, calmly watching the three assassins now emerging from the woods.

Creed asked, "Who has this boy offended that it is necessary to send Hearts, Boars, and Oath Bound out to slay him?"

A gruff laugh came from Gideon. "Master Loftlin, your shaft went astray. Allow me to show you how to properly slay an Elven Lord!"

The Dwarf leaped forward, his battle axe raised above his head. In those brief seconds, Creed noted the Dwarf's leather armor interwoven with links of silver mail. He calculated where his blade would deliver the severest blow. The mail links covering the Dwarf's upper body ruled out that area. Arms or wrists were not out of the question for an enemy axe wielder, but Creed did not target those areas either.

Gideon's axe came sweeping down. Creed dodged the swing, dropping to one knee. The Elven Lord's blade barely moved as he deftly shifted out of the path of the Dwarf. However, when Gideon twisted about to deliver another attack, a thin line of red ran from the Dwarf's forehead to his left cheekbone.

Creed remained crouched with one knee to the ground, one leg drawn behind him. He still maintained a two-handed grip on his long sword. The blade stood out from his hip where his hands were planted. He shifted slightly, slowly bringing the sword up to slant in front of his face. "Arrr!" screamed the enraged Dwarf as he charged, swinging his axe with brutal strength.

Once again, Creed slipped to the side, his blade gliding through the Dwarf's guard. Rising swiftly to his feet, the agile Elven Lord stepped past the attacking Dwarf and executed a smooth but savage back swing. The long sword sliced the air, the leather collar of Gideon's shoulder cloak, and came to... a screeching halt!

Looking behind him in surprise, Creed saw that the steel collar concealed beneath the Dwarf's cloak had just saved his life. The powerful back swing would have taken the assassin's head from his shoulders. The stroke was stopped short by the collar, and Gideon was knocked unconscious by the mighty blow to the back of his neck. He went cartwheeling head over heels and landed in a bank of snow.

As if on cue, Loftlin glided into the fight, pressing his attack with both dagger and long sword. The woodland clearing was filled with the clanging of steel as Creed parried and matched each stroke the Elf delivered. Their blades wove silvery and blue patterns in the frosty air, as the three bars of steel blurred into one. The Elf executed expert moves with a combination of wild, erratic jabs that would have proven fatal to a lesser swordsman.

But Creed was no lesser swordsman. Like a dancer, the agile Elven Lord met each attack, sliding his blade back and forth at just the right angle or height to parry the assassin's attacks. Wherever Loftlin's two blades went, Creed's bar of blue steel was there to meet them.

It soon became maddening to the Elf of the Black Hearts. He was finding this fight not at all to his liking. Determined to win against the legendary Elf Lord, Loftlin pressed on with a fierceness that surprised even himself. Veteran of over a hundred or more such duels, it would be Loftlin of the Black Hearts they talked about in the Great Hall of the Elven kingdom of Mint. The Elven Lord of Erin would finally be slain by an Elf of the Black Heart assassins. Loftlin was sure of it.

Seeing an opening between long sword and Creed's chest, Loftlin swept high with his dagger and drove his sword forward into what he thought would be soft flesh.

Creed, having planned the move and baited his Elven adversary, parried the dagger with his slightly raised sword. He turned at the last moment, feeling Loftlin's sword blade skim his leather jacket. He then brought his sword slicing down through the Elf's neck and chest.

Loftlin staggered back, mortally wounded, and dropped silently to the ground. Before Creed had a chance to draw breath, a long sword came snaking its way over his extended blade, grating against the steel with an ear-piercing Shhrinng! Raising his sword to ward off Garth's attack, he held his ground. Over their crossed blades, Garth pushed his face forward, and hissed, "Did you think you might die today when you arose from your bed?"

Creed simply gave Garth a mocking grin. "It won't be an honorless fool like you who sends me to my grave. But if you truly wish to try, then come! We shall see who will watch the sun set tonight!"

29

When Creed Blackstag rode out of the wooded vale, he left behind Loftlin of the Black Hearts and Garth of the Wild Boars. A sword was planted at the head of the dead man; a sword and dagger were driven into the earth beside the Elf. Between the two dead assassins lay Gideon of the Oath Bound. Planted in the snow near his head was his battle ax. Hanging from the end of the haft was the iron collar that saved the Dwarf's life.

As Creed rode up the steep hill before him, he smiled. The Dwarf behind him would be forever amazed at the mercy that was shown him. Glancing down at Alex, head resting in the crook of his arm, legs and feet dangling over his saddle horn, the Elven Lord's smile faded. He was worried about the unconscious boy, wondering if he had saved him only to lose him.

An irritable growl caused Creed to peer over his shoulder towards Racket who followed his big stallion. His white head sticking out of the stag's saddle bag, Range gave another angry growl. After he had nipped Creed's fingers for picking up the Gypsy boy, he had been placed there none too gently. The pup growled again when he saw that Creed was grinning at him.

On the other side of the saddle, in the opposite bag, Falcon gazed over at the wolf pup. "Fear not, prince of wolves, we've been delivered by the greatest swordsman in the realm of Valasar! Even stuck in a wolf den for sixty odd years, I've heard wolves speak of the commander of the Wolf Lords of Shadow!"

At this, Creed set his heels to Craft's flanks, and the horse and the wyndar stag kicked up snow as they galloped on through the winter-touched woodlands.

When Alex woke, he found himself lying on a couch before crackling flames. Looking to the ornately carved mantle above the fireplace, he thought he was back at the Emerald pub. But as he studied the white-washed walls on either side of the hearth, he decided this was someone else's home. The walls appeared rounded, like something he imagined the inside of a mushroom would look like.

"You're awake!" greeted him. "Awake at last! You took a nasty knock, lad. I imagine you'll not be wanting a lot of noise just yet."

Alex settled back on the couch as a small figure kneeled before him, offering him a concerned look. For a moment he just stared blankly at the face hovering before him. Slowly, however, his eyes adjusted to the fiery glow in the room, and he could clearly see he shared the room with a member of the Jewel Folk.

"Peyton Ring is my name," said the small fellow standing at the edge of the couch. In his long, black overcoat and knee-high boots, he stood only an inch taller than three feet. He had long raven-colored hair and his green eyes sparkled in the dim light as he quietly looked down on Alex. "Did you meet Rifkin?" he asked.

He adjusted his leather headband and feathered back his black hair. Removing his long overcoat, still damp from the evening's snowfall, Peyton said, "I'm impatient. I've traveled far on the trail of Rifkin the Mink. Sorry to be so blunt in my questioning. I am on a mission of utmost importance!"

The gold bands on his bare arms and the ring dangling from the lobe of his left ear glistened in the firelight. Clad in a leather vest, suede slacks and doe-skin boots, there was an untamed look about this dark-skinned Chaykin looking keenly at him as he said, "I've heard you've had quite an adventure."

Alex gingerly touched the bump beneath his right ear.

"Adventures make one late for dinner," he declared, forcing a smile.

Peyton said, "From what I've heard from this enchanted blade, it sounds like I'm in the presence of a real live hero! A great deed it is when a child of the Horse Lords slays a demon from the Realm! From what Falcon has told me, it sounds like you've confirmed yourself as a rightful Advocate."

Alex searched the dimly lit hall. "Where is that babbling blade, anyway?" he asked. "And just where am I? And how did I get here?"

Peyton answered, "Falcon is with the Elf Lord who brought you here. Creed had questions he wished to ask the blade in private. And as to where we are, this is Hickory Hollow, home of the exiled Elf who boldly spoke on behalf of Chaykins before the High Elven Council. Because of his defense of the Jewel Folk, he is no longer welcome in the kingdom of Mint. He abides here now in the Blackwood in this underground Hall."

Alex accepted the cup of orange-spice tea offered him by Peyton, and asked, "What's happened to Rifkin the Mink?"

"That scoundrel!" snapped Peyton.

He seated himself on a footstool near the couch. He said, "On my hunt for the Mink, I was met at my campsite at the Fox Briars late this afternoon by Creed. He urged me to join him, for assassins lurk in these woods searching for me. Evidently, someone else has heard of my mission. Unless, Rifkin hired them to hinder me as I chased him. Of course, I find it hard to believe that Rifkin would contact assassins. Especially those of Elven or Dwarven blood. They'd more than likely assassinate him!"

Alex sat for a moment allowing the sweet scent of spiced oranges to drift in his face. After a long sigh, he asked, "Who saved me? I'm afraid I've lost a piece to this puzzle."

The Chaykin kindly chuckled. "According to the long-knife, you were set upon by assassins. Your savior was Creed Blackstag the Wolf Lord of Shadow. He's also Bard Chieftain of the Order of the Lion, who serves King Corum of Rockhaven."

Alex sat his cup on an end table near the couch. "When Cain Synn came after me, Creed and one of your kind, Tanner Silvertree—"

"You've met Tanner?" Peyton asked. "The Huntsman has crossed your path? I wondered how it came to be that you were riding Racket. Why, Tanner has had that wyndar since he was just a boy back in

Hawk's Hollow."

Alex gave Peyton a curious look. "Good friend of yours?"

"The best," Peyton said. He turned to look as the oak door of Hickory Hall swung open. Creed stepped through the round opening of the Hall. Behind him, two large forest cats slipped in out of the black-ness. The panthers continued on into the Hall. One curled up beneath a dining table. The other cat padded off into another room. Removing his hooded shoulder cloak, Creed stood then, his long, dark hair thick about his shoulders, his clean-shaven face creased by a slight smile. Closing the door behind him, he removed Falcon from a sheath at his waist and hung the long-knife from a peg on the mantle.

He then said, "Fear not, Child of the Woods. You are safe from harm this night. Talon and Storm will serve as your guardians while you take shelter here at Hickory Hall. The assassins who were sent after you have met my sword. All eighteen of them."

"Eighteen?" gaped Peyton. "Who wants me dead so bad?"

Alex slowly swung his legs off the couch and tried to stand. He faltered and staggered. Creed was at his side within moments. "Rest, Alex," he urged as he lifted Alex back onto the couch. "It wouldn't do for the Advocate of the Jewel Folk to faint on my hearthstones."

Alex smiled sheepishly. "Why do you call me Advocate?"

Creed offered him a slight smile. "Just as I am bound to serve the Kings of Erin, you, the kit of Gypsies, are bound to serve the Jewel Folk. Seven hundred years ago, the line of Erin would have ended, if not for the courage of the Jewel Folk of Hawk's Hollow. You are now called to be a mediator between this line of kings and the race of Chaykin. You are to remind the Lion King of the history they share. I am pledged to do all in my power to see no one harms you while you accomplish your task."

Falcon squawked, "And great is that power. I've heard Blackstag has won every Blade Tournament for the past ten years! I've heard you even bested the Lord Jaxton of the Brotherhood of the Blade! Why, the Wolf Lord of Shadows slew a hundred demons at the battle of Sentry Pass!"

"Rumors," Creed said. "I won the Blade Tournaments besting Lord Jaxton in a sword duel? I believe that story came down to the taverns after our battle against the beings of Darkness in the Thunder-Rock Mountains. It was Jaxton, who joined me at that battle. A long night of sword work. When the Dark Ones retreated back into the Passage, Dwarf Watchmen took a count of the dead. Jaxton had slain forty of the beings. I had slain sixty. Some said that the Wolf Lord of Shadow had bested Jaxton of the Brotherhood of the Blade."

Peyton knew he was in the presence of greatness. Here standing before them, was a legendary figure he had heard tales of since he was a wee lads sitting round the fireside. It seemed with his small size and stature that he was a mere boy playing at war, while the dark-clad Elf was a true warrior. While he was seldom caught up in important quests, this Elf was on one every day of his life.

Creed said, "A week past, word reached Rockhaven that the Lion War had been stolen from the vaults of Hawk's Hollow. Messengers informed my King that a Black Fox had been sent after the thief. A day later, my woodland sources came to my hunting lodge on the south edge of this forest. They told me of seven bands of assassins traveling in groups of three through the Blackwood."

Peyton muttered, "But my mission was to be a secret."

"A secret that was not kept well," said Creed. "Rifkin the Mink hired the assassins to hinder you. Sad as it is, you Jewel Folk have many enemies. An Advocate of Woodwalkers will change that."

And as he looked deep into Alex's eyes, a string of sentences came together in his thoughts as he heard Lucas's words: *"Peyton Ring was there to greet someone known as an Advocate for the Woodwalkers. Even as Peyton walked me back to the door of the Lodge, he said, 'You are not the one I have come here for. It would be far too dangerous for you here. Your raw emotions attract evil beings of all sorts. You would be like a magnet.'"*

And then it all began to make more sense as Alex recalled the words of Tanner when they'd first met:

"You are of the Cingane, the Gypsy-born who inhabit the realm of Valasar, fierce horse lords who have been allies to the Lion Kings. We of the Three Races call the Gypsy-born the Clans. Your full title is Alexander Blackthorn. Your ancestor, Arron Blackthorn, was a wizard-warrior, who aligned himself with the Guardians of the One to call the Seven Kingdoms to war. It became known as the Lion War. To read more about him, the book would be a good place to start."

30

Creed Blackstag, Bard Chieftain of the Order of the Lion, closed the large oak door of Hickory Hall behind him. The Elf, his unruly tangles of dark hair falling thick about his shoulders, mounted his sable steed and began his journey back to Rockhaven to make his report to King Corum there at that solitary fortress on the edge of the Blackwood Forest. He pulled the ample hood of his cloak into place. Beneath his cloak, he wore a down-filled jerkin over his black Elven mail. On the belt at his waist was a plain, unadorned sheath. Within the sheath was the sword Silverflame.

The rolling hills below were blanketed with fresh fallen snow. The forest beyond was stark, the naked branches of its trees resembling the twisted fingers of elderly beggars beseeching the sun for a morsel of warmth. Rivers were frozen like snakes of ice entwined within the forest, coiled about the base of the highlands, and looped in and out of lowland valleys. The dark rider and his black steed rode away from the haven of Hickory Hall, the icy winds of midwinter forewarning the storm that was soon to break upon the realm of Valasar.

Behind him, Alex stood at the round, wide window of the Hall, which allowed a view of the snowy forest beyond. An hour before Creed left, Peyton Ring, the Black Fox, had ridden out on his wyndar stag to take up the chase after Rifkin.

Peyton had relieved Alex of his self-appointed quest to retrieve the Lion War book, and assured him that he would do all in his power to stop Rifkin before he left the Blackwood. He also assured Creed that if he took the book from Rifkin he would return to the Hall, so that he in turn could give the book to his king. There was the significance of a king using the words of power to defeat the Dragons of Dread that the Chaykin was considering, and he vowed he would see that the book was placed in the right hands.

"Feeling left out?" came from Falcon resting in his sheath above the mantle. "Blackstag rides to the Rock, leaving you here alone."

Alex turned from the window, looking across the room to the long-knife inside his sheath. Below him, on the fire-warmed hearthstones, Range sat up and looked directly at him attentively. He woofed in greeting, still a bit woozy after his long nap.

Alex crossed the den and kneeled beside the wolf pup, running his fingers beneath his chin and ruffling his fur. "Well, staying cooped up here," he said, speaking to Falcon, "sure doesn't help us find the wolf escort said to be coming here to the forest, either. So exactly what purpose am I supposed to serve?"

Falcon clacked his beak, his twin sapphires glowing in his eye sockets. "And imagine my disappointment, too," he said. "To be confined to that wolf den for sixty-odd years, only to be passed up by a Chaykin who determined that I wasn't meant for him. The prophecy made it quite clear that I was to be wielded by one of the small folk who would slay the Dark King! And even the Wolf Lord of Shadow agreed with this woodwalking imp! And he left me here!"

Alex scooped up Range, cradling the pup in his lap as he settled down in front of the crackling blaze in the fireplace. "I agree with them that the Huntsman is the most likely candidate to become your new owner. I've seen him wield jewel-blades, and I know he's a most competent swordsman. I'm thinking that you were forged for the express purpose of becoming the blade of Tanner Silvertree, Legend Weaver of the Jewel Folk. Trust me, Falcon, you would like him."

Falcon clacked his beak. "Well, how about a little surveillance? No sense staying cooped up beneath the ground again so soon after I've been freed."

Alex felt Range's little teeth graze his chin as the held the wolf pup against him. He lowered his head so that the pup could nibble on his chin. "You heard Creed. Stay put and stay safe, until he returns in three days time. If we go traipsing around out there in the woods, who knows what trouble we might stumble upon?"

"Yeah, who knows," Falcon retorted, "we might even spy the wolf escort searching this forest for the wolf prince soon-to-be-king."

Giving this some thought, Alex shook his head. "Too risky. I don't even feel safe hidden away in here. All that talk of assassins slinking through the woods, has me a little creeped out. At least we have a barred and locked door between us and whatever is out there. And the two forest cats to guard us."

He glanced back to see Talon, the female panther, curled up beneath the dining table. He had no idea where the male cat, Storm, was at inside the underground hall. Still, both cats gave him comfort.

With a soft, Hrrumphf! Falcon said, "I said surveillance, dear Alex. The Elven smith who forged me linked me with the spirit of a falcon, which I am named for. I have the ability to fly from here in spirit-form, if I had an open door or window to do so. My radius is two miles in any direction, and I can send back images through the fire that you can look at during my flight. Care to give it a whirl?"

Staring at Falcon in amazement, Alex asked, "Why didn't you use this gift before when I was searching for Rifkin?" he asked.

"I figured the Mink," Falcon said, "was so far ahead of us that he was out of my range."

Thinking on the long-knife's ability a little more, Alex said, "How long might you be gone for?"

Falcon made a soft clicking noise with his golden beak. "Two miles to north, west, south, and east? At swift speeds as falcons are well-known for? No more than two hours."

Shaking his head ruefully, Alex settled Range on the rug before the fire and crossed the den to the door, unlocking it when he got there.

Seconds later, Range let out a shrill bark and chased after an ethereal form of a scintillated golden sparrowhawk as Falcon sent out a projection. The sparkling winged form flew so swiftly across the room that it passed through the open door and was gone before the little wolf pup was halfway across the den. Stopping the rambunctious pup before he launched himself out through the door of the Hall, Alex picked him up, and peered out into the blustery snow for several moments, watching the ethereal sparrowhawk as it vanished into the falling snow. Tucking Range's small head beneath his chin, Alex closed the door. He carried the pup back over to the fireplace, where images of the dark woodland began to appear.

Far below Falcon's projection, silver shafts of moonlight pierced the frosty air of the Blackwood Forest. Deep snow and dark branches were cast in an eerie shade between deep purple and royal blue. Beneath the black limbs, plunging through knee deep drifts, was a young boy who had been running for miles through the dark wood-land. Long ago, he had lost all sense of direction. Now, in desperation, he ran aimlessly onward. The ravenous beasts that hunted him were closing in on him. The crusty layer beneath the powdery snow suddenly broke, and Briar Erin of Castle Rockhaven stumbled, falling face first in a deep drift.

Frantically, he struggled to his knees and pushed himself forward. His face met abruptly with a tree, and with a whimper of pain, he rolled onto his back, cupping his frozen cheeks in his numb hands. His knees came to his chest and he curled up into a ball. A deep sob of hopelessness escaped from his cracked lips.

Briar stopped himself, refusing to give in. A release of sorrow would have to wait for another time. He hugged the tree before him and slowly pulled himself to his feet. Taking a deep breath and holding his head high, he began to walk through the sparkling snow with all the dignity of a woodland king. His long, dark hair whipped past his shoulders. His sky-blue eyes, yet misted with tears, were filled with a hopeful, fierce light of determination. Briar was going to live.

With numb fingers, he tugged on the drawstrings of his rabbit-fur cloak, pulling it tight against his shoulders. His right hand then dropped to rest on the hilt of the short sword sheathed at his waist. "Twelve-summers," Briar said. "Twelve-summers-old. Too young to die by the attack of hunger-mad wolves."

31

Chapter Thirty-One

The wolves howled. Mournful, hideous wails that traveled far on the icy winds. They were on the hunt. The hunger in their empty bellies drove them on. From dens beneath frozen ground they came. From rotted stumps of fallen trees. From stony caves in the hills. All of them gathered at the call of their leader who led them on the midnight hunt through the snowy woodland.

Ronan and his pack topped the rise of a low hill. From below them in the dense forest, the scent of blood rose in the sudden gusts of icy wind. It stung their nostrils and drove them mad. Like a rolling, gray wave, they shot down the hillside, following their black leader. They darted from tree to tree, sniffing, searching, swiftly moving forward.

Ronan was the first to break into the clearing. The blood smell was so strong that he reared back on his hind legs. Warily, he dropped to all fours, staring at the grisly scene of battle before him. On the red snow of the forest floor were twisted bodies of men and horses, all of them mangled and torn. All of the victims bore the wicked markings of some monstrous set of claws. Some Thing had attacked them. Some Creature with a ferocity that frightened even the wolf.

While the pack looked on, Ronan cautiously skirted the edge of the clearing. The banner and armor of the warriors bore witness that the men were from a fortress on the southern edge of the forest, a place that man and wolf both knew as The Rock. The two figures sprawled in the center of the circle of dead warriors, wore the colors of royalty; one was a He, the other a She. It appeared the warriors had died defending the two. At the northern edge of the area were a set of deep prints. From the succession of adjacent paw markings, the wolf surmised that the Creature had two feet, walking up-right like a man, but having paws three times the size of a wolf. Another odd discovery by the wolf was that the Creature's prints led to a certain place and then vanished. Ronan concluded that the Creature had wings. It had walked a few paces from the kill, and then flew away.

The most disturbing discovery was made after a scent-check on the mutilated horses and warriors. It was a repulsive stench that emanated from the mangled bodies, an odor not totally alien to the old wolf. The rank odor brought back vivid memories of his western trek to the Dark Mist Forest where he had witnessed the Robed Ones slaying their own young beneath a blood-red moon. He remembered the horrid howling of the druids. He could still see their shadowy figures in the firelight. He then recalled that which had made his blood turn cold. Flame had streaked from the hands of these Robed Ones, consuming their young. They had sacrificed their own children.

The memory caused Ronan to shudder even now. The smell was the same. It reeked of the thing known as sorcery.

Ronan barked the message of warning to his followers. At a lope, he bounded away from the slaughter in the clearing, picking up a fresh scent of a young one, the only survivor of the attack by the Creature. Not only was the young's scent heavy in the air, its footprints trailed out of the clearing. Not a meal for the whole pack. But at least Ronan would not go hungry for the night.

Briar tumbled down a thick drift that sloped down to the bank of the frozen river. He sprawled beneath a slender birch stretching from bank to bank. He wondered if it would support his slight weight or if it would snap in two, sending him down onto the ice which might crack, opening a dark, watery hole for him to slide down into.

As he struggled to his feet, Briar could see that the birch was indeed thick enough to scurry across. With an audible sigh, he stepped out onto the ice-crusted bark. With his arms flung wide and his legs bent at the knees, he forced the birch bridge down for a final test. A creak and a groan came from the white sapling.

Briar stepped back onto the bank, taking a last minute inspection of where the birch met with the far bank. It stretched two horse lengths. He could not waver with uncertainty. He must move quickly, leaving no margin for error. Prayers offered, he leaped onto the birch and pivoted about like a puppet on a string. His mouth as wide as his eyes, his arms stretched outward for balance, he shuffled, danced back and forth, and darted for the far bank.

One yard from the opposite bank, his foot skittered off into empty air, and with a cry of alarm, Briar lunged for the bank. He landed heavily on his side, expecting at any moment to be swimming in icy black waters. But the bank was beneath him, the frozen river behind. He offered thanks and scrambled to his feet.

The wind brought to his ears the horrible sound of howling. He winced fearfully at the nearness of the call. They would be following the river by now.

Climbing the bank, branches slapped at his face, stinging his cheeks, causing his eyes to mist over. The sudden pain caused Briar to struggle with the urge to break down and cry. Painful memories wormed their way into his thoughts, visions unraveled, sights and sounds flooded his mind. He knew that if he dwelt on the memory he was holding at bay, the sadness would overwhelm him, and Briar of Rockhaven would become the feast of wolves.

The wolves barked behind him. They were close now. So close, he could hear them panting. The wolves on the far bank stopped in their tracks. Thirty sets of green eyes focused on him.

Briar met their silent stares with a look of defiance. Twigs snapped behind him. With a startled gasp, he whirled about. On the bank above him, was the largest wolf he had ever seen. Black as a midnight sky. Shoulder high to his father's tallest horse. Eyes that glared with intense hatred.

Briar spun about and began running downstream. Ahead of him, he saw a dam that stretched from one bank to the other. It was constructed of thick branches but it was narrow, and the ice that formed around it was thin and brittle. He leaped over a large stone and a fallen tree, and reached the dam seconds ahead of the wolves on either side of the river. He ran out onto the middle of the structure, and there he stood his ground. Ronan came to the dam and howled in triumph. He hunched down, preparing to spring.

Briar's hand flew to the sword at his waist. He clutched the hilt and gave a swift jerk to pull it from the sheath. But the blade refused to budge. The breath of winter had locked steel sword and metal scabbard together. Ronan sprang onto the dam. A large gray wolf from the opposite bank, followed his example. Both wolves sniffed at the branches and tested their footing.

Then, with snarls contorting their faces, they moved in for the kill. In desperation, Briar ripped the scabbard from the bindings at his belt. With all the strength he could muster, he swung from left to right, striking both beasts on their snouts. He twisted about again, and with a shout of rage, slapped the sheath up under the chin of the huge, black wolf. Back and forth he began to swing, using such wild, frantic movements that the two wolves were struggling to keep their footing.

In one last attempt to knock Ronan from his place, Briar struck the wolf a stunning blow to the side of the head. He brought his weapon back to swing again and lost his balance. The ice cracked loudly as it broke beneath him.

Chilly waters clutched at him. The strong pull of swift currents allowed him only seconds to catch air. Sucked below the surface, yanked under the ice, Briar fell helplessly into a swirling vortex of freezing darkness. Icy needles pierced his skin in a thousand different places. He turned, twisted, cartwheeled, and somersaulted helplessly within the currents that forced him into deeper water.

The cold, the darkness, and the turbulent storm beneath the surface of the river, swallowed him like some monstrous beast. Arms flailing, legs churning, he struggled in vain. Panic gave way to despair. Blindly, he was sucked to the muddy bottom. His knee's skimmed the slippery surface, and he tried desperately to push himself upward. He felt himself pressed to the unyielding surface of the ice above. His chest ached. His head throbbed. His tightly pressed lips began to give way to the force within his bulging cheeks. Blackness swirled at the edge of his mind, and Briar broke through the ice overhead and shout-ed into the misty air. He clawed frantically at the edges of the opening he had created. He stretched out his arms to the bank only a yard from his face. Digging his fingers into the icy crust, he crawled forward. The ice groaned beneath him. Like a snake, Briar wormed his way forward. Ice shifted beneath him but it held. He sighed with relief as he clambered up onto the solid bank.

Wolves howled behind him. Woodenly, Briar twisted his head to gaze downstream. They were there, moving gray bodies on both sides of the river. A tree! he thought. Got to climb out of their reach!

Safe and warm inside of Hickory Hall, Alex witnessed Briar's wild run through the snowy forest. Through the images Falcon sent back to him, he cringed, wishing that he could somehow help the boy escape the wolves chasing him so relentlessly through the woodlands.

He was startled by Range's sharp bark as the little wolf, too, peered into the flames, watching Briar's dilemma unfold. Alex heard the soft growl of Talon as she crept up behind him there before the fireplace. When he glanced back, Storm had joined her, as well, and the two forest cats peered intently into the fire, both growling softly.

Alex gave a startled gasp as the ethereal form of Falcon swooped down the chimney, passed swiftly through the dancing flames in the hearth, and slipped back into the long-knife hanging by its sheath from the mantle piece.

"Take me to hand!" Falcon squawked. "Let's save the prince!"

32

Chapter Thirty-Two

The tree Briar set his sights on stood only a short distance up the bank, but his numbed fingers slipped off the ice-riddled bark, and Ronan barked as he lunged at the tree.

Suddenly, Briar saw a solid line of golden flame passing before his eyes. Startled, he discovered a lean, black-haired boy close to his own age standing on his right. Gypsy-born! sprang to his mind. A boy of the Horse Lords! But what is he doing so deep within the Blackwood?

Alex swung the luminous blade of Falcon up between him and the wolf pack. The golden blade dipped to brush the chest hairs of Ronan. He said, "He is not for you, black wolf! I have spoken!"

Alex snapped, "Back off, now or I'll take the fight to you!"

Ronan stiffened. The ring of wolves about the tree growled among themselves. Facing them, Alex and the two forest cats formed a defensive line, offering protection to the badly shivering boy. Storm's fierce rumble gave warning that things were about to turn deadly. Talon lowered her sleek, black form to the snowy ground, preparing to launch herself directly into the center of the relentless wolf pack. Range scrambled out of the saddle pack where Alex had hastily placed him, for the pup refused to be left back at the Hall.

Ronan bristled with anger at the wolf pup now standing before him. He growled.

Falcon said, "If you pursue this, I shall light you up from nose to tail-tip with golden fire!"

Ronan lunged past Range to attack Alex. Briar fell against the tree, watching fearfully, sure that his defenders were about to become wolf-feast. He then gasped in surprise. The dark-haired Gypsy boy's golden blade sang as it sliced the air. And then, in a blur of blinding speed, golden fire arced through the frosty air and the flat of the blade slammed into the side of Ronan's head. The beast fell in silence, and the ring of gray wolves found themselves surrounded by the ghostly forms of enormous white wolves slipping silently out of the forest.

"The White Wolves of Masgar!" Briar whispered in awe.

The gray wolves turned tail and ran off. The leader of the white wolves eyed Range as he approached the little wolf pup. He was a big fellow and missing one eye. A scar ran down through his empty left eye socket, giving him a rather rugged look.

Standing there holding Falcon up between them, Alex watched a bright aura from the blade bathe the big wolf in golden light. He lowered Falcon at once, slipping the blade into the sheath at his side. "I am friend, not foe. And the pup is yours to escort—"

His words caught in his throat. To escort where? It had just occurred to him that these wolves had come to take Range away. These are the wolves Falcon spoke of, coming from the Masgar mountains. But I am not wanting to part with the little guy so soon. I wanted a few more days before the pup meets his own destiny. Who am I to stop that? These wolves have a history I know nothing about. I can't keep the pup like he is some sort of pet. That's nonsense. Still...

"Good, boy," the grizzled old wolf said. "I wouldn't want to pit myself against such a skilled Sword Lord, and end up like nasty Ronan here. Stupid fool that he is, should have known better than to attack a Gypsy-kit wielding a jewel-blade. Looks like you and the wolf prince are traveling together, which I am sure is a story in itself."

Alex, feeling quite foolish to be outright talking to a talking wolf, said, "Oh, I am no Sword Lord—"

"Gypsy-kit," the big wolf said, "don't forget the demon you and the prince slew together. I checked that dark being over, and although you might have delivered the killing blow with that magic blade of yours, I saw the teeth marks on that nasty creature's leg."

He shook from nose to tail, sending snow scattering from his large body. "You must be destined to be an amazing warrior one day."

Alex did not know how to respond. *I often suspected*, he thought, *that Lucas could hold some kind of secret communication with Grunge and Goblin. I think he could even talk to Reason's dog, Lobo, as well. But this? A wolf who speaks out loud? This is so weird.*

"I am Grizz," the old white male said, "warlord of Masgar. We must be off and away with this little prince. We have a council to take him to. There is some beast that hunts these woodlands, and we must avoid it all costs."

Briar trembled with cold, his clothing still soaking wet from his fall into the river. "It is a demon," he said. "It killed my father, mother, and all of our homeguard."

Grizz looked intently at the boy. "You are the son of the King of the Rock. Let's hope you make as great a king as your father was. He forbid his huntsmen to kill us for our white pelts. Sorry for your loss. Your father was kind. I hope you have the same heart."

Briar shivered uncontrollably and sank to his knees beside Alex. Talon and Storm sidled up to the boy, the female nuzzling his neck. Briar draped his arms about the two cats and said to Alex, "How you travel with Blackstag's panthers is a mystery. I hope we are not far from his underground hall. A hot fire would be good."

As Alex moved to help the distressed boy to stand up so that he could mount Racket, Range spoke for the first time. "I'm sorry to be leaving you," the little wolf said, offering Alex an earnest look. "Our battle against the demon bonded us in a strange way. But here our paths veer off in different directions."

His eyes going wide, Alex said, "You can talk, too?"

"Yes, of course," Range said in a voice that sounded so child-like that Alex felt tears rolling down his cheeks.

"Will I ever see you again?" he asked, sadly.

Range moved forward to nuzzle his lowered hand. "If our paths cross again, I will be much older. And a wolf king."

Grizz peered up into the gently falling snow. "Let us go from here, my prince. We have many miles to travel this night."

Alex kneeled down, gave Range a swift hug, and the white wolves and the prince were gone, vanishing into the black trees beyond.

Wiping tears from his cheeks with the back of one hand, Alex turned to help Briar climb up into Racket's saddle.

Briar stopped him with one light touch on his outstretched hand. "Wait," he said.

Alex, Storm, and Talon then looked on curiously as Briar turned to kneel beside the fallen Ronan. The boy placed his hands atop the black wolf's shoulder, and at once a green-tinted mist drifted off of his palms, slowly undulating all across the unconscious wolf's large body. Ronan stirred quite suddenly, letting out a low whimper.

By the time, the old black wolf arose groggily to his four paws, Alex was leading Racket out of the clearing, Briar clinging to him with both arms, while the cats trailed behind them.

They rode for some distance before Alex finally said, "That was justly done. I'd say you definitely have the heart of your father. You will make a great king one day."

To which Briar quietly whispered, "We shall see."

As they moved toward dense forest, Alex reached back to gently pat Briar on his leg. Briar was painfully reminded of his ordeal that began shortly after sundown. And then like a vessel that was broken, his strength shattered. Sadness welled up inside him, and he pressed his face against Alex's back and cried without restraint.

33

Night. Bitter winds. Another storm brewing. These all made for difficult traveling, but Racket carried them on through the Blackwood to their intended destination.

The moment the small stag cleared the wooden bridge, Alex guided her beneath the archway of an oak arbor, and rode on to the snow-covered greenway before the underground haven of Hickory Hall. The black stag's hooves cut through the white carpet as she came to a halt on the cobbles of the Hall's front walkway. With a snort, the wyndar stamped at the stone walkway and reared back as the oak door swung open at the center of the green, grassy mound before them.

Briar felt the stag rising. He quickly shoved himself off its hindquarters, landing feet first on the snowy ground. The blanket fell from his shoulders, and as he stepped back to avoid the stag, he tripped over it, falling into a drift behind him.

Stepping out through the open door situated in the hill that housed the Hall, was Creed, all clothed in white. His apparel sparkled as he moved swiftly across the snow. Upon his brow he wore a silver circlet, a green jewel at its center. He peered with deep sympathy at Briar. "Forest messengers let me know the Rock has fallen. I am glad you survived the assault of the Karth!"

And the memories of his earlier encounter with the demon that had killed his parents came washing over him:

The Karth attacked Rockhaven in the middle of the night. Rockhaven had been a stronghold between the invading Karth and the Seven Kingdoms beyond. This night, the Rock had at last fallen.

Briar saw the dark trees beyond the rear gate, the only avenue of escape. His father's household guards were beside him on skittish horses. His mother, Queen Lorinda, was behind him on her golden mare. His father circled in front of him, hesitating to ride to the forest, reluctant to desert the men who remained to fight. At last his father cried out, "Ride!" But as the King led his white steed through the rear gate, a hooded man in black robes barred the path of escape. It was Zagar the Druid. The Druid snatched the reins from Briar's hands. He hissed, "Of you the Fallen has spoken! To Zagar his High Priest, he has foretold the coming of the future Ard Ri! Dark of hair. Eyes like the sea on a fair day. Fine features, a slight cleft in the chin. I have seen you in the reflection of the Serpent's Eye! And you, can-not be allowed to live. It could mean defeat for the Darkness!"

Zagar lunged at him and Captain Random was suddenly there between him and the Druid. Random fell with the dagger buried in his chest and the next thing Briar knew, the small company of the King was entering the Blackwood Forest.

The black shape descended into the forest clearing, attacking with lightning-like speed. In the chaos of battle, Briar was thrown from his horse. His mother urged him to flee. And the Homeguard circled the King and Queen, and the winged Thing was upon them. As Briar fled, he begged the One that they would have a swift, merciful death.

Creed reached down and helped Briar to his feet, his earnest gaze fixed on Alex. "The Arshzar is coming behind you!" he said.

Creed drew Silverflame from its sheath. He ran to the pathway that led beneath the arched arbor. There, he planted his feet firmly, grasping the sword in both hands. The wind swept his dark hair over his rigid shoulders as he prepared himself for battle.

The horrid scream of the Arshzar came from the open sky beyond the clearing. There, skimming the thin fingers of the tree tops was the winged being Briar had encountered earlier that night. It screamed again. Red flame seared the night sky. With slow wingbeats, the demon descended into the clearing, landing just beyond the bridge. The huge, bare-chested, black-skinned creature drew a sword from the sheath at its waist. Briar shuddered when he realized it was gazing at him, its bat-like face, twisted in a wicked grin. The Arshzar spat flame at Creed. The stream of amber snapped at the Elf like a striking serpent. Creed drove Silverflame up to ward off the crackling tongues of flame. Fire and blade met, and a silent explosion of red and blue light burst and showered down, scorching the snow.

Creed aimed his sword and lightly pressed a small sapphire in its hilt. Blue flame curled down the edges of the blade, gathered on the tip, and erupted in a silver burst. Trailing translucent smoke, a shaft of turquoise shot through the frosty air, striking the Arshzar in the center of his breast. Before he could fall, he caught himself and raised his red bladed sword. He pointed it at Briar. "Ard Ri! You are marked for death! Surrender yourself into my keeping. Come, there is a place for you in the Halls of Death!"

"Kazz the White!" Creed cried when the armor-clad Rock Troll lunged from the trees directly behind the demon. The Troll's snow-white hair trailed over his broad shoulders. His jutted brows were also crested with white, and the weathered skin of his face resembled sun-bleached parchment. Despite the Troll's uncomely face, his deep-set blue eyes sparkled like sapphires as he hammered away at the Arshzar with his war-mace, sending his sword flying from his grasp.

Beautiful, thought Alex, as he watched the black-haired lady coming up behind the Troll. Gypsy-born, also came to mind upon seeing her long, dark hair cascading to her shoulders in rivulets and waves. He heard Creed whisper, "Loriel the Lady of the Woods!"

With a battle cry, Kazz brought his mace crashing down on the Arshzar's head. The blow caused the demon to stagger back. Taking the mace in both hands, the stout Troll swung with all his might. The iron head caught the Arshzar under the chin.

Upon impact, flame shot from its mouth, causing Kazz to duck out of its path. The Arshzar drove its gnarled hands down into his backside. The blow was so fierce that Kazz was driven face down in the snow at its feet, knocked senseless. Loriel took aim with her throwing dagger and let it fly. The knife hissed, splitting the cold air.

With a hollow Thud! it pierced the demon's chest and sank so deeply that only the haft protruded from the wound.

Loriel held high a red rose. She gripped its thorny stem in her right hand and began to move toward the trellis archway. As she went, she poured a crimson liquid from the head of the rose. It flowed down from her hand, staining the snow with a thin line of scarlet. At once, a band of amber light began to radiate from the white forest floor, a florescent glow that rose like a wall before Hickory Hall. With the light pouring from the red rose, she drew a shimmering red line from the top of the archway to the ground, and encased the line within a phosphorescent silver circle. She then brought the rose round in a horizontal sweep, causing it to pass through the midst of the circle, through the center of the vertical red line. When she had finished, the pattern of a circled cross hung in the air, spinning in place.

The Arshzar lashed out at the whirling web of incandescent light with a clawed hand. At once, his huge, black body was sucked into the glowing net. Slowly, as if engulfed in deep water, the demon struggled against unseen forces within the center of the swirling conflagration. Loriel jabbed the Arshzar with the oak wand she drew from her belt pouch.

The wand came alive in her hands and twisted from her grasp, separating into a myriad of spastically lashing roots that snaked out, wrapping themselves about the Arshzar's wings, chest, and neck. As the demon struggled, the roots began to multiply, so that he was soon entangled in their fierce grip. When he realized he had become trapped in a holding, the fury of his anger erupted in a blaze from its gaping jaws. The Arshzar struggled vainly against the roots that imprisoned it. And in his wrath, he set the roots on fire.

Kazz pulled Loriel away from the scene of the battle, even as the Arshzar became engulfed in an inferno of its own flames.

34

Inside Hickory Hall, Alex and Briar sat huddled on a stool before the fireplace. They dozed sleepily as the fire crackled and the sweet scent of cherry wood filled Creed's underground home.

Spacious was the room, with white walls resembling the insides of a giant mushroom. Tapestries hung everywhere, among them the standards of the kings, the lords, and the bannermen of the Three Races of Valasar. At the round oak table situated at the center of the room Creed sat talking to the two travelers who had appeared at the Hall and aided him in killing the demon. The pair were stunned by the news that King Corum had been killed fleeing from Rockhaven.

The huge Troll seated across from Creed said, "So do our plans fail before we even undertake the first step on the long road ahead?"

"Kazz is right," said Loriel. "The Enemy has slain two members of our Order. What do we do now?"

"Humph!" muttered Kazz. "Creed is capable of protecting the boy. Our main concern is assuming guardianship of the little Black Rose."

Placing a hand on the big Troll's shoulder, Loriel said, "Has anyone explained to the boy the matter of the Ard Ri? I deem it time to reveal the truth to the lad."

"As do I," said Creed, reaching down to the small wooden chest situated on the table before him. "It is time Briar knows his heritage."

Briar looked up from the stool before the fireplace. "Ard Ri?" he said. "I heard the Arshzar call me that outside in the yard, and now you speak of it again. What is an Ard Ri?"

Loriel stood up from the table and gently ruffled Briar's shaggy hair as she seated him in her vacant chair. "Ard Ri," she said, "in the old language, means High King. I am Loriel the Lady of the Woods, leader of the Order of the Lion. The other members are Creed, Bard Chieftain. Lord Kennon Moon, Elven Priest. And Kazz the White, First Knight of the Stone Bears. In time, Briar, you'll make a fine Ard Ri. This past year, King Manix of Castlelan disbanded the Council of Kings, removing the ruling kings from their thrones in five of the Seven Kingdoms. Lorne. Cornum. Renford, Corse. Kamber. Only your father defied Manix, determined to serve as King of the Rock. Seven times the Karth invaders have crashed on the Rock, your father defeating each invading horde. It was then that he formed the Order of the Lion, so that his line would continue to rule at the Rock."

Creed removed the lock from the chest and opened the lid. The Elf Lord removed a tightly bound package from the depths of the chest. Facing Briar he held it aloft, softly saying, "The standard of the Kings of the House of Erin. As Bard Chieftain, I will lay the ground work for this coronation by reciting the history that you are connected to.

"In the year 100, Varr the Song Lord attempted to cast down the High One from his throne. In turn, the Shining Host cast Varr from the Bright Realm, down to Valasar, where he became Lord of Shadows. In the year 102, Varr, the Fallen One, hatched a plot to exterminate all Elves of Valasar by sending a plague that spread among the Race of Man. Elvenkind was blamed for this plague and were slain on site. In the year 103, the Elves, aided by Dwarven allies, built a fortress in the forest of the Whispering Timber. Elves and Dwarves settled there in Mint. An alliance was formed and kings and queens of both races shared a joint rule there for the next 500 years.

"In the year 596, a dragon, Drakvoren, ravaged Mint, capturing the Dwarven King Graenor and the Elven Queen Chaylendriel. Drak set a high ransom, demanding payment from the alliance. During the month it took for the two races to put together the ransom, imprisoned there in Drak's den, Graenor fell in love with Chaylendriel, and upon their release, they married in secret on the shores of Moon

Lake.

"In the year 597, the first child of Dwarven and Elven blood was born, and Graenor taking a portion of Chaylendriel's name gave name to the race itself, and thus the Chaykin began."

Creed paused for a moment, allowing Briar to absorb what he'd just shared. The fire crackled in the hearth. Fierce winds tugged at the solid oak door across the room. Sleet and snow pelted the twin round windows on either side of that door. A long silence followed. Creed waited a moment, his eyes straying to the flames burning low in the fireplace. When he spoke again, Briar sat forward, now caught up in the history of the realm of Valasar.

"In the year 2,000, the Crusades to exterminate the Chaykin began. Rorin Erin of Rockhaven, your ancestor, Briar, declared the Black-wood a sanctuary for Chaykin. In the year 2,230, a Demon Horde from the Shadow Realm invaded Valasar, and thus, the Unseen War began. Rorin raced to the Seven Kingdoms of Men to invite their kings to the First Council of the Unseen War. Rorin also summoned King Finn of the Elves and King Bronn of the Dwarves. Even as Rorin and his allies met, Drakvoren attacked them before they rode out to war. Rorin sent up a prayer to the High One, asking him to intervene. In the Bright Realm, the One heard his prayer, and seven blue stars fell from the skies and seven guardians appeared among their smoldering fragments.

"El Dantar the Stag.

"Solomon Temple the Wolf.

"Soren Elryad the Owl.

"Kestral Veren the Falcon.

"Brax Morr the Boar.

"Bres Loren the Bear.

"And Tawn the Lion.

"Tawn declared, 'Among the Races of Valasar, Rorin Erin, your line will forever battle against the Shadow. In the House of Erin a torch will forever shine.'

"Tawn then gave a mighty roar, and in his paw appeared a burning ember, pulsating with bright blue Star Fire. He turned it into a black jewel, placing it in the hilt of Rorin's sword, naming it the

Lionstone. Using the Lionstone, Rorin produced a horde of jewels filled with incredible power. They were placed in the hilts of the swords of a band of Chaykin Black Foxes, and wielding their jewel-blades they soundly defeated the demons of the Horde. And from that day onward, the Chaykin were known as the Jewel Folk."

As Creed finished reciting, he handed Briar a mail shirt. As it unfurled, the bold figure of a white lion was revealed upon its front side. He proclaimed, "Behold, Briar, High King, Lion of the Rock!"

So it was that Briar accepted his calling to be High King.
And he smiled.
And he prayed.
And he silently wept.

In the quiet hour before dusk, they left the Hall. The snow had ceased to fall. The air was crisp and clean. Earlier that morning, the Chief Bard had reached an agreement. Loriel advised that if Creed planned to take Briar into hiding elsewhere, they had better move while they had the advantage. So it was, the small party left the Hall shortly before sunrise.

Mounted once more on Racket, Alex gave a wistful sigh as they rode out of the clearing. Creed had chosen to leave Falcon with the Lady of the Woods, and despite the loud protest from the long-knife, Alex had no choice but to accept Creed's decision. Falcon last words now echoed in Alex's mind: "Sad to be parting ways with you, since we just met. But Creed and Loriel are on different path. Creed's mission is to see to the welfare of the boy prince, and Loriel's quest is to travel to the Emerald Glens. It is there that the Legend Weaver, Tanner Silvertree, lives. You and I will meet again one day, if Destiny is kind to us. Fare thee well, Alex Thorn."

Alex twisted round at the sound of Kazz's deep voice behind him. The huge Troll looked about warily in all directions, muttering under his breath, "As soon we see to the boy's safety, our own quest must be set in motion."

"Kazz," Loriel quietly warned. "Be patient, you big brute. We'll be on our way soon enough. What could be more crucial than seeing to the well-being of this boy-king?"

The white-haired Troll nodded respectfully yet continued to mumble under his breath. The two companions had other matters to attend to, and though they had not shared the secret of their quest with any of them, Alex was grateful they had agreed to accompany Briar and Creed part way to their destination. Afterwards, he guessed from snatches of conversation from Kazz, the two were destined to venture to the Lodge to carry on some secret mission of their own. Kazz grumbled once more, "I am not used to sneaking about like a mole in a mink's territory. This waiting grates on my nerves."

The entire party fell silent as Talon and Storm suddenly appeared in the undergrowth to one side of the trail, their keen, green-eyed gazes fixed on Creed.

Nodding at the silent communication the cats conveyed, Creed looked to the Lady of the Woods, saying, "I will escort Briar into the Blackwood. But, I would urge you to leave this forest by the quickest route. On their return to this birch grove, the cats spotted a Karth war band riding this way. Nearly a hundred strong. It would be best if you ride to your mission in the Glens."

They then said their farewells in short order. Alex sadly watched Falcon being carried away in the sheath at Loriel's shoulder. He waved hesitantly at the long-knife, and in a matter of moments, Kazz and Loriel rode away into the forest.

35

Later that evening, upon reaching the ridge overlooking a deep vale, Creed reined in Craft. He searched the moonlit valley of the forest below. Beside him on his mare, Briar peered down through the shadows of night. Alex nudged Racket forward to join the two. In the center of a grove below, a roaring fire illuminated the white bark of the birches. Around the fire, danced a host of Karth warriors. Their chanting echoed throughout the forest. A number of the savage warlords were charging their screaming steeds through the center of the fire. Wild shouts rang out as horses kicked burning logs into the midst of dancing warriors who crowned themselves with the antlers of deer and elk, and wore capes of bear, wolf, and badger.

    A tall warlord forced his horse through the fire, a white wolf pelt trailing over his bare shoulders. Othgar, Chief Warlord of the Karth gestured at the shadows at the edge of the birch grove. A tall, hooded figure clad in dark robes approached the fire. Zagar the Druid towered above the Karth standing near the fire. Those on horses formed a circle about the grove. The mounted warriors ran their fingers through their strands of hair and suddenly, their wind-blown locks glowed bright amber with the phosphorescent mire from the Fell Marsh.

    Karth horsemen were riding in from every angle of the forest vale.

Drawn swords glinted in moonlight. Bright, luminous hair whipped wildly about in the freezing winds. Antler-crowned warriors screamed angry oaths to the pale gray sky. Forming a constantly moving ring, the mounted warlords hemmed in the Druid and Othgar.

Zagar growled, "Ten-thousand warriors, you vowed! But where are they? I see merely a thousand. Too few to storm this realm! Broken vows! Unfulfilled oaths! You swore by blood that I would have ten-thousand at my command by the moons of winter. What have you brought me? A raiding party! A war host is what I demanded!"

Horses began to restlessly stamp the frozen earth. Othgar had only to nod or gesture, and a thousand steel blades would be drawn against the Druid. With one vicious look, the warlord could easily have signaled his men to hack the Druid into a thousand pieces.

Othgar said, "Blood and words have little power over the silver ice of the black sea. Ships of the Karth cannot come near this land when the sea is filled with sunken mountains of a thousand blades! When the spring thaws begin, you shall command ten-thousand!"

Creed turned Craft to the trail beyond the ridge. Racket and Briar's pony followed behind the Elven Lord, and they silently left the grove of the Karth behind them.

In the amber light of morning, Creed, Briar, and Alex rode through an aspen-lined vale. Creed smiled and said, "I am pleased to be your guardian, Briar. You've been a quiet observer of the chaos that has come raging into your life. A child of lesser strength would have succumbed to terrible bouts of despair. But not you. You are filled with an earnest desire to stand firm, to conquer, to become what you must in order to save the land. You've seen and heard enough to cause a grown man to tremble in fear. But you've accepted the truth of how matters are to be. No one could accuse you of rejecting your calling. Quite the opposite is true. As King, you shall greatly be loved by your people."

The trees began to thin on either side of the trail. Creed slowed Craft to a gentle trot. Directly before them lay the place of refuge. The ride had been long and wearisome, with the constant, nagging fear that they were being followed. But now, in the brightness of the winter morning, Creed sighed in relief. He had been right to choose this place. They had traveled so far north that not once did they see enemy search parties. If by chance, one appeared now, Creed was confident they were going to simply vanish from the face of Valasar.

Ahead, in the distance, between two massive elm trees, lay the waters of a crystal-clear lake. Creed spurred Craft to run between the twin elms, directly toward the clear water.

"Creed! There is a lake there!" Alex cried in alarm as he followed closely behind him.

"There seems to be," laughed Creed. And then they were on the surface, but their mounts did not sink, nor could the sound of splashing be heard. The two horses and the wyndar simply ran as if on solid ground, and the mist swallowed the three riders.

The blue-tinted haze before them opened like a swiftly drawn curtain. Before them stood a castle formed of sparkling white stone. Creed said, "An illusion, Alex. Despite what you saw, the lake was not there. In fact, there are no lakes in the Blackwood Forest. There is however, a Crystal Castle in a deep wooded glen, with twin giant elms that stand at the beginning of its greenway. Though no man sees it that way, now."

The moment they entered the large courtyard of the castle, they were embraced by a gentle breath of clean air. Winter had no grip on the Crystal Castle, for it was held now in the grasp of spring. Rolling, green berms met them on all sides, and the cobblestone path that opened onto the courtyard was lined by twin flowerbeds of marigolds, purple begonias, bluebells, bleeding hearts, and lemon-yellow lilies. Subtle hints of their fragrance lingered in the air.

A paved lane ran through the center of the central courtyard, splitting in three different directions. To the east, past an archway of smooth granite, was a manor house, with oaken doors, stained glass windows, and white walls interlaced with dark beams. Rounded eaves graced the roof of the third story, and a hedge of glazed marble encircled the front lawn. The lane that turned to the west, swooped down to the stables where even the kennels and stable house were formed of white-washed stone. Ahead and to the north, was an open field and an orchard of fruit trees. Beyond these was an enormous oak tree. Bright green were its leaves, and its wide-spread crown stood out against the sky, and dwarfed the seven central towers of the castle.

Creed suggested they dismount. They did so, and after removing their cloaks and winter jackets, they made their way down the lane past the kennels and stable house. As they passed the open door of the stables, they spotted a shaggy brown pony. Upon rounding the corner of the stable house, they saw thousands of roses trailing back into the vale, forming a barrier before an iron gate. Beyond the gate stood seven tall, white stones forming a circle on the edge of the vale.

A Chaykin appeared there with thick, maple-colored hair. He stood no taller than Creed's waist. "Greetings," he said. "Welcome to the Vale of Roses. I am Niffit Oakleaf. I am the Faith Holder. I simply believe and therefore, I may move mountains."

"Mountains?" asked Briar.

Niffit chuckled softly. "Well, that of course, is a figure of speech. I've never moved a mountain. I wouldn't know where to put one even if I did."

Briar eyed the Chaykin skeptically. "Faith Holder? What do you mean? Do you call an act of magic a working of faith?"

"Magic," Niffit said, "and faith are one and the same thing, Briar."

The small Woodwalker gestured to the enormous oak, its widespread crown standing out against the sky and overshadowing the central courtyard. Bright rays emanated from the center of the courtyard. At the core of the wildly shooting beams of light was a spinning sphere of amber.

And in front of this, kneeling before a forge, was a Dwarf

36

Within the stocky fellow's blistered hands, he held a finely crafted sword. His red hair, burned in a dozen places, hung loosely about his broad shoulders. His long beard was singed and darkened with soot. With a reverent whisper, he tossed the sword into the depth of the flames. Then, the brawny Dwarf turned to face them. Staring intently at the standard of the White Lion on the front of Briar's Elven shirt, he said, "Lion of Rockhaven, I am Gideon Rockbrow. I have forged the Talisman's of Erin for you and I will soon present you with your sword!"

A hiss filled the air as Creed drew his sword, blue light glowing within the blade. "The last time we met," he said, "you served the Oath Bound assassin's guild! I thought by leaving you alive, my mercy would mean something to you. What are you doing here?"

Gideon made a deep and gracious bow. "Ah, Blackstag," he said, "your mercy was not taken for granted. I shall tell you the tale of how I ended up here, but first let me attend to the young king."

Nodding, Creed sheathed his sword. He skeptically eyed the seven items set before them on an oaken table. The first was a black breastplate. "The Breastplate of the Bear," proclaimed Gideon.

Briar stooped over, placing his hands on his knees to study the breastplate more closely. Within the silver sheen of the black armor, he saw his own reflection. Staring back at him was a boy, his long dark hair held in place by a band of leather. A boy whose blue eyes matched those of the bear upon the armor.

Briar moved over to inspect an ornate key with fine engravings of vines and roses up and down its length. Out of this pattern of thorn-laced vines emerged a leaping wolf with bared fangs. These fangs formed the teeth at the end of the key. "The Key of the Wolf," stated Gideon.

Briar glanced over at a bone-white horn inlaid with golden bands. Gideon said, "The Horn of the Stag."

Next to the horn lay a silver ring with an owl at its center. Gideon declared, "The Symbol of the Owl."

Briar looked down at a pair of fingerless gloves made of fine black leather. Upon each one, where the knuckles of a hand would fit, there were four silver emblems of screaming falcons.

"The Gauntlets of the Falcon," Gideon said.

Briar peered down at the round, black shiny shield with a rampant wild boar engraved on its sleek surface. "The Shield of the Boar," Gideon declared.

Briar moved to stand over a circlet of black metal. At its center was a lion's head. Within the open mouth of the lion was a small black jewel. "Behold," proclaimed Gideon, "the Crown of the Lion."

He then added, "These are the Talismans of Erin. They will be most necessary in your battle against the Shadow. They shall ward off spells, protecting your mind, and shielding your soul, Briar."

The stout Dwarf kneeled before the forge and sorted through the seven objects lying before him. He held up a golden torch, alive with flickering tongues of flame. He then picked up a fist-sized ball of pulsating light. Still before him was a lantern. Tiny bursts of green light flickered like fireflies within its glass cage. Beside the lantern was a cylinder that spun round with a power of its own. Next to this, were two bricks, one of gold, one of silver. And last, was a slender white strand of long hair. In turn, Gideon took each of them and cast them into the spinning sphere of amber brilliance, naming each item:

"First, the Torch of Sunflame!

"Second, the Orb of Moonshine!
"Third, the Lamp of Stardust!
"Fourth, the Rod of Lightning!
"Fifth, the Bar of pure Gold!
"Sixth, the Brick of pure Silver!
"Seventh, a strand from the mane of the White Lion!"

A radiance filled the courtyard. The sphere of spinning amber slowly settled upon the forge. Sparks began to fly in a fierce wind. The sphere began to brighten with each passing moment. Sparkling dew drops of each color fell like transparent rain, and suddenly, all color vanished, leaving points of light dancing in the air.

"Briar," Gideon said, "I present you with the sword, Sunflame!"

The Dwarf softly quoted an ancient verse:

The sword of light shall assail
    the realm of the Dark Domain,
    searing night, cleaving shadows,
    splitting darkness,
    it shall end the Dark One's reign.

Through battle he will ride to the Dark One,
    the sword shining brighter than day.
    He will set free those who are bound,
    when the Evil One he does slay.

By the hand of the King who wields it,
    great victory shall be won.
    And he that was bred of the Darkness,
    shall be consumed by the light of the sun.

Briar reached out to the long sword, and grasping it with both hands, lifted it in the air. He examined Gideon's craftsmanship, saying, "Sunflame is the work of a true master. The blade is finely wrought, and gleams with streamers of both silver and gold. The guard is arched properly, and these twin lion heads on each end are beautiful.

The pommel is evenly wrapped with this blue leather binding, and the prophecy of Sunflame is etched with precise detail down both flats, but what about these claws on the hilt?"

Gideon responded. "That spot is to be the final resting place of a fabled jewel. The power of the sword cannot be released until this jewel adorns its hilt. The jewel was given to me two nights past by Tawn, King of the Guardians. It is known as the Lionstone."

Gideon then produced a fist-sized black gem from his belt pouch, saying, "Once attached to your sword, this gem will activate the spells that enchant Sunflame. The Lionstone holds the power to restore or the power to destroy."

Gideon attached the Lionstone to the open claws on the sword hilt.

Taking the hilt in both hands, Briar leaped from one sunny spot to another, playfully avoiding the web-like shadows created by sunlight shining through branches overhead.

Creed, Niffit, and Gideon smiled at the boy's antics as he twirled his new sword around and over his head, feinting and mock-fighting invisible enemies.

It was Alex who spotted the trouble coming from above.

He gasped, "Dragon!"

37

Far above the Blackwood Forest, Drak had been flying toward the mountains of the Whispering Timber when flashes from the forest below had caught his eye.

Down from the skies he flew, making his way in ever-smaller circles, watching with keen interest as the dark-haired child danced beneath the giant tree. Drakvoren eyed the shimmering gold sword in his grasp, a treasure free for the taking; a trinket to add to his horde at his den in the mountains of the Sun-Cast.

The moment his shadow fell on those below, he spelled Creed, Niffit, and Gideon with such intense terror, that they became helpless to his attack. Drak landed, whipping his tail out to send the Elf, Chaykin, and the Dwarf sprawling to the ground.

The dragon kindled flame to burn the life out of the three.

Yet, even as fire began to swell within his chest, a devastating bolt of power shot through him, racking his black body with so much pain that Drakvoren cried out. Fire died within his open maw. His eyes widened in alarm. With a stunned look to his hind quarters, Drakvoren saw the cause of his sudden agony.

Standing there, his hands gripping the hilt of Sunflame, Briar had slapped his blade down hard across the dragon's tail, willing the black Lionstone to activate its killing force. Uttering a painful cry, the dragon crumpled to the ground, and slowly began to die.

Briar knew then that the force that moved through the sword had struck the dragon a blow, mortally wounding it. He knew that death was creeping over the dragon's prone form as it lay there moaning in pain. Taking a firmer grip on the sword hilt, Briar prepared to send the force shooting forth once more. He knew Gideon had said it had the power to destroy or restore, but Briar wanted to make sure the dragon died. As he tried to rekindle the power within the sword, the dragon did a strange thing. So strange, in fact, that Briar was smote to the heart with pity for the pain-wracked creature. No scream of agony came from its parted jaws. No wail of horror did it give as it faced death. Drakvoren, murderous beast that he was, simply cried.

It was a sound so foreign to Briar that he froze, undecided about what to do. The cry had been like the mournful cry of a lost kitten, like the soul-stirring yelp of a cuffed puppy, like the heart-rending cry of a lonely child. Briar knew that if the dragon had made an ugly, gurgling sound, he could have easily slain it. Or if it had given a venomous hiss of defiance, he could have blasted it away without a second thought. But, it had not.

Instead, the fierce, foul-smelling beast had sadly whimpered.

And Briar had not the heart then to slay it.

Already, Briar could feel power surging through the sword. It was building in force, like a storm about to break. Extreme potent power was on the verge of bursting forth, and Briar felt it was too late to stop it. As power streamed forth to the already dying dragon, Briar willed the force to restore, not destroy. His pity for the poor creature would not allow him to slay it. He swung the blade down on its tail for a second time.

Expecting sudden death, Drakvoren shuddered as the power surged through his weakened body. He squinted his large yellow eyes, and prepared to cry one last time before darkness descended. Yet, suddenly, his eyes opened wide, his jaws gaped. He lifted his massive head and neck in astonishment. He was restored, brought back from the brink of death to the bright borders of life.

Drakvoren rose on his four claws. He roared fiercely, looking about the clearing for the boy with the golden sword.

Niffit suddenly appeared between the boy and the dragon. "Fly away!" he commanded.

At once, Drakvoren rose skyward. He spread his long black wings and flew away. Why he flew, he did not know. He only knew, in his small brain, that he must leave the Vale of Roses at once. He flew north in a state of utter confusion. He did not comprehend what it was that controlled his will or diminished his wrath. He knew only that flying away was what he must do. As he flew, he was also confused about the fact that he still lived. A dragon such as he, cruel, evil, savage, wicked and full of blood-lust, could not quite comprehend the act of kindness that had been shown. It saddened him, which was odd. He had never known sorrow; only hatred and deep-rooted anger. He had never before encountered mercy. The memory of the merciful man-child, and how he had healed him, would remain with Drakvoren for a very long time.

Back in the Vale of Roses, Briar asked, "How did you do that? How did you just command the beast to fly away, Niffit?"

Niffit said, "Faith. I simply believed he would fly away more than he believed he wouldn't!"

Rain began to fall before evening, and Creed led the others inside the Great Hall of the Crystal Castle, where they built a fire in the Hall's massive hearth.

The five of them gathered round the large oak table situated before the roaring blaze, and over a meal of bread and cheese and a pot of buttered mushrooms, Gideon told the others his tale.

Creed kept his gaze locked on the red-haired Dwarf during the entire time he spoke, while Alex and Briar went right on eating the food placed before them by Niffit, who turned out to be a most gracious host.

Gideon swallowed a mouthful of hot mint tea and then said, "When I woke up back there in the grove where we tried to slay you, Master Blackstag, I found I was not alone.

"I sat up between my dead assassin companions to see a lion-man holding the metal collar that evidently saved me from your blade. He looked up from studying the intricate metal work, and fixed me in his blue-eyed gaze. 'Do you wish to atone for past deeds?' he asked me. 'Now that you've been given a second chance, do you want your life to be something more meaningful than that of an assassin?'

"I had no sooner told him that I did, when he suddenly transformed into a winged creature, that looked more like a lion than a man. He spread his wings wide, launched himself from the snowy ground, and clutched the back of my collar in his talons. Up, up, and away, he carried me far above the forest.

"When he at last set me down it was here within the white-walls of this castle. His wings vanished, he transformed back into a tall, man-like figure. He said, "Tawn is my name. I am King of the Messengers. I serve the Light, and as such, I have a task for you. I know that before you became an assassin you were a talented blacksmith in the dwarf kingdom of Quain. I have need of your skills. I want you to forge a sword.'

"He supplied me with all the items I would need to forge this particular sword. He asked me to swear a vow. I did so. He then flew away to see to some other quest. I remained here to forge the sword."

Creed asked, "This oath? What did it pertain to?"

Gideon drank another swallow of tea. He looked across the table directly at Briar. "I swore to serve the new king, Briar of the House of Erin. I vowed to be his smith and his bodyguard in the days to come. And I intend to fulfill my oath. Any objections, Elf?"

Shaking his head, Creed said, "No. Not from me."

With a mouthful of food, Briar returned the Dwarf's intense gaze and mumbled, "I accept your service."

38

The next morning, as boys are inclined to do in such circumstances, Alex and Briar went exploring the grounds of the Crystal Castle.

Bundled up in thick furs against the icy sleet that had been falling since early morning, the two boys walked round the entire battlements, climbed to the guard stations in six of its towers, ventured down into the dungeons below the keep, and ended their three-hour excursion by butt-sliding across the smooth, black ice of the castle's small pond situated before the giant oak tree in the central courtyard.

After running directly at the sleek surface, Alex launched himself from the snowy ground and slid for quite some distance across the ice. Briar, being a quick study, watched him perform the sliding maneuver three times, before he, too, took to the undignified position of sliding across the ice on his butt.

After laughing breathlessly over his own antics, Briar slid directly into Alex in front of him, and the two ended up in a tangle of arms and legs, their thick fur coats and hoods causing them to look like two bear cubs sprawled on the ice-covered pond.

"I'm not sure," Briar said, his words coming out in vapors leaking from his lips, "I am ready to quit my boyhood so early. I wonder if being a king can wait a bit longer, that is, until I am done being a boy. There will be no time for such play, when I am king."

Alex reached out and patted him gently on his fur-covered arm. "Well, don't let me stop you from playing, your majesty."

Briar reached out and latched onto Alex's gloved hand. "Please, never call me that, Alex Thorn. To you, I shall always be just Briar."

Their eyes met as they scrambled back to their feet, using each other's support to keep from slipping and sliding on the smooth surface of the pond. "Okay," Alex said. "Briar it shall be between us."

Smiling warmly at him, Briar looked across the pond to the faint outline of a doorway within the base of the massive oak tree. "Come," he said, "let's continue our explorations. As a king I could command you, but as a friend, I simply ask you. Will you follow?"

Nodding, Alex followed Briar across the ice and the two boys found themselves standing before the gnarled roots of the giant tree, with the criss-crossing roots creating a stairway up to the round outline of the door. They searched around the tree for several long minutes, unable to find a way to open the door which would certainly open a way inside the massive tree. Confounded and frustrated, they both returned to the root stairway, mounting it one more time to stand before the outline of the doorway.

Alex took a hold of Briar's right arm. He removed the glove from his hand and said, "Perhaps it's like the sword in the stone of the King Arthur legend. Maybe it takes a certain touch."

He raised Briar's hand and placed his palm into a slight indenture beside the door. Both boys gasped in surprise when a golden light traveled around the outline of the door, and with a slight whoosh of sound, the door swung outward.

Peering down at his hand, Briar said, "Tell me more about this King Arthur, if you please."

They rode an elevator up inside the giant tree and it took them far, far above the castle's walls and even its tallest towers. On the ride up, Alex shared with Briar the King Arthur legend, and yet before he could conclude the tale with its tragic ending of Lancelot and Guinevere's betrayal, the small cabinet they stood inside stopped, and its door opened onto a round, dome-shaped tree house nestled within the topmost branches of the oak tree. The dome consisted of a chamber filled with a council table covered almost entirely by an enormous leather map of the realm of Valasar. A woodstove stood in one corner, and beyond that was a sleeping chamber with a large bed inside. Beyond the bed was a giant glass window revealing the snow-touched forest beyond and below.

Briar walked over to the table, placing his index finger down on the map tracing a path from Rockhaven into the Blackwood Forest. The map came alive with a gold illumination, and one location lit up with green sparkles of light. Alex stared down at the focal point far to the south, deep within the Emerald Glens. He narrowed his eyes as the bright glow from the Lodge lit up his troubled features.

"What is wrong?" Briar asked him, concern showing on his own face. "You look like you've lost your way, Alex."

Alex frowned. "I have, Briar. I am from outside of this realm. My homeland lies beyond the door of the Lodge. That at least is where my friend, Lucas, came to the first time he visited Valasar. I believe that is where the one known as the Celtic Chieftain first entered the realm, as well. If I am to find him, maybe the Lodge would be a good place to start."

Briar shook his head. "You'll not stay to see me crowned?"

Offering him a sad look, Alex started to respond, when Niffit stepped from the shadows in one corner of the dome-home. The small Chaykin said, "Such are most quests, Briar. One person starts one, and steps aside to allow someone else to take it up. For the time being, Alex's quests he started here are over. Time to let someone else take up the cause. Yes, Alex saved Range from Dariak by wielding Falcon. Rifkin the Mink intervened on his behalf, weakening the demon even more, and yet he stole the Lion War book, and now Peyton Ring has taken up the chase after Rifkin. Alex parted ways with the little white wolf pup, destined to be king, when Grizz escorted him away. He once again wielded Falcon when he rescued you from Ronan. So, you see, Alex may have stumbled upon another's quest, only to take it up himself, only to pass it onto another. Such are the way of quests."

He paused, his hand hovering above the Lodge on the map spread before them. "Alex may return one day, and find that many of those quests have ended, or he may find himself right back on track to finish them. Who knows? But, you will not be left alone on the next leg of your journey to be king, Briar. Creed will be a good friend to you. Gideon, too, and me. And although the King's Company has very few members now, with Loriel the Lady of the Woods and Kazz the White, when Alex returns here, you will have a large following of your special company."

Briar stared down at Niffit's hand held only inches from the table. "But how will he, who is inside, travel back outside?"

Niffit turned his hand palm upward, indicating that Alex should reach down and clasp it in his own. Alex lowered his hand and the Chaykin connected his palm with the Lodge. A brilliant flash burst from beneath their hands and a sudden green wind sprang up from the face of the map, swirled around and around Alex, and carried him back down to the round, open door of the Lodge.

A gust of the green wind thrust Alex forward, so that he literally flew through the Lodge and passed through the doorway that would take him back to the dragon chamber inside the Emerald Pub. Behind him at the council table, Briar's eyes filled with tears and he stood there weeping for a long time after Alex was gone from the realm.

Reason, Boone, and Celeste, having finished their heated conversation with Nate, Gypsy, and Diesel, stepped back inside the Emerald. Boone snorted in disgust. "We tried, didn't we? If the Den wants to cause any more trouble over this, I've a mind to just put Dad and the Outlaws in their path. Maybe you should make sure Nate knows Lucas is safe and sound, or they'll likely come back here and tear the dragon room apart."

Pulling the door of the pub closed behind him and locking it, Reason said, "Lucas is fine. Celeste is, too. I have no intention of using either one of them to test the game play. Alex is still my key player when it comes to testing the game."

Boone skidded to a stop beside the fireplace. Behind him, Reason ran into him, and the two brothers stood staring at Alex exiting the dragon room. He had removed the fur coat and the gloves, but he was still dressed in the sleek and shiny brown leathers he had dressed in when he first entered Valasar.

He staggered down the hallway, and Reason rushed forward to catch him before he fell. He held him up with both hands and asked,

"What are you doing dressed in those leathers, Alex?"

Alex coughed and spluttered. "Time must pass differently between the two realms," he said, coughing once more. "I've been gone for over four days inside Valasar."

"And we," Reason said, "have been outside for maybe ten minutes talking to the Den."

Seating him in a chair before the fireplace, Reason examined his features and the leather outfit he wore. "Do you want to tell us about it, Alex? Sounds like you've got a story to tell, right?"

Alex exchanged uncertain looks with Reason, Boone, and Celeste, and let out one long breath, saying, "Boy, howdy!"

39

Having picked up Lobo an hour ago, Lucas was hot on the trail of Hunter Synn. He had brought the dog to the window at the Emerald through which the boy had escaped. Once the award-winning pit bull picked up the scent, he had led Lucas through the park, down three blocks of residential streets, past Ballard ball field, and to the bike trail running east and west out of Havelock.

Lobo stopped there, looking toward the right.

There, the old Santa Fe railroad tracks once passed through downtown Lincoln seven miles to the west. Those tracks connected with the rail yards there and split into, not one set of tracks to carry trains out of the city and into the country beyond, but nine different tracks that diverged at a place known as the Hump. It was named for the observation port that thousands of trains passed over to be inspected before being sent on their way out west. Although the Hump was still in operation, the tracks that connected Havelock with the downtown yards were now gone, having been turned into a hiker/biker trail. The trail ran east into the country, following the rail lines that connected Lincoln to Omaha sixty miles away.

Lobo turned from staring off to the west, and focused on the trail running east. He lowered his head and sniffed the ground. With an excited huff! the big pit darted in that direction, pulling Lucas behind him. "Here we go!" Lucas said, glancing back at Grunge and Goblin who quickly caught up to them. The dogs kept up a steady trot as the four of them traveled down the trail leading east and out of the city.

Grunge sent, *Celeste asked you to head for home, Little Luke. She's depending on us to get you there safely. Whatever this crazy loon is up to, it's not our business. Time for home.*

Lowering his hand to pet Goblin's head, Lucas said, "Yes, guys, I know. Wanting to protect me like a mother hen. But where's your sense of adventure? Lobo is tracking the loon who attacked Celeste earlier. Don't you two want to be there when the kid goes to ground? Don't you think El Lobo would appreciate your help in case the kid goes hostile?"

No, came from Grunge.

No, said Goblin, giving Lucas a gentle headbutt.

Beef, Grunge said, *will serve as backup for whatever trouble that kid gives Lobo. It's late, Little Luke. Let's head for home like Celeste suggested.*

Lucas shook his head, causing his long blond bangs to fall down over his eyes. And then he shook the tangles back from his face, for he thought he saw something move at the periphery of his vision.

Grunge growled. Goblin turned to face the ballpark as a dozen white-furred baboon creatures emerged from a ring of bushes at the far end of the field. The thickly-built beasts ambled forward on all fours, their heads four feet from the ground. One of them gave a low hiss, and they stopped there at the edge of the ball diamond, glaring at the dogs, yellow eyes shimmering in the moonlight.

"Home," Lucas said, softly, "is no longer an option."

Lobo led Lucas and the other two dogs three miles out into the country east of Havelock. The dog had caught the spoor of Hunter Synn and it became stronger as he closed the distance between the kid and himself. The pit bull had busted millions of dollars in cartel drugs during his service as a sniffer dog, and Reason had trained him in nose-work, which meant El Lobo was not only an expert in tracking drugs, but could find people, bombs, and particular items when presented with them. Following the scent of one psychotic kid was an easy task for the dog, and he led Lucas far out into the country to a hollow between two hills past an old railroad bridge that spanned a creek. There before the kid and three dogs stood Wounded Arrow dog rescue ranch, owned by Lakota dog handler, Benjamin Black Bull.

Lucas stood there looking at the large dog barn, the berm that housed Ben's underground home, and the dark trees north of the property. Nearly a year ago, Ben took him in as a foster kid when the courts removed him from his home after a violent dispute between Stone and Maggie. He had at first been placed with a husband and wife team, both police officers. Ben had been there the day Lucas nearly threw himself off of a sixth-story parking garage, desperately threatening to end his own life. Later, Ben claimed it wasn't him that saved Lucas from launching himself from the top of that building, but instead Goblin, who had been thrown out onto the downtown street by dogman Duce Hammer.

Spotting the pit bull pup far below him on the sidewalk, Lucas scrambled off of the sixth-story ledge, no longer determined to take the hard way down. He not only rescued Goblin, preventing him from getting run over on the busy city street, but Hammer came back around the block in his car and dumped Grunge out onto the street in front of them, then drove away. It was on account of Goblin being chipped that Hammer rid himself of both pit bulls. He feared the tracking device embedded beneath Goblin's skin would lead the cops to his dog fighting set-up.

Ben was good for Lucas. He took in troubled dogs at Wounded Arrow and allowed vets suffering from PTSD to work with them here at the ranch. The Lakota dog handler paired Lucas up with Grunge, a notorious fighter on the Nebraska circuit, and the experience transformed both of their lives.

Ben used Native medicine to tame dogs, then paired them up with distressed vets. Those relationships between dogs and vets conjured up heavy magic. Taming the wild beast. Healing the broken-hearted. Stepping onto the Red Road. Entering into the Medicine Circle. There was magic at work out here at Ben's place.

Lucas had continued to glance back as they made their way down the bike trail, staying ahead of the creatures trailing them. There was no sign of the beasts now. They had either broke off their stalking or were hidden now in the bushes to either side of the trail. Grunge continued to softly growl. Goblin remained on high alert, constantly checking the trail behind them. He was hoping to maintain a good distance ahead of them. He'd counted twelve of the lumbering white beasts, and though Grunge was the fiercest dog he'd ever met, he knew that he, Lobo, and Goblin would not stand a chance against so many of the thick-limbed baboon beasts.

At a whisper of sound behind them, Lucas wheeled around to see Colton Lone Wolf emerging from the trees beside the trail.

"Wolf!" Lucas said, excitedly. "The Dog Soldier!"

The massive Lakota ambled forward and gently ruffled Lucas's shaggy hair. "Maybe the Thunder Dreamer could explain all this to me, since he's got a better connection to the Otherworld than this old Injun. An award-winning sniffer dog? And the backup of these two fine-looking pits? Is there a story to tell?"

Lucas said, "We're out hunting some psycho kid who tried to attack my sister with a knife. But, some baboons are following us."

"Baboons?" Wolf said, frowning.

"Yeah," Lucas said, defensively. "Only they were all white."

Wolf peered back at the bike trail.

Lucas asked, "Where did you come from?"

Wolf kept his dark eyes fixed on the trail behind them. "I was out doing recon, when I happened upon the Thunder Dreamer, who tells me he and these dogs are out hunting?"

Lucas nodded emphatically. "Yeah, the kid who pulled a knife on Celeste and Alex."

Wolf said, "I heard your dad and Khalid flew all the way over to Egypt to find the nut job Waziri. Only thing is, Waziri ain't even over in Egypt. He's still here. Somewhere. More than likely planning some other kind of terror attack. Finding a terrorist over there in the Middle East is the last thing I would want to tackle. I wish Khalid and your dad all the luck in the world if they return here and find Waziri."

Lucas said, "Only one will walk away from such an encounter. Khalid's a Phantom agent, and they have an unspoken code regarding extremists. Only a bullet to the head will cure the radicals. I heard him telling my dad that millions of dollars have been wasted on de-radicalization programs over in Europe. Programs that don't work."

Feeling a powerful tug the leash, Lucas was led onto Ben's main property and stopped, peering earnestly up into the forested hill to the north of the ranch. Lucas knew by Lobo's excitement that Hunter was soon to be found.

"Lucas," Wolf said, "it was a bad idea for you to follow this kid."

"You think," Lucas blurted, "I might be in danger? On account of some nutty kid?" He pointed down at Grunge. "He'll be the one in danger if he tries to attack me."

Lobo whined and strained at his leash. Lucas allowed him a little lead way, and the big pit started up the hill toward the tree line above them. "See," Lucas said. "Lobo is hot on the trail. We wouldn't want to interfere with his sniffing now, would we?"

He gave Lobo free reign to proceed. Taking one last look at the dark and silent mound of earth housing Ben's underground home, he said, "Come on, Wolf!"

As they exited the trees and stepped onto the former farmstead of Kooper's Steading, Lucas said, "This land was deeded to Ben by a former dogman named Kooper. He felt bad about his grandson and his pup dying out here in a fire one night, and to ease his conscience, he deeded this steading over to Ben."

He gestured at the enormous dark and shadowy building before them and muttered, "But what the hell is that?"

Peering hard at the dark stone walls and at the six towering turrets blocking out the night sky, he said, "A castle? Looks like Game of Thrones meets Nebraska cornfields!"

40

They stood there staring at the lowered drawbridge and the arched opening beyond. The walls and towers took up nearly half an acre of land, stretching before them to the left and right, with the six turrets pointing toward the sky. It was indeed a magnificent looking castle that would have looked normal in Ireland, Scot-land, or Great Britain, but yet there it stood in the middle of the heartland of America.

Lobo, too, seemed to be confused by the sight of the huge, black castle, and he whined softly as he studied its open gates. At a slight sound behind them, Grunge and Goblin slowly turned their heads and glanced back at the forest of trees they'd just passed through to reach the steading. Goblin narrowed his eyes and let out a low Grrrrr!

All of them, the two humans and three dogs, turned to peer hard at the darkness beyond the right side of the castle, when a commotion erupted within the forest of trees lining the far edge of the steading. A moment later, an entire troop of the white baboons emerged from the shadowy trees there, and stood staring at them from two-hundred feet away. "Holy Moses!" gasped Lucas, as he glanced behind them to see another large troop of thirty or more of the large, white beasts flitting through the trees and undergrowth of the forest they had just passed through to get to the steading.

Lobo, Grunge, and Goblin took up defensive stances in a bold move to protect the humans. Lobo faced the troop to the right of the keep, and Grunge and Goblin turned to face the creatures now gathering just outside the trees behind them.

Wolf quietly said, "No need to play hero just yet. Not unless they find a way to storm the walls!"

The big Lakota then herded the others toward the lowered drawbridge of the castle. And both troops of white baboons gave chase.

Boom! reverberated throughout the entire keep as Wolf finished cranking the drawbridge up and into place at the gate below him. The moment they had entered into the main courtyard, he had ran up a set of stone stairs leading to the gatehouse above the gateway. Although the old Dog Soldier was turning seventy, he was still strong as an ox, and he used that great strength to crank the drawbridge up into place seconds before the baboon beasts reached the castle.

Lucas stood there on the battlements, peering inside the dark gatehouse in case Wolf had needed his help. "Did any make it inside?" Wolf asked him as he emerged from the gatehouse.

"No," Lucas said, turning to peer down between the crenelated battlements to study the yellow-eyed creatures milling around before the keep. "Thanks to you, we seem to be safe for the moment."

He looked down in wide-eyed amazement at the horde of strange-looking beasts. "Tried to tell you," he said, "that I was being followed by them. Just what in the hell are they? I mean, they have the bodies of great apes, yet the heads and faces of baboons."

Wolf continued to stare down at the milling beasts. "Gelch," he said. "Creatures from another realm, and they are many. We managed to trap some of them inside the cells beneath this castle. The entire troop is weakened due to the Sacred Medicine Wheel that surrounds this keep. Days ago, when this castle suddenly appeared here within the steading, Ben and I created a medicine wheel out of stones."

Lucas leaned out a little too far between the crenelated battlements, and Wolf latched onto him and pulled him back before he fell forward and over the wall. "What are you trying to prove?" he said. "Next thing you know, you'll be monkey meat!"

"Trying to see," Lucas said, "if any of those things can climb."

Wolf said, "Oh, they can climb like the monkeys they are related to, but not these walls. On the first night they arrived here, some of them got blasted from some inner wardings intertwined within these stones and since then, these walls have put forth an invisible field of force to keep them from coming over the battlements. The only way in for them is through the open gate. The reason it was open, I had thought those beasts long gone from here. Something attracted them, something called them back from wherever they had gone."

Checking on the dogs positioned below inside the courtyard, Lucas then looked out into the close grouping of dark trees. "Could it have been him?" he asked, pointing to the pale figure standing amongst the black trees. Wolf looked to the forest one-hundred yards from the castle. There, Hunter Synn stepped out of the tree line, dressed in white leathers, sharply contrasting with his bright red hair. Two silver hoops glinted in the lobes of his slightly pointed ears, and he smirked as he moved in between the hulking bodies of the Gelch.

"Do you think these walls," Hunter snarled, "will prevent me from freeing those bound beneath this keep, old man?"

His words were directed at Wolf, and the Lakota Dog Soldier and Boy Wizard locked gazes for long moments.

"Kid," Wolf said, amused at his arrogance, "be my guest."

Hunter gave a stern command, and at once, the entire mass of Gelch darted to the foot of the thirty-foot wall and prostrated themselves one on top of another, building a white-furred ramp so that the boy might reach the top of the battlements. As agile as a monkey, Hunter climbed the stacked bodies of the baboon beasts, his green eyes fixed on the top of the wall before him. He drew a slender dagger from a sheath at his belt, slipped it in between his clenched teeth, and kept on coming.

As he neared the top of the pile of beasts, Lucas looked over at Wolf and said, "He's coming, Wolf! He's coming!"

Wolf simply stood there, his arms folded before his thick chest, grinning down at the potentially dangerous kid only six feet below. When Hunter reached the topmost beast stretched out below him, he launched himself up toward the wall, drawing the dagger out between his teeth even as sailed toward the battlements.

"Oh, my," Wolf actually chuckled as the knife-wielding boy flew through the air toward him. And then, he laughed.

The moment Hunter's free hand came down on the stone battlements, a bright blue explosive force struck him and flung him back as if he were a rag doll. His dagger flying from his grasp, his arms flapping, and his legs spastically kicking, he slammed into the dog-pile of white-furred Gelch, knocking them over and joining them as they fell and went sprawling across the lawn before the castle's gate.

Wolf laughed, "I just love magic!"

Hunter picked himself up, clambering to his feet amongst the fallen Gelch. "I've been sent to free them, old man!" he snarled. "And I will not leave here without them!"

Lucas said, "He's the son of an Elven wizard named Cain Synn, and in the realm of Valasar, he's supposed to be really powerful."

Wolf asked, "You've been to Valasar? Only in your Thunder Dreaming, right?"

"No, not really," Lucas said. "I mean, I don't think I was dreaming. I was really there. I was running from old man Connors and he chased me into this room down the hall from his fireplace. And I ended up seeing demons and dragons, and some lion-man named Tawn."

"Tawn?" Wolf gasped in amazement. "You've met the Guardian of the One?"

"Do you know him, Wolf?" Lucas asked in disbelief.

"No," Wolf said, with a frown, "but I've heard Ben speak of him. Guess he met him on his own trip to the far off realm."

"Ben has been to Valasar?" Lucas asked.

Peering down to Hunter Synn, Wolf said, "A story for another time. I fear we need to deal with him."

41

Standing at the forefront of the troop of sixty-odd white-furred baboons, Hunter removed a golden band from a pouch at his belt. He tossed it on the ground before him, and facing the front gate of the castle, he began to cast a spell. He gestured wildly with one hand. At the end of an erratic fluttering of his fingers, a burst of white smoke shot up in a geyser from the center of the band. From out of the smoke emerged a man-sized bat-like creature.

Above on the battlements, Wolf whispered, "Morgothan Bat Lord? That took some skill to conjure! This boy is dangerous!"

Hunter leaped up and latched onto the creature's ankles, and the Morgoth rose into the air, swinging the boy up and over the gatehouse. The Bat Lord carried him up above the courtyard of the keep. As he hung suspended forty feet above the stone paving, Hunter eyed the metal door at the center of the tower at the far end of the keep. He ordered the creature to fly him to the door.

Behind them on the battlements, Wolf drew a blue-tinged Bowie knife from a sheath inside his left boot. He brought the glowing blade up over his right shoulder, and sent the knife flying through the air. The blade struck the Morgoth Lord between his shoulders, directly where his wings sprouted from. The bat beast exploded into a scattering of red-hot embers, then drifted away in the evening breezes.

Hunter plummeted to the courtyard, falling through thirty feet of empty air. He landed on both feet, but driven by the force of his fall, he sprawled forward onto his hands and knees.

"Don't allow him to reach that door!" Wolf shouted to the three dogs directly below him near the gate. "Stop him! Stop him, now!"

Lobo and Goblin barked excitedly and tore off after the boy still dazed from his fall. Grunge, however, passed the other two dogs within seconds, his gaze locked on the slender Elven boy at the far end of the inner court. Taking one alarmed look at Grunge swiftly closing in on him, Hunter scrambled to his feet and ran unsteadily toward the iron-bound door twenty feet away. Spurred on by the threat of the menacing dogs coming up quickly behind him, he bolted across the paving stones, latched onto the handle of the door, swung it open, and darted inside.

The door closed behind him with a solid clang!

By the time Lucas and Wolf reached the dogs, the entire keep was rocked by a sudden explosion from deep within its walls. The detonation came from behind the door the wizard-boy had passed through. An airy whuff of sound and force seeped from the seams beneath the iron door, striking each of them with a hot wind that traveled up from deep inside the castle's dungeons.

"What was that?" Lucas asked, blinking away dust particles.

Wolf leaned forward, placing both large hands on the closed iron door. He said, "That kid came here for a purpose!"

The three dogs whined as they nosed the closed iron door, disappointed that Hunter had escaped them. "Yes," Wolf said, "we should pursue him. But we might be walking directly into a trap."

Retrieving his blue-tinged Bowie knife, Wolf said, "We will both need to be armed with magically enchanted weaponry. The eagle feather that Cora gave you is all you will need, Lucas."

As the big Lakota approached him, Lucas withdrew the necklace from beneath his shirt, displaying the feather that had once belonged to American Horse, a distant relative of Cora Red Cloud.

Gently shoving the three dogs aside as he stood before the door, Wolf said, "Thunder Dreamer, when the medicine is needed most, you may be very impressed with that feather you carry."

"You," Lucas said, "mentioned the kid came here for a purpose. What did you mean by that?"

"Yes," Wolf said, with a deep frown. "The kid may have freed from their cells. And that would be Molech and Baphomet just sent here from the Valley of Kings over in Egypt."

The moment Wolf opened the door that led inside the inner keep, they were met by a barrage of screaming spirits that came roiling up from deep inside the castle proper. The entire mass of wailing souls of dead people that Molech had fed off of in his short rampage upon the earth had been set free, and all of the tortured individuals were barely visible as they swarmed their way through the door.

The dogs, with their finely tuned senses and their Sight into the Otherworld, were able to clearly see the struggling mob of ghosts as they pushed and shoved to get outside. To the eyes of the two humans wheeling away from the door to get out of the path of the swarm, they appeared as unsubstantial forms, wearing barely visible robes as they exited the stairwell.

Lucas held up the eagle feather of American Horse. "They mean us no harm," he said. "They are just looking for a way to pass on. They want nothing to do with us, just simply to die in peace, instead of being savaged by the god, Molech."

The dogs moved to stand beside Lucas, all three growling at the apparitions hovering outside the open doorway. "Hush," Lucas said, "they don't want you guys neither. They just want to be on their way."

The feather in his hand suddenly evolved into a long, oak staff, and at the top of the staff, a wolf's head, a black gem sparkling within its open maw, the eagle feather trailing from its brow. Lucas gripped the staff just beneath the wolf's chin. "How could you know," Wolf asked, "what they want?"

"He told me," Lucas said, gesturing at his seemingly empty left shoulder. "He's the eagle this feather of American Horse came from. He's sent to instruct me, to give me directions, for magic is not to be trifled with. He's come to make me a Master of the Thunder."

As the sparkling form of a bald eagle suddenly appeared there on Lucas's left shoulder, Wolfe stared in amazement. Lucas cocked his head, listening to the shimmering raptor as it whispered into his ear.

Lucas raised his staff. "Go!" he ordered the spectral forms. "Time for another plane! Go, before Molech returns!"

At the mention of the brutal god's name, the transparent spirits made a terrific lunge toward the star-glazed sky, and as one, the entire mass of beings flew up and away from the castle, disappearing into the dark skies. Wolf looked to Lucas, as if expecting him to know what to do next. Lucas was listening to the shimmering eagle. He tapped his staff on the ground, and the black gem embedded in the wolf's mouth lit up with a violet glow, sending out a pulsating luminance in a six-foot circumference. At the center of what appeared to be an enchanted screen, a vision rolled across it:

Khalid, Stone, and Agent Raynes came rushing into an under-ground tomb. Before them, three small figures stood cowering in one corner of the chamber, trapped there by the goat-headed Baphomet. Loki, Puck, and Coyote quailed in terror as Baphomet glared at them with his goat-like slanted eyes and inched his way closer to them.

Behind the fire god, shards of the broken imprisonment gem lay scattered where Loki had dropped it onto the stones of the tomb's floor, allowing the soul of Baphomet to escape.

"Tricksters?" Baphomet growled. "The dark gods of the universe sent Tricksters to the tomb of Tut in the Valley of the Kings? Where is the gem that holds Molech's soul?"

Cringing like terrified children, Loki, Puck, and Coyote let out pitiful cries as Baphomet conjured up a handful of glistening black snakes. Clutching them in his hand, he raised them above the heads of the three lesser gods. Each snake had long fangs that dripped with poison so vile and harsh, it sizzled as it fell to the stones of the floor.

"Stop this!" Khalid shouted as he stepped over the glittering shards scattered beside the gem that imprisoned the soul of Molech, for it did not break and shatter when it struck the floor. It was still intact, with the soul of Molech trapped within it. Unaware of the gem laying on the floor between him and the sarcophagus of the boy-king, Tut, Baphomet continued to advance on the three lesser gods.

Swinging his black walnut staff up above his head, Khalid whispered a spell, and brought the sleek, black staff down hard on Baphomet's horned head. Thunder rumbled from somewhere outside the tomb in the Valley of Kings, and sheets of blue lightning rained down on the fire god even as he tormented the three lesser gods. Bolts of thin shafts of the lightning struck each snake, ripping them from the fire god's hand and pinning them to the floor. Each tendril of the wicked blue lightning penetrated the heads of the snakes and tore through their long, slender bodies, killing them within seconds.

Enraged at the damage done to his snakes, Baphomet cast a barrage of fiery pellets at the Mage Lord, ripping the staff from his grasp. Khalid was struck in the chest and hurtled back off his feet. He slammed into the sarcophagus of the dead boy-king, then flew back against the stone wall beyond, striking it with a sickening thud.

Baphomet drew a dagger from a collection of relics hanging on one wall of the tomb, and charged Khalid even as he tried to weakly rise up to meet his attack. It was Stone Holland who saved the Muslim man from the wrath of the goat-headed god. The biker swept up Khalid's staff and launched himself at Baphomet, striking him with the tip of it. In an explosion of glittering sparks, Baphomet was catapulted off his feet. Stone stood there, holding the staff before him as a burst of greenish light shot from its tip, hammering the fire-god back against the stone wall, causing Loki, Puck, and Coyote to scam-per out of the way. In one last pathetic attempt to ward off the magic washing over him, Baphomet lashed out, a dispersal spell flickering weakly on his fingertips.

And yet, before he could activate his own magic, an explosive concussion of power and light came shooting through the air, plowing into the fire-god, blasting him with crackling green fire. Engulfed in the emerald shades of power, Baphomet let out one last whimper, and collapsed there on the floor of the tomb. Khalid, Stone, and Raynes turned and with uncertain looks, they watched as Billy Connors stepped in between the realms, his sizzling staff held before him.

The old Irishman twirled the staff with a dramatic flourish, and greenish sparks rained down on the form of Baphomet sprawled before him on the floor. Loki let out a shrill giggle, gesturing at the unconscious fire-god with a one-fingered salute. Coyote and Puck danced around his downed form, kicking at the incapacitated Baphomet as payback for tormenting them.

"Stop!" Billy said in commanding tones. "You three tricksters have already done enough damage!"

Offering the Mage Lord contrite looks, the three lesser gods crept out of the chamber of the dead boy-king. In seconds, Billy conjured a second gem of imprisonment and with a flourish of his hands, re-captured the soul of Baphomet.

Raynes picked up the leather pouch from the floor, opening it so that Billy could place both gems inside.

The old Irishman walked toward the shimmering portal connecting the tomb with the dragon chamber back at the Emerald pub. "Sorry," he said, "if I had the power, I would tele-port the three of you out of the Valley of Kings and back to the Emerald, but that is beyond me."

Khalid asked, "What will you do with those gems?"

Stepping through the portal, Billy said, "Place them in a secure place out at Wounded Arrow. Someone from beyond, has conjured a castle that was designed to hold the souls of the two fire-gods."

With that, Billy Connors was gone.

42

"They're gone," Lucas said. "With Hunter's help, they've blown their way out of the basement of this keep."

He held the glowing staff up, and by its illumination, they could see past the landing inside a set of stone spiral stairs leading down into the belly of the castle. Wolf asked, "Blown their way out? Into this world? Or into the world beyond?"

Lucas stood staring at the large hole in the deepest dungeon of the castle. Hoping to see far beyond the ragged opening, obviously made by a powerful explosive force, he raised the staff above his head. The dogs peered into the undulating silver mist beyond the broken stones still left in place at what had once been the back wall of the cell they all huddled in. Wolf took two tentative steps forward, intending to step beyond the hole in the wall.

Lucas, however, stopped him by saying, "No use tempting fate, Wolfman. Who knows what is out there in that mist and fog?"

"They are out there," Wolf said. "We should hunt them down before Molech regains his strength. Once he comes back into full power, there will be hell to pay."

Peering out into the thick mist, he added, "The two weakened gods are being led by the kid. Even now, they are traveling deeper and deeper into the realm of Valasar, and farther and farther away. God help that crazy kid when Molech turns on him."

"How do you know this is Valasar?" Lucas asked. "This could be any realm out there. And what do you mean, turn on the kid?"

Shrugging his large shoulders, Wolf said, "A god who thrives on child sacrifices? He has an unknowing victim as his traveling companion! He will crave the power his sacrifice would gain him."

Lucas and the dogs saw a flicker of movement from deep within the thick mist roiling out there beyond the hole in the wall. Suddenly, a rider appeared there and the mists parted to reveal a wide open field. "It's Cora!" Lucas cried. "She's being chased by a pack of wolves!"

And they watched as Cora Red Cloud came racing toward the opening in the castle wall on a sleek black stallion, her long raven hair streaming over her slender shoulders, her finely-featured face set in grim determination.

Casting one last harried look at the black wolves closing in on her, Cora dug her heels into the flanks of her running mount. Bent low in the saddle, she slapped her reigns to the left and right, urging the swiftly running horse to put on one last burst of speed. The stallion complied and leaped through the opening in the wall before them.

Wolf used one arm to plaster Lucas against the wall in the small cell, and they watched in silence as Cora's horse sprang past them and passed into the hallway beyond.

Lucas used his staff to herd all three dogs out of the opening even as Cora made her last effort to outrun the wolf pack. Once she entered the hole blasted into the wall by Molech's escape, Lucas used his staff to cast a warding in the gap, preventing the pursuing wolves from following Cora into the basement of the castle. More than a dozen wolves literally bounced back from the field of force, and they all limped away in sullen defeat, snapping and snarling at each other.

A moment later, Cora appeared at the doorway on foot, having left her mount out in the hallway. She shared a grim look with Wolf, nodded to acknowledge Lucas, then said, "Ben is back there, lost in that realm. We need to go in there and rescue him."

And yet, despite their urgency to go beyond the cell of the castle, either to rescue Ben or to hunt down the two fire-gods, they could not get beyond the field of force Lucas himself had cast to keep the wolves from following behind Cora. When Wolf attempted to step through the shattered wall of the cell, he was blocked from doing so. Cora tried next, and she could not pass beyond the barrier either.

Blaming himself for creating such an obstacle, Lucas took his staff in a two-handed grip and hammered at the barely visible shimmers of power keeping them from passing between realms. Upon seeing that Lucas was working himself up, Grunge moved in between his faintly glowing staff and the field of force he was trying to get past. *No,* sent Grunge. *None of us are able to pass through the realm of Valasar at this time. That barrier remains in place for a reason. For now, let us retreat, and try another route to enter that distant realm.*

After a lengthy discussion, Wolf made the decision that Lucas and the dogs should leave the castle and return to Havelock. He assured Cora that he was working on an alternate route to get into the realm, he had no intention of leaving Ben trapped in there.

While Wolf set himself up as the guardian of this particular gateway closed to them for the moment, Cora agreed to drive Lucas and the three dogs back to Havelock.

Celeste had been woken from a sound sleep when Reason entered the house, ranting and raving about Lucas and the three dogs now missing. She had gone to bed a short while ago, agreeing with him that the missing Billy Connors was a mystery desperately needing to be solved. The old Irishman had vanished shortly after his encounter with Lucas, and now that they had confronted Nate and the Den, they had not heard the last from them with their threats to either blow the Emerald up or burn the pub to the ground in order to prevent Reason from allowing Lucas anywhere near the dragon room.

Celeste knew Reason well enough to know that he would never harm her little brother, nor would he do anything as rash as abducting him in exchange for his grandfather. She also knew Reason was genuinely worried about Billy's strange disappearance. Just as he would be over Lucas's vanishing act.

She'd hated the youth worker ever since he'd been assigned to her case, but over the years, she had to come to respect him. He of all people, was the real deal. He not only talked the talk, he walked the walk, and she had found him to be a strict and caring shepherd to her extreme lost-lamb act that she had pulled over and over again, while trapped within the juvenile justice system.

Reason Nelson never gave up on her. And nor would he give up on her little brother. In fact, with Lucas's extreme rage-fests that he was prone to throw, digging himself into a deeper hole as far as the courts were concerned, Reason might be Lucas's only answer to finding his way out of the system.

If he could only save him in time.

To calm Reason down, Celeste assured him that she would join the search for her wayward little brother. It was after all 4AM in the morning and Lucas had no business sneaking out of the house at such an hour. Even if he did have the dogs as protection.

As Reason and Alex speculated where Lucas could have gone in the kitchen, Celeste started toward the Emerald pub. The least she could do is eliminate that location as to where her little brother might have gone to.

She had just wrapped her long, black duster around her slender frame to ward off the chill of the wee hour of the morning, when Jango sprang from an overhead branch, landing on her left shoulder.

Startled by the spindly black monkey, Celeste gasped, "Geeshsus, you damned monkey-beast! You trying to give me a coronary?"

You search for Lucas, Jango sent. *I know where he is.*

Celeste glanced sideways at the little black, bald-headed creature as he curled his skinny fingers into the strands of her short hair. "You gonna tell me?" she asked. "Or play games with me, like usual. This is serious—"

Yessss! he said. *Hunter Synn has allied himself with Baphomet and Molech. Already, those three have carved a bloody path through the marshes, the fells, and the commons just south of the Sharmin Bogs. They are savagely slaughtering on a path to Dun Galvin, Queen's Tor, Andarin Keep, and down farther south to King's Hall. If not stopped, they will leave no one alive.*

Celeste was not overly concerned with a savage slaughter taking place in Jango's homeland of Valasar. Yes, she had studied the map he'd produced of the realm, and she knew the importance of key locations such as Castelan, Kallador, and the Seven Kingdoms, the fortress cities of Men. Mint and Quain, the homes of Elves and Dwarves. And Hawk's Hollow, the Tree City of the Jewel Folk.

She had listened to Jango explain the history of the realm, of how Elves and Dwarves had sailed there thousands of years ago fleeing from persecution in other lands. She had learned that the two races had set up major kingdoms of Mint in the Whispering Timber in the far north, and Quain in the Thunder Rock mountains to the east. She had been fascinated by Jango's tale of how the Chaykin race had come about, and the Crusades that followed soon after due to racial differences between Elves, Dwarves, and their Chaykin offspring.

However, this realm was far away. She had never been there herself. The Cingane Chieftain who had marked her with her magical tattoos, had mentioned an ancient battle she was to be involved in, but she had no connection to Jango's homeland.

"What," she snapped, "does Molech's bloody raid have to do with Lucas? Are you going to help me find my brother or simply riddle me to death?"

Jango twisted his homely face into an even uglier image than the one he normally wore. He blinked his overlarge blue eyes.

"What?" Celeste growled, irritably. "What are you not telling me, you little bug-eyed beast?"

Jango patted her cheek gently, then sent: *Hunter Synn came here to free Molech. Lucas and the dogs are tracking Hunter!*

Fifteen minutes later, Celeste arrived at Wounded Arrow, the dog rescue ranch owned and operated by the Lakota dog handler, Ben Black Bull. She had been in treatment while her little brother had lived out at the ranch, but she'd heard all kinds of positive stories about Lucas's recovery and rehabilitation due to Ben's care and commitment to him, troubled, angry kid that he was. She had never met the Lakota man herself, but she knew that Ben would never allow Lucas to get himself mixed up in the affairs of demons or gods. Celeste fully believed Jango, but thought perhaps the Mogrim was making some kind of mistake as to what Lucas was now involved in.

As she soared past the dog barn fifty feet beyond Ben's underground house, the headlights of her Volkswagon van illuminated the narrow tracks of a dirt roadway that wound up into the tree-lined bluff some distance ahead of her.

The castle is just beyond that hill, Jango sent to her as he perched precariously on her shoulder, shifting about as she recklessly drove her van up into the black trees.

"Castle?" Celeste asked. "There's a castle out here in these hills?"

Jango slid down into her lap. *Yes. It was sent here from Beyond by Lady Kerrin Skye, Elven Priestess of the Unseen War. It was sent to function as a prison, to keep Molech and Baphomet from entering Valasar, until the White Council could decide what to do with them.*

Celeste shook her head angrily. "Riddles, Jango! Why do you insist on talking in riddles? Kerrin Skye? Unseen War? White Council? A castle meant to serve as a prison?"

Sitting in her lap, Jango peered up over the steering wheel, nodding his small, round head. *Yes. Get inside the castle. You will then learn more. Lady Kerrin can then explain it to you more thoroughly.*

The headlights of her VW van lit up the dark walls before her. Her eyes widened in surprise at the forty-foot high walls and the towers overshadowing them. She then looked to the solid oak drawbridge, which was closed, barring access to the solid-looking fortress.

Celeste stomped on the brakes, causing the van to skid to a halt just before she nosed her way into the large pack of white-furred baboon creatures emerging from the forest beyond the keep.

In seconds, the ape-like beings surrounded her van, and one of the larger beasts began to bang on her windshield, glaring at her even as the windshield spider-webbed beneath his furious assault.

43

The loud crack of a high-powered rifle caused Celeste to flinch, and she and Jango peered up through the cracked windshield to the gatehouse above the castle's closed drawbridge.

There, standing out against a moonlit background, wreathed in silver light, was Cora Red Cloud. She had a large caliber rifle tucked in tight against her right shoulder. Smoke poured out of the barrel of the gun as she worked the lever, ejecting a spent casing and sliding another cartridge into the chamber.

Her first shot took off the ear of the white beast attacking Celeste's windshield. Clutching the bloody crease on the side of his head, the beast yelped and sent the rest of the Gelch scattering in all directions.

Celeste studied the slender Lakota Animal Control officer dressed in her brown and tan uniform. She is beautiful, she thought. A real Native princess straight from the Dawn Time!

As Cora lowered her rifle and held up one finger to indicate she would be right back, Jango sent, *Pretty lady, she is. Long, raven hair. Fine-featured face. Dark doe-eyes. High cheekbones.*

Cora was gone from her place on the battlements for mere seconds when the drawbridge was lowered to the ground. "Drive inside!" she shouted. Celeste gunned her van and shot inside the central courtyard of the castle, even as Jango craned his skinny neck to look back through the back window of the van at Cora working the lever to close the drawbridge. *Very pretty lady.* he sent.

Turning off the van, Celeste took Jango in her arms and climbed out of the VW. She, too, looked up to the walkway above the courtyard to watch as Cora raised her rifle and promptly fired off one more shot before turning away from the gatehouse and descending the stairs to the courtyard. The Lakota woman lowered her rifle as she approached Celeste, her dark eyes fixed on Jango cradled in the younger girl's arms. "Greetings," she said. "You are the sister of Lucas, correct? And this wanagi is your pet?"

Celeste offered her a puzzled frown. "Wana—what?"

"Wanagi," Cora repeated, putting a slight growl in the agi of the word. "It means demon in my people's language. This monkey beast is a demon, no? Maybe its even related to those creatures out there in the forest. They both hail from the same place."

Shaking her head, Celeste said, "No, Jango is merely a—"

I am Mogrim! Jango sent, his thoughts reaching both ladies as they stared down at him. *Yes, my kind has fallen from grace, but I am friend, not foe. We waste time here. Has the council been called?*

Cora offered the little creature a slight smile. "Forgive me, small one, I did not mean to offend. But council?"

In the chamber below, Jango sent. *Kerrin Skye is calling on the champions of your realm to partake of the Hunt! Molech and Baphomet were to remain imprisoned here in this castle, but Hunter freed them from their cells below.*

"Well," Celeste said, "evidently, my little brother, Lucas is somehow involved in all this nonsense, hunting demons or gods who intend on slaughtering folks over there in the realm of Valasar. I am here to stop him. He's already damaged goods due to his anger issues, and hunting demons is certainly not going to improve his behavior."

As she led the way down the stone stairway into the lower level of the fortress, Cora said, "Lucas is now safe at his foster home. I have just returned from driving him and his three dogs back to Reason's house. You need not worry about him."

Soft blue lights embedded in the dark walls added a slight illumination to the shadowy corridors as they traversed them. "I don't know," she said, "anything about a meeting taking place down here. A few minutes ago, Uncle Colton sent me up to the gatehouse to retrieve this Winchester from where he'd left it. I had the sneaking suspicion he was trying to get rid of me, while he tried to determine what he intended to do about our escaped prisoners. I think he wants to leave the safety of this castle and enter into the realm of Valasar. That is where I left Ben two days ago. He and I entered there together to seek advice from the lady who sent us the castle. We wanted to know how to properly imprison the two gods we were receiving as prisoners. I never imagined someone would come and so recklessly free them."

"Hunter Synn," Celeste told her. "He's the devious son of some dead-beat wizard. I only wonder if he knows he's traveling with two evil gods who suck the lives out of their victims like two blood-thirsty vampires!"

A lemon-yellow shaft of light filtered into the corridor ahead of them. It erupted so suddenly, flooding the confines of the tunnel-like shaft that Jango hissed, and Celeste's violet blade seemed to leap into her hands.

"Sorry," came the deep voice of Colton Lone Wolf as he appeared beyond the misty powers swirling between him and the two ladies. "I completed the Medicine Wheel, closing off this realm from the one you are in, my dear niece. Only to protect you. Know that you survived in the realm beyond, now it is my turn. Stay safe, dear Cora. Pray that I return, and bring your young buck back with me."

The elderly Lakota offered Cora a sad smile. He turned and walked back into the large chamber beyond the field of force. There he took his place at an enormous round table, accepting the chair offered him by an Elven lady with short-cropped golden hair and amazingly green catlike eyes. Upon seeing the three Bears and Cat and Cinnamon from the Roaring Lion bookstore also seated at the giant round table inside the chamber beyond, Celeste raised her sword to swipe at the magical currents undulating between the floor and the ceiling of the hallway they were in.

"Wolf!" Cora cried. "What in the hell are you trying to prove? Come out of there, right now! And I mean, now! If not, I am going to royally kick your scrawny—"

"Be still," Celeste said, placing a hand down gently on her forearm. "Wolf has severed their realm from ours. Here, let me attempt to open the way forward. With a little help from my friends."

In a silent explosion of brilliant blue sparks, the stag and wolf tattoos on Celeste's neck and shoulder slowly came to life.

Cora stared in amazement at the three forms as they evolved into phantom-like figures, the two wolves taking up guarded positions on either side of Celeste, while the stag lowered his head and charged. A flash of scintillating light burst in front of the wide-antlered stag as he tore his way through the field of force stretched across the opening at the end of the hallway. The ethereal stag passed through the warding that prevented entry into the chamber beyond. The two wolves ran directly at the currents of magic blocking the way ahead. And they, too, passed through the barrier, penetrating the field of force.

Celeste sheathed her sword.

Jango sauntered up to her. *Shhh!* he sent. *Listen to Lady Skye.*

With the shimmering field of force now gone, Cora followed Celeste as she and the Mogrim entered the chamber where the White Council was beginning to hold a session.

The two blue-tinged wolves and stag took up positions on either side of the three, and soon all of them were intently listening as the council meeting took place before them.

44

Kerrin Skye stood up from the table, her emerald eyes fixed on Celeste standing beyond the table. "I," she said, her voice soft as gently falling rain, "will summon the champions needed to hunt the two gods."

Celeste nodded at the Elven Priestess as she said, "They would have to be powerful champions indeed in order to slay two gods before they come into their full power."

Kerrin picked up a hunter's horn from the table and blew three stout blasts of the curved horn. Thunder of fast-approaching horses came from beyond the hole in the wall created by the risen gods' escape. The champions answered the summons.

Kerrin named these heroes as they sprang from their mounts and entered the chamber. "Torin Redleaf," she said, gesturing at the blond Elven swordsman clad in silver mail who first came through the doorway. "Master of the Brotherhood of the Blade."

Torin's white-blond hair was braided along both sides of his head and ended in a long tail down his back. He smiled and stepped aside as a lady with fiery red hair joined him. "Lady Sendra, Leopard of the Vale of Seven Rivers," Kerrin said, greeting the lady who wore a chain mail overcoat, the emblem of a rampant leopard on her chest. Sendra was shadowed by a large man with dark hair and a full beard. "Grolf the Viking Lord," Kerrin declared his name.

The big, rough-looking man bowed to her and said, "Trian, Gypsy Prince of the Horse Lords," as a small, willowy man followed behind him, his raven hair braided in one long tail down his back.

Five more champions entered the chamber. All wore their hair in wild tangles or plaited braids, and they were dressed in plaids and kilts. Their leader had bright red hair and a full beard. Hoops dangled from both of his ears, and a leather band with a bear at its center rested on his head. "Conn of the Hundred from Les Callas," Kerrin said. "Cullen of Rissen, Sword Lord of Conn."

Cullen, a large man who wore no armor nor shirt, was heavily muscled and stood a head taller than the rest of the men. His long, black hair fell nearly to his waist, and unlike the rest of the heroes, he was clean-shaven. For such a big man, he moved gracefully as he pulled out a chair for Conn to sit in. As Conn accepted the chair, he quietly thanked his Sword Lord, then said, "Finn the White Arrow of the Fife. Liam of Delvaria. And Kellen of the Red Lance."

Finn's hair was golden white Liam's black hair and thick beard gave him a bearish look. Kellen had long locks of fiery red hair and a thick, red mustache.

Filling the shadowy opening to the realm beyond, a band of four men walked in earning bitter looks of reproach from the majority of the heroes in the castle's chamber. Despite the looks of scorn cast their way, Lady Kerrin declared, "Stag-Heart Knights from the Kingdom of Rogues and Renegades, vouched for by Prince Kragnor, pardoned for past deeds by his father the Dwarven King of Quain."

These warriors were all heavily-muscled men clad in leather armor with the standard of rampant stag on their breasts. They all wore leather moccasins that caused them to be as silent as they entered the chamber. All had long, dark hair and were clean-shaven, and were dressed in leather long shirts, belted at the waist and sporting an assortment of knives. "Scouts," said the black-haired, long bearded Dwarf who entered the chamber behind the four sullen men. He was a stout fellow, nearly four feet tall, his corded bare arms clearly revealed in his sleeveless black jerkin.

"Prince Kragnor of Quain," the Dwarf said, grinning. "And just as unhappy about my traveling companions as the rest of you are. But, my father gave them pardons if they vowed to serve us on this dire mission, and as a dutiful prince, I obey his commands."

Kragnor smiled at the other champions. "As far as names goes, until they've proven themselves, Panther, Owl, Falcon, and the smaller one is, Fox. They've promised to serve me. At the first sign of treachery, I give each and every one of you permission to remove their heads. Of course, the King of Quain won't condone such a deed, but I make such concessions on account I know what these dark hearts are capable of. Stag-Heart Knights are not well loved in the Kingdom of the Rock Folk."

Prince Kragnor led the four rogue knights over to the round table, each of them looking at Celeste. The Dwarven prince narrowed his dark eyes as he studied the three spirit-creatures on either side of her. He knowingly said, "The wolves and the stag serve as guardians to the sister of the Thunder Dreamer."

Wolf stood up from his place at the round table, offering Kerrin a frown. "Sorry, my lady," he said apologetically, 'but am I to assume you are asking us to enter the realm beyond to hunt down and destroy these two gods with only a small force of sixteen? I mean, are their weapons powerful enough—"

"I will equip you with an arsenal," Kerrin said. "You will all be armed with swords, shields, bows and arrows, all crafted by the Jewel Folk, all powerful enough to slay these two demons."

She turned her head sideways to look over into the shadows of the large chamber beyond the table. "Will you lead this company?"

To Celeste's great surprise, Beef Tory stepped from a dark alcove as Kerrin said, "Your grandfather and father belonged to the Order of the Templars, and though you were only a shadow at some of those meetings, you've never sworn vows to that order. And yet, you are a Keeper of the Ring."

She reached inside a pouch at her waist and placed a single ring on the table in front of her. "The rings of the Celt, the Saracen, the Hebrew, and the Norseman. The rings that have passed down through your family line to you."

Staring in silent wonder at the ring that had been in Reason's keeping all these years, Beef said, "I always knew it was dangerous to trifle with such tokens of power. Each ring contains potent magic that responds to its wearer accordingly. I have wanted nothing to do with such power."

Kerrin picked up the ring, the one belonging to the Norseman. She slid it down the table to him, and as he picked it up to examine it, she said, "You will serve as commander of this small company of demon-hunting heroes. Wear the ring, use its powers, allow its magic to transform you during your time in our realm."

Beef placed the ring on his ring finger. "This is all a little bizarre, to be called to this cause in another realm. I've always been the one with a solid head on my shoulders, warning Reason not to mess with these rings passed down to us from our ancestors. Why me? Why now? Why do you place this in my path?"

Kerrin smiled at him. "Because it is your time to rise to greatness, Brave Heart. Time for you be the Lion Heart you were destined to be. When you see the path of destruction left behind by these two savage and brutal fire gods, you will know why this task has been given to you, specifically. To protect and serve, son of Thor's son."

Celeste still stood there, staring down at the ring of the Norseman on Beef's finger, uncertain about what part she was to play in the events unfolding before her. "What about me?" she asked.

Kerrin, the Three Bears, Cat, Cinnamon, and Beef turned their gazes on her. "It was your little brother who stole the rings in the first place," Kerrin said. "He now wears the ring of the Saracen."

Celeste shrugged. "It once belonged to a Muslim?" she asked. "A Muslim like Khalid or one like Achmed Waziri?"

"And what does that," Kerrin asked, "have to do with a ring of power? It is the wearer who controls the magic, not the other way around. Besides, with Lucas's great rages, do you think he will be able to focus on calling forth the power of the ring, or will his anger block the flow? When using magic, one has to have a clear mind. You may question why I bring up Lucas's fierce temper when the subject of entering the distant realm comes up, but the two dogs, Grunge and Goblin have made it their goal to tamp down his rages, and keep the boy from losing his cool in the heat of battle. I would prefer that he remain safe at home, but he insists on venturing into Valasar. I am well aware that his burning rages may very well attract evil beings with equally hot rages, but the dogs are determined to see that Lucas controls his anger."

She paused, then added, "He should be quite humbled by the fact that he is so well-loved by these two dogs. I pray their loyalty has not been given in vain. I know you want to join this company that leaves here, but I present another quest to both you and Cora Red Cloud."

At this, Cora opened her mouth to protest, but it was Wolf who silenced her by placing a hand on her forearm. "Shhhh," he urged her. "Listen, my niece. Listen to what is said."

Nodding gratefully at the old Lakota, Kerrin said, "Celeste, I ask that you return to your brother and stop him from stepping into the Dragon Room at the Emerald. He listens to you. He respects you. If you do this, you may very well save his life. If he is allowed to venture into our realm, there are legions of evil beings who would be attracted to him due to his rages. If you truly love your brother, you will do as I ask. Understood?"

Brooding there in silence, both Celeste and Cora watched as Beef, Wolf, and the company of demon hunters stepped beyond the force field and exited the chamber. The ethereal forms of the stag and the wolves evaporated there beside Celeste, all three returning to the tattoos inked onto her neck and chest, until they were needed in some other tricky situation. Tears came to her eyes as she watched Beef and his company mount up on the small herd of horses tethered just outside the chamber. Beside her, Cora cursed as they listened to the sound of galloping horses as the hunters rode away from the castle.

Kerrin stood up from her place at the table, her green-eyed gaze fixed on Celeste, then drifting over to Cora. "You two will venture to the Emerald, correct?" she asked, her eyebrows raised expectantly.

Offering her a puzzled frown, Cora said, "The Emerald Pub that belongs to Billy Connors? That Emerald?"

"Yes," Celeste said. "Billy's grandson is dabbling with alternative realms with a video game he designed, one that uses virtual reality to enhance game play. I'm afraid my little brother has done some exploring in Valasar. If Kerrin is right, Lucas is determined to go back in there."

As Cora opened her mouth to respond, Jango let out an alarmed hiss, causing those inside at the council table to look beyond the chamber and out into the clearing beyond the hole in the wall. There, dark shapes began to emerge, evolving from the wintery landscape. They were riders, some with horned helms, others sporting antlers on their helms. Still others wore dark hoods and cloaks, and fiery eyes glowered within their deep cowls.

Celeste immediately thought of the Four Horsemen, and then her mind jumped to the Nine Riders, but there were so many of them she lost count at one-hundred as they milled about, gathering just beyond the opening in the castle wall. Far too many to be trailing behind the small company that had just left there. One of the dark horsemen gestured wildly at the hoof marks leading away from the castle, and soon, the entire mass of riders went racing off after Beef and his company.

Lady Kerrin calmly explained to Celeste and Cora how and why it was important for them to accept the two quests she offered them.

The Three Bears, Cat, and Cinnamon sat there in respectful silence while Celeste and Cora listened to the Elven Priestess of the Unseen War lay out her plans for them. She spoke with such wisdom and authority that the two ladies found themselves, at the end of her talk, nodding in agreement with her.

When certain Kerrin had convinced the two that hers was the best course of action to take, Cat and Cinnamon stood up from the table, silver wands shimmering in their hands. "Come, Cora Red Cloud and Celeste Holland," Cat said, with a warm smile. "Let us teleport you to the Emerald. Driving there would just waste time."

"And," added Cinnamon, gesturing at the empty winter landscape beyond the council chamber, "as you can see, time is most important when Beef Tory, the Dog Soldier, and their companions are being pursued by such a nasty mob of miscreants in the far off realm."

As the two Mages drew a large golden circle on the floor of the chamber, the Bears joined them, each of the large Mage Lords helping them to complete the circle by wielding their oaken staves. In a matter of moments, Cinnamon and the Bears stood at the center of ten-by-ten foot shimmering aura. "Come," said Cat as she joined them. "Simply step into the golden circle. We shall travel swiftly to the Emerald that you two might complete your separate quests."

"Will this hurt?" Celeste found herself saying, her mind putting on the brakes before she leaped from a ledge she might not regret jumping off of. "I'm afraid, I am not yet ready for this sort of magic."

Cora, however, took Celeste by one hand, and making sure she had a hold of Jango, she moved them all inside the circle.

There was a brilliant flash of light, and while Cora whistled in amazement, Celeste let out a gasp of surprise, as the small company was hurtled through time and space.

45

Lady Kerrin's idea proved to be a little too farfetched for Boone, but Reason tracked with Cora through much of her explanation. He had done plenty of research to create his game, and some of it into dark places in the world history. Therefore, what she told them as they gathered there inside the Emerald, made sense to him. At her first pass through, Boone sat there before the fireplace completely dumbfounded, but Reason could not help but agree with Cora's theory she so enthusiastically shared.

"The name Molech came from the Second Temple period," Cora said. "It is based on the root mlk, meaning king. There are a number of Canaanite gods with names based on this root, which became associated with Moloch, which refers to a god of the Ammonites.

"Jewish Rabbinical tradition depicted Molech as a bronze statue heated with fire into which the victims were thrown. This has been associated with child sacrifices in Carthage to Baal Hammon. Baal ammon was the chief god of Carthage. He was depicted as a bearded old man with ram's horns and was worshiped as Lord of Two Horns.

"Greco-Roman sources report that the Carthaginians burned their children as offerings to Baal Hammon. His female cult partner was Tanit. In North Africa, she was known as a goddess of war. There is significant evidence, both archaeological and ancient written sources, pointing towards child sacrifice involved in the worship of Tanit and Baal Hammon.

"Tophet is a Hebrew term from the Bible, used to refer to a site near Jerusalem at which Canaanites and Israelites who strayed from Judaism by practicing Canaanite idolatry sacrificed children. A large one in Carthage, the Tophet of Salammbó, was the location of the temple of the goddess Tanit, where children were sacrificed and buried in the Tophet. The area covered by the Tophet in Carthage was over an acre wide with nine different levels of burials. 20,000 urns were discovered there, containing the charred bones of newborns and the bones of fetuses and two-year-olds. These double remains have been interpreted to mean, the parents sacrificed their youngest child.

"Stele with Tanit's symbol in Carthage's Tophet, include a crescent moon over the figure. Her symbol found on many ancient stone carvings, appears as a trapezium closed by a horizontal line at the top and in the middle by a circle. Tanit is sometimes depicted with a lion's head, showing her warrior quality."

Cora paused then for several moments before saying, "Molech AKA Lord Ammon dominated this duo god-head, but what happened to his goddess, Tanit? A co-star? A silenced deity? Hell hath no fury like a woman scorned, but what about a goddess left behind by her male counterpart?

"What if she wants revenge for being forsaken or cast aside? And that she was considered a war goddess is even more intriguing. A she-lion with an ache to be avenged? What better ally could we have?"

She waited, expecting some sort of support from the rest of them.

"Ally?" Boone asked. "A she-lion with one hell of a temper? How and why would she be willing to help us? I mean, that is what you're saying, right? Where in all the universe would we find her?"

Cora held up one finger. "Hold that thought, while I explain what Kerrin revealed about Baphomet. For one, he is a deity that the Knights Templar were falsely accused of worshiping, that was incorporated into the occult. The name Baphomet first appeared in trial transcripts for the Inquisition of the Knights Templar starting in 1307. The name appeared in July 1098 in a letter by the crusader Anselm of Ribemont: 'As the next day dawned, they called loudly upon Baphometh; and we prayed silently in our hearts to God, then we attacked and forced all of them outside the city walls.'

"When the medieval order of the Knights Templar was suppressed by King Philip IV of France, on Friday October 13, 1307, Philip had many Templars arrested, and then tortured into confessions. Over 100 different charges had been leveled against them. Most of them were dubious: offenses of heresy, spitting and urinating on the cross, and sodomy. These acts were intended to simulate the kind of humiliation that a Crusader might be subjected to if captured by the Saracens, where they were taught how to commit apostasy, with the mind only, not with the heart. The simulated worship of Baphomet formed part of a Templar initiation ritual.

"In the trial of the Templars one of their charges was the worship of a idol known as a Baphomet. The goat pentagram symbol would later become synonymous with Baphomet, named the Sabbatic Goat. Samael is a figure in Talmudic lore, and Lilith is a female demon in Jewish mythology. The Hebrew letters at the five points of the pentagram spell out Leviathan. This symbol was adapted by the Church of Satan and officially named the Sigil of Baphomet.

"Modern scholars agree that the name of Baphomet was a French corruption of the name Muhammad, since Templars believed that Muslims worshiped Muhammad as a god, with mahomet becoming mammet, meaning an idol. This idol-worship is attributed to Muslims and a Saracen idol is called Bafumetz."

Reason had caught on to what Cora was suggesting, but Boone asked, "So, you are saying let's incorporate a female goddess to confront this Molech that Beef and the others are hunting?"

Cora nodded, then said, "Not one female goddess, but two. Lilith is often envisioned as a dangerous demon of the night, who steals babies in the darkness. Lilith is linked historically to a class of female demons in ancient Mesopotamian religion, found in Sumer, the Akkadian Empire, Assyria, and Babylonia. In Jewish folklore, Lilith ap-pears as Adam's first wife, who was created from the same clay as Adam. Lilith left Adam after she refused to become subservient to him and then would not return to the Garden of Eden after she had coupled with the archangel Samael.

"In Hebrew-language the term lilith is translated as night creature, night monster, night hag, or screech owl. In the Dead Sea Scrolls, the term first occurs in a list of monsters. In Jewish magical inscriptions, Lilith is identified as a female demon. Samael is often identified as Malkira, king of evil. During the spread of Islam, Samael appears as the serpent in Genesis, influenced by the Quran, due to its parallels to the Islamic equivalent of Satan. Samael created with her a host of demon children, including a son, the Sword of Samael or Asmodai."

Boone shook his head. "Where would one find a goddess? After all, the worship of goddess figures in the majority of world religions has been literally obliterated by male dominated religions. We've been praying to father figures for the past 2000 years, with hardly any consideration that there might be a mother figure involved—"

"Or wife," Celeste said. "And hell hath no fury like a wife scorred. Tell them where might we find such a goddess."

Cora said, "The Tophet of Salammbó, was the location of the temple of the goddess Tanit. It is located on the eastern side of the Lake of Tunis in Tunisia in northwest Africa. It is bordered by Algeria to the west and southwest and Libya to the southeast."

She paused, then added, "I've spoken to Khalid over in the Middle East. He believes Lilith can be found somewhere in Jerusalem, where a band of rabbis actually bound her in a tomb 2000 years ago. He and Stone and Raynes are now traveling to Lake Tunis. All three have agreed to meet me there to try to awaken this goddess, Tanit.

"As a Phantom agent, determined to make a difference on the war on terror, Khalid also has contacts with descendants of the very rabbis who bound Lilith to the tomb in Jerusalem. Khalid is our man in the Middle East."

Celeste smiled and said, "Karma is a bitch in heat, ain't it?"

Cora looked to everyone gathered in the pub and said, "Yes, and if we pull this off, two red-hot bitches are going to be a very unpleasant surprise that the two fire gods did not expect."

46

Celeste left Reason, Boone, and Cora deep in discussion about plans to send Cora to the Middle East to complete the quest Kerrin had given her. Boone was still having trouble wrapping his mind around the fact that the plan was to incorporate two goddesses into the war on Molech and Baphomet. First, he could not fathom how Khalid was supposed to summon two female godheads to the realm of the living. Or better yet, how he and Cora were supposed to invite Lillith and Tanit to join them in a scheme to confront the two fire gods wrecking havoc in the realm of Valasar. It was all too far fetched for him.

Besides, Boone was still troubled about the disappearance of his grandfather, and he chided Reason for not being more committed to finding and locating Billy, even if it meant that one of the Nelson brothers enter the Dragon Room, and venture beyond this plane of existence. Boone couldn't shake the feeling that the old Irishman was on one last desperate mission before he left this planet.

Reason held no less love for the old man, and yet, he assured Boone that sooner or later, Billy would return to the pub, whether by stepping in through the front door, or entering via the chamber down the hallway, where the words of the sign stood out in bold letters, saying, "Here, there be Dragons."

Celeste Holland would have been the last person Reason Nelson would have trusted to save his grandfather's life. He knew that, and what's more, she was well aware of that fact herself. During his time as her truancy tracker, Celeste had been a most belligerent brat. She had not cooperated with any of his well-laid plans for her, being the defiant, rebellious teenager that she was. But Reason was desperate and had seen her grow up some over these last several months. He knew he could not give up on her now.

And yet, Celeste knew she could not allow him to use her little brother as a guinea pig play-testing the game. Kerrin was right about the rage-fests of Lucas and just what his frequent outbursts might attract in a realm where dark beings, demons, ghosts, and evil spirits ran rampant. If Lucas ventured back into Valasar, he was setting himself up to be a magnet for such entities. Celeste could not allow that.

And while Lucas slept safe and secure at Reason's house during these last few hours before sunrise, she was going to go into the Dragon Room, and examine the portal doorway, hoping she could find a way to control access to the realms beyond. She was planning on using a chain and combination lock to lock and bar the door. If it was used as a safety precaution to keep Lucas from stumbling his way into dangerous territory, she was convinced she could explain her drastic measures to Reason, that he would certainly understand her concerns, combined with the words of Lady Kerrin. As her brother's foster parent and truancy tracker, certainly Reason would agree that some safeguard needed to be in place.

She would, of course, pass along the combination on the lock so that Reason could have access to the portal in order to kick-start game play for Alex when the next session was intended.

Determined to follow through with her plan, Celeste crept silently down the hallway, Jango trailing quietly behind her. Upon reaching the door of the Dragon Room, she opened it, ushered Jango through before her, and slipped inside the chamber beyond. The door slowly swung closed behind her with a soft, Click!

Her eyes were immediately drawn to the six windows above the doorway to the central portal. Images passed by those windows in kaleidoscopic scenes that left her staring up at them in awe and wonder. Dragons, huge, scaly beasts, flew through a sky painted with the amber shades of a brilliant sunrise. There were nine of the winged, serpentine creatures, all blowing flames from their open maws as they flew. They were black, green, red, and light shades of blue in color, their iridescent scales reflecting the sunlight

"Riders?" Celeste said, without realizing she'd spoken out loud. "Those dragons all have riders mounted on them!"

Peering up at the scenery flashing past the window, Jango sent, *The Wind Lords. All nine wizard-warriors trained at an early age to be guardians and Keepers of the Flame.*

Looking down at the Mogrim whose large blue eyes were fixed on the dragons sweeping past the one window, Celeste hesitantly asked, "These Wind Lords? Are they good guys? Or bad guys?"

Jango scrunched up his pug nose. A look of puzzlement crossed his features. *Good? Bad?* he sent. *They are all wild boys whose loyalties have not yet been determined. Very dangerous if they side with the Darkness. Very helpful if they instead chose to serve the Light. A rage festers within their young hearts, for they have seen what few boys have seen: the deaths of their parents, their families, their entire kingdom of Avandia, far to the north of Valasar.*

"Rage?" Celeste said. "Young boys distraught over their loss?"

Nodding sadly, Jango sent, *Rage fueled by sorrow, yes.*

Sounds like Lucas, she thought as she watched the dragons and their young riders become specks in the distant sky as they flew to some unknown destination. Her sights flickered over to a second window and she locked in on a small company of riders cresting the rise of lightly forested hilltop. At the forefront of these riders, a raven-haired girl of 13 was gesturing wildly with the sword she wielded. She stabbed the air with the weapon, directing her companions' attention to the vale behind them, she then slashed the air above her with her sword, pointing her blade at the trail ahead.

Celeste glanced down at Jango, expecting some sort of explanation to be forthcoming from the Mogrim. He looked up at her and sent, *Alicia the Black Rose. Loriel the Lady of the Woods. Kazz the White. Kennon Moon, Priest of the Unseen War.*

And as he named the riders, Celeste looked to the slender, dark-haired lady seated on a golden mare to the right of the raven-haired girl. She then looked to the large, white-haired, ape-faced brute mounted on the massive war-horse to her left. And lastly, she studied the tall, golden-haired rider clad in white leathers at the rear of their formation. Her own eyes widened in wonder as she noted the slightly pointed ears protruding up through the strands of his long blond hair.

"An Elf?" she asked Jango.

The Mogrim sent,*Yes, Elven. But look there, they are joined by the young Ravenhawk.*

Celeste turned her gaze to peer down the trail leading up to the hilltop where the others sat. Riding swiftly up the slope, his long black hair streaming past his shoulders, was a young boy of 14. He was handsome, and had he been born here rather than there, Celeste surmised the kid would have made a great model. He was tall, slender, and his long tangles of coal-black hair made her envious. It was his cornflower blue eyes, however, that caused her to stare overlong at the rider even as he rode up on a black stallion to join the others.

And although he was still a child compared to the other three adult riders, they paid him a respectful deference as he nudged his steed so that it sidled up beside Alicia the Black Rose. Reaching out, the boy took a hold of her sword arm and gently guided her sword back into the sheath at her side. In a playful gesture, the kid tweaked Alicia's nose, then turned in his saddle to speak to the rest of the company.

The other three riders peered back into the forested vale behind them. Celeste found herself rising up on the tips of her toes so that she could see what they were seeing.

There, riding up a slender trail snaking its way up from the vale below, were a rugged-looking assortment of horsemen. Some wore weathered leather armor. Others wore deep hooded cowls and long, black cloaks. And some wore bits and pieces of rusted chain and plate, while others were shirtless, wearing no armor at all. The entire company appeared to be a rough-looking crowd, and as they crested the hill and rode past the black-haired boy, each rider either saluted or nodded their head in a show of deep respect for the boy.

The mercenary companies, sent Jango, watching the horsemen pass by the boy on the hilltop, *have answered the summons of the Ravenhawk. Brennan has called, and they have come. Wolf Lords of Shadow. Badgers of Mosk. Spears and Shields. Ghost Company. Sons of the Hawk. Sisterhood of Song. All have come to serve as riders of the Clans and Companies. They recognize the nobility of the Outlaw King before he assumes his role. It is their service to him that the Black Rose should now be thankful for.*

The boy, Brennan, nodded cordially as each rider passed by him, and at the end of the long line of rugged-looking riders, Creed Blackstag rode his black steed up beside the now smiling boy.

Brennan gestured at Alicia, who all that time, had sat silently appraising the company of mercs as they rode past her and down into the next vale. His eyes bright, he said, "Thanks, Creed, for gathering them. They will make a fine honor guard for our future Queen, Alicia the Black Rose."

Sliding gracefully from the back of his horse, Creed dropped down to one knee, offering Alicia a respectful bow. The Elven Lord then rose to his feet, moving to Brennan's side in one long stride. A look of extreme sorrow in his eyes, he reached out and grasped his left wrist in both of his hands. Solemnly, he said, "It is with great sadness that I received the news that your father had fallen, Brennan. Even now, I have a company of warriors venturing to the keep to retrieve the sword he left behind. Kestrian now belongs to you, and I shall see that it shall be returned."

Brennan simply nodded, tears beginning to stream down his face.

47

Even as she rose up on her toes, Jango imitated her movements as he, too, tried to see down the trail on the vision screen above them. Upon failing to get a better look at the forest beyond the window, both Celeste and Jango rose up higher on their toes. It was just a matter of balancing there on the tips of their toes that sent them staggering off kilter. To avoid trampling on the small, black monkey-beast hunkering down before her, she took two hop-skips out around him and went careening into the portal door.

The oaken door opened on its own accord, and Celeste thrashed madly at empty air as she tried to stop herself from hurtling into the dark chamber beyond. She had nearly righted herself, pivoting back on the balls of her feet, when Jango, not wanting to be left behind, launched himself up and off the floor, scrabbling for a hold on the back of her duster.

Feeling his tiny claws trying to find purchase in the folds of her duster, Celeste stumbled forward once more. She and Jango literally popped into existence in the middle of a forest trail. A bright flash lit up the clearing, and they stepped out of a circle of light and onto a path lining the rim of a forested vale.

Celeste inhaled the chilly evening air and found herself staring at two towering fir trees standing like ancient guardians at the entrance to a valley of pine trees. She blinked in awe as she spied two specks of light within a massive hill nearly a mile away. The luminous yellow circles on either side of the round oak door stood out in bold detail. On one stained-glass window was the image of an open book.

On the other, the symbol of a gold harp.

Pineridge Hill, Jango sent. *Home of Niffit Oakleaf, the Master of the Lodge, housed within the hill.*

Her eyes drawn to the golden windows within the hillside, Celeste moved across a meadow shrouded in mist, and nimbly picked her way along a narrow trail. Behind her, Jango scampered to keep up.

In moments, the two reached the arbor before the Lodge. As they started up the slope to the front door, dozens of horned owls glided out of shadows between the pines on the hillside before them. These birds of the night performed a series of aerial acrobatics that left a fine misting of florescent dust trailing in their wake. Bright red in color, it burst in mid-air as it flew from the feathers of the owls, and the glittering red dust not only left patterns of wide-spread wings in the air, but scintillating particles drifted down, forming radiant clouds that lit up the entire hill.

"Can you keep a secret?" came a voice that startled both Celeste and Jango considerably. Slipping out of the shrubs beside them, a small Chaykin said, "I'll still call them Fire-owls, but I recently discovered the secret of their magical flight. They nest in the fir trees at Boggin Glen, which leaves them with traces of scarlet dust on their feathers. But as to why they perform their aerial ballet above the Lodge every night, is still a mystery!"

Celeste peered into the brown-eyed gaze of the maple-haired Chaykin standing beside her. "I assume," she said, "you are Niffit, Master of the Lodge." She then added, "Dust from fir trees or not, they are truly marvelous to watch!"

"That they are, my lady," agreed Niffit, watching the wind carry the ghostly outline of an amber owl up to the crest of Pineridge Hill three-hundred yards above them. The Chaykin waited until the fluorescent owl dissolved into a fine mist before saying, "I'm with friend."

Puzzled, Celeste stepped into the golden light shining through the large, stained-glass windows on either side of the round portal before them. Without a sound, two Elven Woodmasters slipped through the shrubbery on either side of the porch. Clad in dark cloaks, faces concealed by deep hoods, the Elves appraised her for long moments. Finally, one offered her a cordial nod while the other looked to the forest vale beyond.

"She's alone," Niffit assured the two Woodmasters, opening the door to the Lodge. "No one followed her, except the two Marsh Cats I sent out earlier. And the cats would know if there was a threat to security in the Vale, wouldn't they?"

"They most certainly would, little master," replied one of the tall Elves. He then nodded politely and seemed to glide as he moved back into the thick bushes beside the door. Celeste didn't even see the other Elf fade from sight, but she did catch a glimpse of two shadowy shapes weaving their way back down the slope into the valley. Huge and silent, the Marsh Cats vanished into the mist, leaving Celeste amazed to think they had been her unseen escort.

Niffit said, "Times have changed, lass. Long ago, Jewel Folk were rejected by Elvenkind. Now, they watch over us like we're children!"

"Children of the Woods, little master," came the Elf's voice from deep within the bushes. "Children of the Woods."

Brennan sat alone as Alicia and the entire company rode on ahead to the Lodge. He had served faithfully all 14 summers of his life, preparing for his role as Sword Lord. He had never questioned his destiny, always accepting that he was serving a greater cause, one that was chosen for him by Fate. He had no doubts then that he was doing what was right, had never questioned whether he had a choice in the matter. Ravenhawks served the House of Erin. There had been six Sword Lords before him, and all had done their duty, serving their particular king—and queen—with honor.

But Brennan's failure to save his father caused him extreme grief and caused him to doubt himself. "Can one lose sight of their Destiny," he had asked Alicia as they rode to the Vale of Pines, "if they make a mistake that causes them to stumble and fall?"

Alicia replied, "We all stumble and fall, Brennan. The ones who keep their appointment with Destiny, are the ones who simply get back up and keep going."

But Brennan had not felt like getting back up. He had suffered a deep hurt by failing his father, and as he saw it, failing the High One, as well. He thought maybe he was being punished by the One, and wouldn't be fit for service again until he was thoroughly chastised. "Nonsense!" Alicia had said. "The One doesn't punish us for our mistakes. Life is too short for such. He would encourage you to do as I said: Get back up and keep going!"

Yet Brennan no longer felt like he deserved such grace. His self-doubt tore through his being like a raging wind, and in these past days he hadn't learned how to calm the storm in his soul. And yet, since the fateful incident five days past, Alicia gave him comfort and lent him the support he so desperately needed. And Brennan allowed him-self to trust the Gypsy-born girl. She, too, had been most vulnerable. Alicia's mind-link with birds and beasts might well be considered a gift by some, but her father, Talisdan Whiteheart was convinced that such communication was a curse, not a gift that came from the One. As King's Champion, he lived by a strict code. Faith in a god whose priests condemned such things as sorcery, made Talisdan suspicious of Alicia's talents. He even suggested that Alicia served the Darkness.

Hurt and bewildered by her father's rejection, out of pity and compassion, Brennan formed a bond with this Gypsy girl with such rare talent. And yet, in his heart, he knew she was destined to become queen to a boy named Briar Erin, Lion of the Rock.

Alicia dismounted before the Lodge, and at once was greeted by Niffit. Grinning up at her, the Chaykin extended his hand. As she took the small fellow's hand, she looked past him to Celeste exiting the Lodge before her. She smiled apologetically for she was staring too long at the stag and wolf tattoos showing on Celeste's neck.

"You have the most interesting visitors," Alicia told Niffit. "This girl with the short, boyish hair style, her catlike green eyes, and the most wonderful tattoos I've ever seen, has me quite curious."

Alicia reached out, her fingers coming within inches of the front of Celeste's black leather duster. "May I?" she asked, politely.

Upon seeing that Alicia appeared to be fascinated the long, leather coat she wore, Celeste said, "Sure. Why not?"

Alicia proceeded to examine the lapels, the buttons, and the waist-line of the black duster. "If I had to guess," she said, "you are the daughter of a Warden of Kallador. Though why you're wearing black is a mystery. Wardens love their whites, as in armor, capes, cloaks, and steeds. Does your father ride a white horse?"

Finding herself drawn to the young girl's innocence and her child-like manners, Celeste said, "My father rides an Iron Horse."

Both girls looked out to the greenway before the Lodge as the large company of mercenary riders rode past the hillside haven. "Isn't that a sight to behold?" Alicia said. "Each of them seek to restore their honor with the pardons I offer them."

As the mercs guided their mounts around the side of Pineridge, Loriel drew rein before the front porch. Kazz joined her, drawing a packhorse behind him. In moments, the big Troll busied himself removing six little wolfhound puppies from the ample packs of the packhorse. Carefully, the Troll placed each pup down on the porch, shooing them toward the door with a gentle push on their rumps. "Sorry, my lady," he said. "Are they allowed inside?"

Alicia said, "Niffit loves hounds. Beware though, that our little charges don't stain a few of his rugs. Keep an eye open for such."

"Oh, I will, my lady," said Kazz as he set the last pup down and followed it into the Lodge.

Alicia looked to Brennan as he rode up onto the Lodge's front lawn. She saw at once the troubled look on his face. Sighing heavily, she whispered to Celeste, "It saddens me to see one so steeped in legends so crushed by sorrow. He grieves for his father recently fallen on his last mission. They were ambushed by a company of Stealth, and only five survived, Brennan was one of them. He saw his father and his band of heroes cut down before his eyes."

The shadowy creature that dropped from the branches of the maple tree directly above her never made a sound. The sleek, white-scaled, ape-like being drew twin red blades as he passed silently through the air. He was tall, lean, and moved with the speed of a viper, landing behind Alicia as she descended the steps.

Brennan lunged from his saddle to face her attacker even as the assassin's red-bladed sword pierced his left shoulder. He groaned in pain yet raised his right arm to deflect the second blade descending towards his face. The sword hissed as it sliced through his gauntlet, cutting through the leather and raking a bloody gash across his forearm. The lean assassin drove his one sword deeper into Brennan's shoulder, and swung his second blade at his unprotected head.

Shang! echoed through the forest clearing air as Celeste threw herself between Brennan and his phantom attacker. Moving like a wraith herself, she parried the white-scaled creature's swift strikes with her violet-bladed sword, distracting the assassin long enough for Brennan to pull free of the blade piercing his shoulder. She executed a leg-sweep and sent the assassin sprawling.

The wiry figure touched the ground for only seconds, though, and launched himself back onto his feet with surprising agility. He came directly back at Celeste, and she delivered a stunning blow with her extended elbow. The assassin staggered back. It was then that Brennan slid in between Celeste and the ape-faced being, and sent his sword cleaving through the assassin's chest.

The white-scaled attacker glared at him, hissed two angry words, then fell dead without a sound. Alicia moved to Brennan's side. "What did he say?" she asked, examining the gash in Brennan's shoulder. Her eyes widened in alarm when she noted blood mixed with a strange black fluid streaming from the wound.

Brennan slipped to one knee and answered, "Too late."

He then fell to the ground unconscious.

48

Chapter Forty-Nine

Night fell soft upon the woodlands. Owls hooted in the distance. Nighthawks twirred quietly to their mates. Fireflies drifted lazily through the moonlit glade of the Lodge.

"Back on Lady Kerrin's farmstead, I used to catch those dazzling fliers and put them in a jar," said Alicia, kneeling amongst puppies milling about inside Niffit's den.

Turning her gaze from the fireflies drifting through the woods just beyond the den's window, Celeste said, "I used to do the same. Once, when I was reading my little brother a story, I had so many jars filled with fireflies I needed no light to read by."

"Fireflies to chase away the gloom of the night," Alicia softly said. "Brennan still sleeps. He is fighting a battle. Those blades were cursed by a Varr enchantment. Kennon and Loriel do not know how to dispel it. The Wolf Lord claims Brennan has a powerful venom flowing through his veins. All three of them have spent hours searching through the archives of the Lodge. Still they could find nothing to break the spell of wyrm-blood contaminating his system."

She frowned and added, "Brennan barely hangs onto life."

Celeste picked up one of the puppies and cradled him against her chest. The tiny hound snuggled up in the warmth of her embrace. "I heard Creed say the assassin was a hybrid, a cross between the Trake lizard-kin and the white furred Gelch, part baboon, part ape."

Alicia looked to the fireflies in the deeper woods beyond the open window of the den. "Talisdan, King's Champion," she said, "is my father, a hero of great renown. He and a band of Horse Lords once ventured to the fortress of Trakes in the Sharmin Bogs. It is said, they slew a thousand of the lizard-kin, and that my father killed their king in single combat. Although Creed did not say it, he knows that assassin was sent for me. Brennan just happened to get in the way of the foul creature. I know those blades were enchanted by a Trake shaman, destined to be used on me, not Brennan."

Celeste placed the nose of the pup she was holding close to her chin. As she kissed the tiny hound's head, she breathed in the sweet smell of puppy breath. "Brennan won't die," she said. "I heard Loriel say there has to be a talisman to lift the curse, an antidote to burn out the venom, a charm to reverse the spell, or a remedy."

She listened for a moment to the owl-song drifting through the dark woodlands, then solemnly said, "Let us keep searching. We will not stop until we find it."

Alicia and Celeste were seated together in the Lodge's den. For the past several hours, the two had been reading musty tomes and faded scrolls. Both had joined forces after Loriel had examined Brennan given her assessment of the wounds and the enchanted blades that had caused them. Alicia sat between twin lanterns, a heavy book in her lap. She was the less confident of the two, having little knowledge of healing arts. She just didn't believe they would find what they were searching for by looking through Niffit's many books.

But Celeste had sensed her distress at the grim prospect of losing Brennan, and even though she'd just met Alicia for the first time there at the woodland haven, she knew that the girl loved Brennan dearly. She'd been in a surly mood, too, since she had learned the assassin was more than likely sent her way because of past deeds of her father, Talisdan Whiteheart. The two young girls now sat across from each other, yellow lantern light illuminating the massive tome in Alicia's lap while a green gem on Celeste's ring lit up the page of the booklet she was diligently studying. "Anything useful?" asked Alicia, noting the intensity within Celeste's emerald eyes as she read.

Brushing aside a loose strand of her dark hair, Celeste quietly said, "Dragon burns, Grunge bites, poison from the claws of a Gelch, and even a theory on an arrow that sapped forty years from its victim. The little master of the Lodge has quite a collection here, but as yet, I can find nothing on the evil we seek to learn about."

"Maybe the healers of Greenbriar have more knowledge about that which we seek," said Alicia, her eyes straying to the many shelves around them as she wondered what book to search through next. "This is a hoard of knowledge. I've never seen such a collection in my life. Besides, these Varr-enchanted blades come from a distant realm. The cures that we seek might be far from Valasar. Cursed blades that infect victims with black magics or sorcery. We are seeking a cure to the devastating effects of arcane forces.

"'Powers of Darkness,'" she said, grimacing as she recalled words her father had once shared with her about the deadly enemies that one day might come for him. "'Hunters of the Fallen,' Talisdan said to me. 'They will challenge me one day, and I must always be prepared to face them. Do you see why I can't allow you to dabble with magic words that tame birds and beasts? It would be letting my guard down to have my little girl conspiring with evil spirits. The One forbid that my own flesh and blood would open the door to such a betrayal. You must cease this nonsense.'"

Celeste offered Alicia a sympathetic smile, but at the mention of evil spirits, she shook her head. "I know a little about such spirits," she said. "In my world, we call them demons."

She reached out for another dusty book. Alicia picked up the book that Celeste was reaching for and passed it to her.

The two shared a smile and continued to read.

Fireowls soared above Pineridge Hill, the muffled murmurs of their calls drifting in through the open window of the Lodge. There in the guest room, Brennan heard the owls, and for brief moments, he looked out through the window to see dozens of the owls scattering shimmering red dust in the air.

He dozed once more and continued to wage a fierce battle against the curse that ensorcelled him. Drifting off into fitful slumber, he was immediately assaulted by a horrid dream in which an ape-like demon pinned him down, fiercely mauling his damaged shoulder where he'd been stabbed by the cursed blade of the assassin.

In his dream, he saw a long, thin, vertical shaft of violet light some distance ahead of him, shining like a beacon. He reached out for it, whispering, "Kestrian?"

Suddenly, Brennan heard a strange, female voice: *Ravenhawk! Cain Synn has sent the assassin, Rasp, to slay you here at the Lodge.*

He was buffeted by strong winds of enchantment, and like a leaf in a gale, he went spiraling down where arcane forces beckoned him to embrace sleep. He told the unseen speaker, "I have waged this battle too long. I am weary of the fight. Leave me be."

I will not! the speaker declared. *You are not yet finished. You must not quit. Rise, Brennan.*

He peered warily about the dark room, slightly illuminated by the low burning fire in the hearth. War horns sounded in the distance. The thunder of rapidly approaching horses echoed through the glens of the Vale of Pines. The clash of steel on steel rang through the hills. The reedy sounds of a lone piper filled the air.

He slowly sat up. Brennan tried to swing his legs out of bed, but instead collapsed and sank back into a mound of pillows. He closed his eyes once more. The lady spoke again: *No, Ravenhawk! You cannot rest now. All you have done so far in your life will be in vain if you do not find the strength to carry on. I can see your inner flame, and though this curse has you convinced that your fire has been dim-med and will never burn bright again, it is not so. You are a warrior, and not insignificant in this ancient war.*

Brennan was then assaulted by a barrage of memories, and he saw:

Himself as a boy, riding with his father the Sword Lord of Erin, and twenty knights of the Order of the Lion.

They had ventured to the highlands of Valasar. It was autumn. Red leaves scattered in their wake as the riders crested a rise. Before them on a high ridge, lay the ancient fortress of Dun Raven, its open gates resembling the black maw of some ominous creature.

Young Brennan did not wish to enter the fallen fortress where an alliance of Elves and Men had died to a man.

He shivered in fear as he recalled the wraith warriors rumored to haunt the deserted keep of Dun Raven. But he was the son of the Sword Lord of Erin, and he was obligated to follow these knights as they entered the dark heart of the haunted fortress.

They were attacked immediately. A swarm of dark-cloaked Stealth flooded the open courtyard of the central keep, wielding ice-white blades and cutting down Lion Knights with savage strokes. Pulsating veins of sorcery rippled up and down the length of their crackling blades, and many of the knights turned suddenly into figures of ice, then shattered into tiny, bloody shards. "Brennan!" his father cried out. "Fall back! Live on to serve our king!"

Brennan's eyes remained locked on the falling and rising violet blade of the ancestral sword of the House of Ravenhawk, as his father cleaved a pathway through the ranks of Stealth, erupting into a whirlwind of fury with his violet blade. But then at last, Mace Ravenhawk was slain, the legendary sword falling beside him.

Bear latched onto young Brennan. The last remaining knights, Govar the Red, Taylor Mason, and Crow Blackthorn joined them as they raced toward the drawbridge. Suddenly, a mob of little Elven ghosts formed a protective ring around the five of them, streaks of lightning sizzling from the thin blades they wielded vaporizing Stealth with each stroke. In one terrific surge, the band of long-dead Elven children cut a pathway back to the violet blade in the center of the courtyard. Brennan twisted out of Bear's grasp and ran back to retrieve his father's sword. Crow Blackthorn ran back to retrieve Brennan. Taylor Mason herded Crow and Brennan out through the gateway, leaving Bear and Govar the Red to bring up the rear.

The five survivors of the battle hastily mounted their horses and rode hard to leave Dun Raven behind.

And the four knights wept for their fallen companions while the boy swore vengeance upon those who had slain his father, even as he wept for the loss of the sword, Kestrian.

49

Brennan was aware that the fighting outside in the vale was getting closer to the Lodge. The piper's sorrowful song still filled the woods. Brennan had no idea how large of an enemy force was coming. He knew only that someone had warned him. He wondered who his unseen, mysterious ally had been and why she chose to intervene. Swaying unsteadily, he shuffled his feet, then swooned and crashed to the hard wooden floor.

The voice slid softly through the darkness: *Brennan? Open your eyes. Raise your head. Do not give up now.*

Brennan remained sprawled there. Weakly, he responded, "I cannot. Why do you ask this of me? I am finished."

The female's voice was insistent: *Finished? I think not. There is more to you than you realize. If you only knew of your potential, you would resist this apathy and rise.*

Brennan shook his sweat-drenched locks out of his face, forcing himself up onto his knees. He willed himself to remain still, focusing on his breathing. He then peered across the room to the ethereal form of a woman floating to one side of the fireplace. The wraith lady's silvery hair cascaded down past her shoulders and fluttered around her slender waist like a mantle, matching the white dress that she wore. Her luminous green eyes shone with a brightness and her penetrating gaze momentarily dispelled the effects of the Varr curse.

I am sorry, she apologized. *I wish I could do more for you. I am not free, however, to leave the confines of my prison. Drak has dispelled the warding surrounding the Vale of Pines, and the Rasp has come to claim you. You have brief seconds before he arrives.*

The ethereal lady gestured with both hands and in a burst of incandescent light, she placed a sword on the mantle above the fireplace. The blade appeared to be lit with a brilliant source of light, and the oak mantle was awash in the deep purple glow of Kestrian. And Brennan wondered if the lady taunted him with an illusion or if she indeed had the power to dispel the warding in the vault at Dun Raven, where his father's sword had been lost to him. If so, he was amazed.

"Who are you?" he hoarsely whispered.

At this, the wraith-like lady's form began to slowly dwindle. He then blinked in stunned amazement as shafts of moonlight illuminated the shimmering form of a silver dragon suspended in the air where the lady had been hovering.

An instant later it was gone.

Brennan suddenly recalled the last time he'd seen those sorrowful green eyes. Pulling himself to his feet, he remembered the silver dragon and said, "Elendriel?"

Staggering unsteadily toward the fireplace, Brennan could only wonder if the ghost lady and this dragon were one and the same. He reached out, fully expecting Kestrian to be an illusion and that the lady had played a cruel trick on him.

Astonished, his hand closed around the familiar hilt of the jewel-blade. And as he lifted Kestrian from the mantle, he heard her gentle voice once more: *It's not important who I am, Brennan. It's more crucial or you to remember who you are. For that will soon make the difference as to whether you live or die.*

Taking Kestrian in a two-handed grip, Brennan swung the blade point down and placed its tip on the stones of the hearth before him. Slowly he lowered himself to both knees. Tightly grasping the hilt to support himself, he swayed dizzily and closed his eyes. The brilliant light pulsing within Kestrian bathed his sweat-streaked face in its violet glow. He tried then to draw strength from the sword, a mighty weapon that had been passed down through the six Sword Lords before him.

The blare of horns sounded through the deeper woods of the Vale. The urgent blasts signaled a retreat.

Three piercing horn calls echoed from the distant hills. They were followed by two answering calls. The three distant horns were winded once more, and in the middle of the last shrill blast, the call was abruptly cut off. The tune of the lone piper ended on a piercing note, as well, and after that, a brief silence filled the Vale of Pines.

The curse of the poison ignited at that moment, and a fiery serpent constricted around his ravaged shoulder and infected him with such feelings of defeat that he simply wished to just lay down and wait for the approach of his coming enemies. I am done, he thought. I am finished. I have fought the good fight, and now I must submit to taking the Long Voyage.

But seconds later, Brennan opened his eyes and caught a glimpse of his own reflection in the bright blade of Kestrian. For long moments then, the shadows of the curse became like a dark pool of oily black water in his mind. Memories rose sluggishly through those dark depths, shining like silver fish swimming to the surface.

And Brennan saw:

Taylor Mason riding at the head of their small group as they fled from the ruins of Dun Raven. The big, white-haired knight was leading them through the thorny hedges of the woods. The pathway snaking through the spiky barrier was narrow and their running steeds whinnied in pain from the nips of sharp thorns.

Bringing up the rear behind Brennan, Crow Blackthorn, Bear, and Govar the Red continued to glance back to see if they were being pursued. After what seemed like an eternity, Taylor finally brought them to the edge of the woods. The large knight turned in his saddle and met the solemn gazes of the other three knights.

"A victory of sorts," Taylor gruffly said. "I think we lost them back there in the thorns. What say you, Bear?"

Bear said, "Corum will exile us for not fighting to the last man."

Crow said, "Surely, our king will think it wise that we rescued the Sword Lord's son, so that young Brennan can serve him as faithfully as his father did. Besides, how could we hope to defeat those demon knights with their ice-blades? Kestrian was the only weapon among us that had the power to slay those wraiths. If we had all been armed with weapons potent enough to do damage to those demon knights, our battle would have turned out much differently. The sword of the Sword Lord is now yours, Brennan. One day, the four of us will return to Dun Raven to avenge our fallen comrades armed with blades potent enough to slay Stealth of the Unseen War."

And as they made camp that evening, there on the moonlit plains, Brennan sat beside the fire, listening to the four Lion Knights talking in harsh whispers as they speculated where they might obtain jewelblades to exact the revenge that they vowed to take one day.

Brennan staggered across the room, with barely enough strength to raise his blade. As he stumbled, Kestrian scraped the stones beneath his bare feet. Still, he struggled to raise the sword in what would be the last battle of his life.

Despite his pathetic condition, Brennan smiled grimly.

This is how he'd always wanted to die, pitted against impossible odds, sword in hand, and giving one last showing of the gift that had been both a blessing and a curse throughout his life.

He remembered it well, too, the day his gift had come alive and sprang up to show itself in the skills he used to defend himself.

He had been barely ten-summers-old. He had repeatedly trained, learning all he could about blade work from the four Lion Knights, who faithfully served his father.

Brennan gazed at his reflection in the glowing blade of Kestrian, and saw his sweat-drenched raven hair hanging down on either side of his pale face. He peered into his own pain-glazed eyes, and in spite of his cursed shoulder wound, he smiled as he remembered:

Upon their first days at Rockhaven, while King Corum and his father, the newly named Sword Lord of Erin, had gone hunting, the four knights who so faithfully served Mace Ravenhawk, began training young Brennan. Taylor had been jabbing at him with a sword. Bear had been poking at him with his long instructor's stick, shouting out his mistakes, whacking his knuckles when he didn't correct them. And Crow and Govar were shouting out encouragement when young Brennan blocked a strike or parried a jab.

It had been a hot summer's evening, and though the sun was setting in the west, Taylor refused to quit his diligent training for the day. Brennan was sweating profusely and blowing and sucking air like a forge bellows. He had been at this particular mock battle, armed with his own sword, for nearly an hour. His arms were sore. His legs had gone weak. And his head was swimming in a sea of weariness. All he could think of was for this training session to end, so that he could dive into the cool waters of Rockhaven's pond.

But Taylor had another series of lessons to put him through, for as a taskmaster he could be brutal and relentless, driving home tactics until Brennan mastered them to his satisfaction.

Bear laughed loudly as Brennan muttered his complaint. He then poked and prodded him with his stick, yelling at him to raise his sword, slant his blade, reverse his stroke, drive his point home. And a dozen more loud commands that had Brennan's ears ringing.

Just when it seemed Taylor was about to disarm him, Brennan let loose with an overhand stroke that surprised both men. He followed through with a cross-cut and snapped Bear's instructor's stick completely in half before launching himself at Taylor. The white-haired giant had to take his own sword in a two-handed grip to defend him-self. Crow moved in to take Brennan out with a swat to his backside. Brennan slanted his sword down his back, deflected the sword, and wheeled to attack Crow in a full frontal charge.

Taylor moved in to take advantage of Brennan's open backside, then found himself fending off a rapid flurry of strokes as Brennan turned to meet his advance.

Whirling to face him, Brennan parried the thrust, rapped Taylor on the head with the flat of his blade, and turned and jabbed at Bear, sending him stumbling backwards.

"Enough!" Govar shouted. "Stop, now, Bren! Enough! You've given a good accounting of your skills today, lad!"

But Brennan's temper couldn't be cooled so easily. He had reached a point where he did not know how to switch off his fighting mode. He had brought to life a gift that he did not know he had. Until Taylor and Crow were forced to tackle him and take him to the ground. A pail of cold water was finally thrown on Brennan by his father who had watched the entire spectacle in mild amusement from the nearby tourney field.

Mace then stood over him and said, "I don't know where that came from, Brennan, but you, little Lord Ravenhawk, are a marvel with the blade!"

To be continued in Book Four, Thorns of the Black Rose.

The Havelock Emerald series . . .

Broken Road, the Prelude: 13-year-old Reason Nelson finds himself entangled in a web of treachery over the evidence that would solve the murder of a young female informant. As he flees from both drug dealers and a persistent private detective, Reason ends up at the Emerald Pub where he is confronted by the old Irishman, Billy Connors. Reason refuses Billy's help and continues to play a game of keep-away from those who murdered the narc. Despite the intervention of his mother, Rose, director of a drug program, and his brother, Boone, a youth advocate, due to his behavior disorders and his addictions, Reason remains defiant and refuses to accept help.

Book One: Wounded Arrow: When 11-year-old Lucas Holland, the son of the president of a notorious biker club, is placed in foster care he ends up at Ben Black Bull's dog rescue ranch, where the Lakota dog handler works with some of the most damaged dogs on the planet. Ben incorporates a company of veterans who suffer from PTSD, pairing each dog with a wounded warrior. It's there that Lucas learns that dogs and people all need healing of some sort.

Book Two: The Saracen: Shortly after his mother is killed in a car accident, Lucas returns home to Havelock to live with his dad. At his school, Lucas stumbles upon three boys recruiting another young boy to carry out a school shooting. Lucas comes away from the encounter carrying a pistol. Hidden in the butt of the gun is a flash drive containing the directives to terrorists to infiltrate Wounded Arrow, where 200 Military service dogs have been returned from the war overseas. Their goal is to place a chemical agent in the ventilators of the compound, eliminating these retired service dogs awaiting adoption as a reward for the service they provided to the US.

Book Three: Here, there be Dragons: In this Sci Fi thriller, the Emerald Pub is a way station between realms. Reason Nelson has finally grown up and is performing youth work with kids who are as troubled as he once was. In his role as a foster parent, he takes in Lucas Holland and Alex Thorn. Breaking into a relic collectors house one night to retrieve a set of rings that Lucas's older sister, Celeste, has stolen from him, the two boys set off a chain of events that releases a demon into the world. To destroy this Prince of Darkness, Alex Thorn, a child of Gypsy blood, is chosen to enter the chamber inside the Emerald to retrieve a weapon that will annihilate the demon.

Book Four: Thorns of the Black Rose: Lucas, Alex, and Celeste find themselves back in the realm of Valasar. They find themselves in a quest to not only slay a dragon, but a conspiracy to save one, as well. When a lesser king and his two Sword Lords refuse to slay the dragon, Elendria, in order to steal her Star Fire, High King Manix declares them outlaws. When he orders that their three children are to be executed, Lucas, Alex, and Celeste become determined to rescue them, for one is to be a legendary Sword Lord, the other is to become the Lion Lord, and the third is destined to become the queen, Alicia the Black Rose.

Book Five: Jewels of Kandahar: Jenna McGuire is a specialist in the Mind over Martyr program used by the US Military. When faced with the reality of 500,000 Caliphate kids, she travels to Afghanistan to save a 14-year-old charismatic boy who may set off a raging firestorm. She is escorted by a group of Delta Rangers, who travel with her into the Kandahar Mountains. There, Jenna and her team discover a mysterious treasure of gems and jewels.

Milton Keynes UK
Ingram Content Group UK Ltd.
UKHW022209030324
438776UK00012B/1975